JERICHO ROAD

FERNANDO J CAMPO

1

RELUCTANT RECRUIT

APRIL 2001

The sun was setting behind the mountains west of Palo Alto, transforming the view from inside the sixth-floor conference room from a beautiful purple sky to a reflection of the scene inside. Nick Aday had been using the conference room as his office during a visit to his company's Bay Area office.

As Nick slid his laptop into the top pocket of his Tumi bag, he caught a glimpse of his reflection on the window. He wore the software executive uniform of a Hugo Boss charcoal gray suit, Ferragamo black loafers, striped Brooks Brothers baby blue-and-white shirt with no tie. Nick was of medium build and height and had characteristics of his ancestral lineage from Northern Spain – fair freckled skin, thick brown hair, and hazel eyes – but aside from those, his facial features were Eastern Mediterranean. He had a prominent nasal bridge and eyes close together. His looks did not make him stand out in a crowd, but he made up for it in smarts and a mysterious, yet charismatic personality.

Nick ran Global Sales for Macro Insights, a Virginia based software company, with its Americas headquarters located just off Highway 101 in Palo Alto. It was a Friday night after a three-day trip, and there was one last thing he needed to do before heading out to the San Francisco airport for his redeye flight back to Dulles. It was actually the main reason he had made the trip to the Bay Area, a trip that was disguised with client meetings and a dinner with a handful of members of his West Coast team.

He took a deep breath and walked over, pulling his carry-on suitcase, to the corner office at the opposite end of the hallway. Pete Kalimeris, who ran the Americas Sales team, was the only other person left in the office, responding to emails, while he waited for Nick to leave. Had Nick not been there, Pete would have been wrapping up a round of golf near his home in Pleasanton. He was happy to hear Nick's footsteps approaching his office, an indication that the day was finally coming to an end and he could go home.

"Do you have a sec?" asked Nick, who came in and sat down on the couch next to Pete's desk. He leaned forward, resting his forearms on his knees and clasped his hands, signaling he was about to say something.

Pete missed the cue, and as he turned away from his laptop, said, "Sure thing. By the way, I just got an email from Rod, the CIO at Kaiser, and guess what? They got the funding! Cha-ching! The Board meeting..."

"Pete," Nick quickly interrupted, "My car service is on its way, so I only have a couple of minutes." Pete's enthusiasm was quickly replaced by a tinge of concern based on Nick's tone. It was dark, forceful, and efficient. He had seen it before. "The time has come for us to part ways. Your team's performance during the last two quarters has been...disappointing. You have no idea how much time I've spent with Rich explaining the Q1 meltdown. I know it. You know it. We're done."

"Nick, this is a bit of a blindside. I mean...we just spent the last three days meeting clients and the team, as if nothing was wrong." Pete paused to collect his thoughts. The reality of the situation started to sink in as Nick remained quiet, giving him time to process the news. "I mean...what the fuck? I've worked my ass off trying to get back to pre-dot-com crash levels, but the economy isn't cooperating. Nick, this is not an execution issue. If you give me one more quarter, I'll show you that..."

"Pete, it would be best of you picked up your things and left. I'll have someone get the rest of your belongings from the office and ship them to your home. Just, don't make this more awkward than it has to be."

After a brief period of silence, Pete finished packing up his briefcase, put on his jacket, and hung his bag on his right shoulder. He walked toward Nick, who was already standing, extended his hand, and shaking his head said, "I'm sorry I let you down." The act of humility, particularly given the circumstances, did not even register with Nick. All he was concerned about at this stage was to get it over with. The conversation had worked as planned.

Even though it was almost 11:00 pm on the East Coast, Nick stayed in Pete's office and made several phone calls to notify each member of Pete's direct team, as well as his own. This was the third time in the last two years that Nick had fired a member of the team he inherited from his predecessor, but in this case, he felt no compunction about it. He wasn't sure whether this was a good or a bad thing, but for now he was relieved that Pete was out of the way, and it was time to upgrade the position.

Less than three hours later, Nick was on his flight heading back home. The Business Class cabin was full, and most reading lights had already been turned off after a late dinner service on the redeye from SFO to Dulles. Nick had been lucky enough to get a last-minute upgrade, which made the inconvenience of the window seat a lot easier to deal with. The expense controls that the company had implemented the prior year, after the dot-com crash, were still in effect, and that meant that only Senior VPs could book business travel. Nick was still one step away from that.

When he was done with dinner and the flight attendant picked up his tray, he pulled out his laptop to finish drafting an email he had started earlier. He wanted to capture his thoughts while fresh in his mind, but there was no rush, since he could not synchronize email until arriving at home. Nick had been in his current role for the last five years and was itching for the next move, where he could consolidate several functions currently run by two of his peers and become the first COO in the history of the young, but quickly growing company. Among many things that would improve his life once promoted, he would qualify for Business Class travel and not have to rely on the occasional upgrade to come through. A big deal for someone that traveled almost every week.

Nick took the last two sips of the chardonnay he had ordered with dinner and got up for a final trip to the bathroom before attempting a couple of hours of sleep. He had to perform some gymnastics to climb over the legs of the semi-reclined seat next to him, where a middle-aged woman that worked at AOL was already deep asleep. He had met her upon boarding and struck up a quick and superficial conversation about what both did for a living. As Nick walked along the narrow hallway to the front of the plane, he noticed the couple seated in front of him, the man already with his sleep mask on, and the woman reading a paperback, which from what he could discern appeared to be *Tuesdays with Morrie*. He then turned his gaze toward the end of the hallway, where one of the crew was standing next to the partially opened cockpit door having a conversation with one of the flight attendants. It was a smooth flight, and most people were in their seats trying to get as much rest as they could considering its less than five-hour duration. Such was the fun of the dreaded redeye flights.

The moment Nick opened the door on his way out of the bathroom, he noticed it was unusually quiet in the galley area. The crew member and the flight attendant had left, and there was no one else around. The conversation must have ended shortly after he went in, he thought. Then, another realization – it wasn't only quiet. The hiss that is ever-present inside the cabin of a jet was gone. Instead, there was absolute silence. It was peaceful, not eerie, but very unusual. He turned, started walking along the aisle, and once he got past the first bulkhead, noticed something very unusual. He scanned all seats, starting from his left, and did not see a single passenger. Out of the corner of his eye, he noticed a light source coming from the right side, as if someone had opened a window shade, but it didn't make sense that light would be coming in at night. He turned his gaze to the light source, and there, standing in the aisle in front of him, near his seat, was the only person within sight. He was looking at Nick, his gaze piercing. Yet, Nick did not feel scared. On the contrary, there was a certain magnetism about the man Nick found interesting...and familiar.

Nick knew that this was not normal, most likely not natural. After the initial shock, he stopped and focused again on the man. He was at least six feet tall with broad shoulders and an athletic build, short wavy dark hair, and big green eyes that were framed in a youngish face with no facial hair and a smooth complexion that appeared to have a golden hue to it. The most striking features were his attire and body language. He was wearing a linen robe, and underneath, was clad in what looked like an ancient warrior's armor that glowed in its own light. There was a certain confidence that he projected in his posture and in the way he immediately locked eyes with Nick. It was not a threatening stare, more like a friendly one of someone that he knew but had not seen in years. Yet, Nick had no idea who he was, and the awkwardness of the moment put him at a loss for words. All he could think about was to keep walking in the man's direction to see if he could understand better. As he took his second step, a light of indescribable brilliance shone on Nick and lit up the entire cabin of the plane. Then, in another flash, the light went out and Nick was back in the Business Class cabin with the original passengers. The only difference – he was now on his knees.

He thought, "OK, what just happened?" Did he trip and fall, and the shock of the fall had him suppress the memory? Were the wine and the altitude playing tricks on him? Nick had only had one glass of wine and had never experienced issues of this type in the past. So, what was it? Had the man in the ancient-style clothing really been there, or was it some sort of hallucination? The questions stayed with him as he got up and continued to slowly step toward row five. Maybe there was something in the bathroom that triggered this episode, so he went back there and looked inside. Nothing. No clue. After taking a couple of deep breaths and realizing he was not going to find an immediate answer, Nick walked back to his seat, did the gymnastic move over the extended aisle seat, and sat down.

The excitement from what he had just experienced kept him awake for the remainder of the flight, even though he reclined his seat and closed his eyes. Nick kept trying to find a logical explanation that would categorize the experience as something he imagined, and the questions kept circulating in his mind for the next two hours. By then, the flight was less than an hour from landing, so Nick proceeded to go to the bathroom to splash some water on his face and brush his teeth. This time, his aisle seat neighbor had already moved the seat to the upright position, so he did not have to engage in the circus-like contortions again. He got to the bathroom, and upon sliding the door lock, the lights came on revealing his reflection on the mirror. He was immediately drawn to examine the redness in his face, as if he had been out under the sun for hours. Finding it hard to believe, he wiped the mirror clean with a wet paper towel and took a closer look. His face was uniformly red, including his forehead, all the way to the hair-line. That was strange! He had hardly been outside during the trip and hadn't noticed it the last time he was in that bathroom. He turned around and saw no redness on the back of his neck.

To add to the strange happenings that morning, there had also been a thought cycling through Nick's mind as he tossed and turned on his seat. Could it be something he read recently or heard on TV or radio? It was very persistent, to the point of almost annoying him. The thought went something like: *Go back to your roots. Let your curiosity guide you…*and there was a third phrase that he could not recall. He was not sure how this could relate to him, but now that he was looking at his sunburned face in the mirror, there seemed to be a connection. Was the stranger on the plane real? Was he the one that said this? Did he plant that thought in his mind? How? What was the point of the encounter?

2

BLOCKING THE TRUTH

Once he arrived at his townhouse in Old Town Alexandria, Nick took a nap to try to recover from the jet lag and lack of sleep on the flight. After a restless three hours, he got up and walked over to the kitchen to get something to eat. His wife, Shannon, was already there, working at her computer on a design project for a friend's business. Shannon was slender, of medium height, had beautiful light blue eyes and dark brown hair, which made a great contrast with her cool fair skin. She was a graphics designer who had started her career in an advertising agency after college, but for the last few years had slowed down, only doing freelance work for a few clients, mostly friends. She was now balancing her time between the ten to twenty hours a week she devoted to work and as a volunteer at her neighborhood church, the Basilica of St Mary.

Upon Nick's arrival, she said, "Well, good morning, or… afternoon! How was the trip?"

Nick walked over behind her, gave her a kiss and a hug, and while still having his arms wrapped around her shoulders, said, "Morning, baby. I didn't sleep on the flight. Got the upgrade, but...I don't know. I guess too much on my mind...good flight, though. What are you up to?" He then walked over to the fridge to make himself a sandwich.

"Oh, Seema asked me to re-do her homepage. It's not due for another week, but I thought I'd work on it now before a meeting I have at church...which, by the way, is in fifteen minutes. The way you were sleeping, I thought you would be going longer, so I started with this."

Shannon had met Nick during a time when his external appearance gave the impression that he was completely together. He was financially successful and highly respected professionally, stayed in good physical condition, had a great sense of humor, and even in his humble demeanor was always upbeat and assertive. He succeeded in hiding his struggles from her, and to some extent, had been able to cope with them by blocking the tormenting thoughts and displacing them with things that kept his mind busy. One of those blocking strategies was his maniacal focus on his career. He felt it was justified on the basis of being a good provider and offering Shannon the best possible life. The truth was that he was not maintaining a balance that worked for her, as she would have traded the financial success for more time and attention from her husband.

After a brief pause, Shannon asked, "So how is Pete?"

"Well, he may be the reason I wasn't able to get any sleep on the flight. I had to let him go..."

"What?!" Shannon exclaimed, "Pete Kalimeris? Wow! I didn't see that coming!"

"Neither did he." Nick took a deep breath, then continued, "He said it was a *blindside*. I don't know. A senior guy at that level needs to recognize when something like this is coming."

"Nick, he has been on the incentive trip every year that you've been in this role. That's how I met Maria. Oh my God! I guess I will not be seeing them again either," and after thinking some more about it, "Isn't that trip for the top performers only?"

"He attended as an executive host, but it is true that his team has kicked butt." Nick had not expected Shannon to be the source of questions that would indirectly challenge his conscience. She was always supportive, and on his side, so her reaction was unexpected, and he felt compelled to justify the decision to her. "Baby, I gave this a lot of thought, and trust me, it's in everyone's best interest. Pete went into *excuse-mode* ever since we had the meltdown in Q1 of last year because of the dot-com crash. I don't know what happened there, but he never recovered, and I can't have an *Eeyore* running my largest Geo."

Shannon looked at her watch and realized she would need to leave now to make the meeting in time. The Basilica was only a five-minute walk away, but she wanted to get there early since she was hosting the meeting. Before leaving, she said, "Sorry for all the questions, Nico. This one just feels different...but I trust you did the right thing," and as she was about to close the door, she walked back toward Nick, hugged him and said, "This was probably the last thing you needed to hear after a tough trip and a sleepless flight. Sorry, let's do something fun tonight! I should be back by 3:00, OK? Love you." She kissed him, playfully pulled on his right ear lobe, and left.

Nick, now by himself, was confronted with a reality that Shannon had unknowingly exposed. There was no way he could justify the firing, and he knew the real reasons behind his decision. For starters, he never clicked with Pete, even from the time he was promoted into the role and inherited the sales organization. Their styles and management philosophy were very different – Nick, a much more-hard driving, no-nonsense East Coast guy, and Pete, a softer, more idealistic Silicon Valley type. But the other thing that Shannon sensed immediately was that it must have come as a surprise to Pete. Nick had made no attempt to coach him, manage his expectations, much less try to help him, while his team struggled. So, instead of an act of strength, Nick had just committed an act of cowardice.

Nick was also faced with another truth about his behavior that was making him feel even guiltier. He did not make any mention of the other-worldly episode during the flight. This was the real reason he could not get any sleep, and as much as he was trying to brush it aside as a product of his imagination, it was a big enough deal that he should have at least mentioned it to his wife. This was yet one more example of inner struggles Nick had been going through but had never brought up with her.

Aside from the events of the last twenty-four hours, Nick's most persistent and concerning struggle over the years was a question about his own existence – *is this all there is?* Being smart, analytical and curious can have its advantages, but it was also a curse in posing questions of existence, meaning, and purpose that were not easily answered. During Nick's early teenage years, one of the biggest realizations was how fleeting the *present* was. Events he had highly anticipated eventually arrived and then flew by, sliding as if pulled by gravity, to the past. That slide was a force that was not controllable, and everyone moved at the same speed within it. Even things that he started to anticipate when they were years out, like graduating from high school and the first day of college, eventually arrived and passed. Nick thought most or all people around him were not bothered by that dynamic, or maybe were oblivious to it, so he thought it best not to talk about it, not even to his best friend and soulmate, Shannon.

After the quick snack, Nick became sleepy again and returned to bed for what he hoped would be a power nap that would help him re-set and ease the jet lag. Before going to sleep, Nick opened the drawer of his nightstand and pulled out his Game Boy. He had not had much time to play Super Mario during the last few weeks, and the last time he did, he came to within one level of reaching the eighth world and facing the real Bowser. Retro video games were Nick's escape, and this one could be addictive. He knew they were a total waste of time and was not particularly good at them, but they brought back good memories from his teen years. He swiftly moved through the first four worlds in almost mechanical fashion, and in that brief period, his racing mind took him back to the tormenting thoughts that persisted.

There were a new set of questions now, related to what he had experienced on the flight. His mind went into replay mode on its own, and Nick relived the walk out of the bathroom and back to his seat. He remembered the face of the stranger and the interesting attitude he conveyed with his gaze and posture. Nick started to realize that there had been more to the encounter than he immediately remembered, as if he actually had some sort of exchange with the stranger. He knew there was more but could not replay that part, could not retrieve it, as if it had been erased from memory or stored in his mind in an unreachable place. He remembered concepts and even feelings from the encounter, knew the stranger was someone that knew him well, that he never felt threatened, and even felt there was a purpose in the encounter but could not unpack it. Then, the thought that had been playing in his mind came back – *Go back to your roots. Let your curiosity guide you*, now with the recollection of the third segment: *Will you let God act through you?* It became a constant repetition, particularly the call to action at the end. Why would he need to allow a god to act through him? This god, if almighty, should have the power to do whatever he wanted without permission. And why the need for Nick to even be involved? If this was some sort of supernatural event, and there was really a god involved, he would surely pick someone that was religious, well in-tune with his teachings. While Nick had a relatively good base of understanding of Catholic teachings, he was no expert, and no longer believed in it. But...was it possible that this was real, and that somehow, he was supposed to play a role in some sort of supernatural intervention? If so, what was it? Did he even have the skills and knowledge to help?

It took a few more minutes, but the temporary distraction made him lose focus, and Mario lost his last life to the fake Bowser in the sixth world. Nick put down the Game Boy and eventually fell asleep. No more than twenty minutes later, he abruptly woke up from what he sensed had been a very vivid dream. Without even opening his eyes, he became aware of being awake, and immediately tried to bridge back to the last recollection he had from the dream. In it, he was all by himself facing an invisible evil presence. He could not see or hear it but knew it was there. He knew this was someone that absolutely hated him and wanted to do him harm.

Instead of being intimidated, Nick felt a certain power that he had over that entity, and that spiritually he was not alone. As he was recalling the dream, all of a sudden, he felt a sense of warmth all over his body. It felt like being hugged spiritually, to the point where he felt his body vibrating from the energy he could sense. He felt the presence directing this embrace, and that it wanted Nick to feel loved and protected. He then heard the same message being delivered within his mind – *Go back to your roots. Let your curiosity guide you, Will you let God act through you?* Then, gradually, the embrace faded.

Every cell in Nick's body pointed him to the truth of what he just experienced, while his mind told him to deny it and file it away as an imaginary concoction. He was not sure whether to think that this was as direct as it gets in delivering a message, or if it was a vague imagination, this time magnified by a bad case of jet lag and possible dehydration. His skeptical inner self was popping questions, like: "If this is God, why can't he communicate more clearly and directly?" But upon giving it more thought, how else could it have been communicated to compel Nick that this was real? Someone in a suit walking up to him and telling him? In writing, like a letter? In less than twenty-four hours, he had experienced two events he could not explain. There was always the possibility that he was hallucinating, though that seemed even more far-fetched than trusting what his senses told him. He kept replaying it in his mind, trying to make sense of it and what it meant. He also reflected on how willing he had been to accept everything he learned while in school, trusting that all of it was true, but was being a skeptic with himself. Then, an interesting thought crossed his mind, and he felt almost embarrassed to accept that it was true – he did not want to believe!

How else could he explain ignoring all the evidence in front of him and filing this away as an unimportant, hard to explain *episode*. What if it were true that God had pierced through the boundaries of the material world to deliver a message to him? What logical argument could stop him from believing that? At that point, Nick made the conscious decision that, while the experiences had been extremely vivid and triggered all of his senses, they did not conform with his belief that there was nothing outside of the natural. Therefore, these would just be labeled as fabrications of his mind. He needed to move on.

3

TRAGEDY AND LIFE

May 13, 2001, al-Eizariyah, West Bank, Palestinian territory of Israel

The dark, poorly illuminated apartment room seemed like a cave, as the young Palestinian couple dealt with the dramatic delivery of their firstborn. Based on their calculations, the woman was late by almost a week. They had a pretty good idea that late July or early August of the prior year was when the child was conceived, as he was working on a construction project near the Dead Sea and that was the last time they were together before she found out that she was pregnant. They expected May 8th to be the date, and Ghassan had taken time off from work to be at Layla's side during the delivery.

Their only family was his sister Reema, a fifteen-year-old who lived with them but was not allowed in the room during the delivery. Instead, Sister Lucia, a midwife from the nearby convent of the Sisters of Saint Joseph, was in the room with them making every effort to manage what had been a very difficult delivery. While the couple had access to Makassed Hospital nearby, they preferred to deliver at home with the help of a midwife. It had been their family's tradition, and they understood it had worked without incident at their respective births. This time, though, it had been a grave mistake.

The expecting mother's blood pressure was increasing at an accelerated pace, bordering on eclampsia. Sister Lucia's anxiety grew as every time she checked the woman's blood pressure, the numbers kept inching up, her face was getting redder, and she was starting to complain about a strong headache. As she was not in a hospital, she did not have the basic medication that was necessary at the time. Intravenous magnesium sulfate therapy would have been enough to mitigate the risk of seizures, but even something that basic was not part of the arsenal at Sister Lucia's disposal. She had to act fast to get the baby out, then stabilize the mother.

Ghassan could see in the midwife's eyes that things were not going as planned and started to regret and blame himself for not having taken Layla to the hospital. They had not even gone to routine visits to monitor her progress. Had he been more supportive in taking the time to bring her to see a physician, her preeclampsia would have been diagnosed in time, and preventive measures could have been taken to mitigate the risk of complications during delivery. Instead, they had learned about the volunteers from the Sisters of Saint Joseph, and while they would have preferred not to have a Christian perform the delivery, they thought they could trust them. After all, many of their neighbors had delivered the same way without any incident. It was also free and could be done at home. All of these factors drove his decision, and now he was sorry for that terrible mistake. In his limited way, he attempted to help Sister Lucia.

The baby's head had already cleared the birth canal and was starting to show. One more push could completely clear the head, after which Sister Lucia could, with some effort, manipulate the baby out. The shoulders would be the biggest challenge, but something she could handle. As the woman made a last push, her body began to convulse, and she lost consciousness. In the middle of that chaotic situation, with the husband yelling at her, Sister Lucia began to feel a sense of calm that surprised even her.

As she grabbed the infant's shoulders, she looked up to the husband and said, "We both must pray. Your wife and child are in grave danger, and their only hope is the intervention of the Almighty. Please join me in praying to the Virgin. Today is the anniversary of the first apparition in Fatima, so let's pray to her."

Surprisingly enough, Ghassan dropped to the floor and joined the nun in prayer. He was not very devout, but at this stage could use all the help he could get. He started to pray to Allah, but also followed her as best as he could as she recited the Hail Mary, "...Holy Mary, Mother of God..."

His attention was completely focused on the tragedy that was about to happen at breakneck speed in front of him. The stress and desperation were such that he felt detached from himself, as if he was a spectator watching the entire drama unfold. In the middle of the fear and chaos, he also began to sense a feeling of peace and calm that he thought might have been the influence of Sister Lucia's calm demeanor at the time. He was able to breathe again, even as he watched his young wife convulsing uncontrollably while the nun remained focused on turning the child's shoulders and pulling with all her might. He buried his head between his arms and continued to pray.

From near darkness, Ghassan suddenly became aware that the room was full of light. The next time he looked toward the head of the bed, he saw a young woman, perhaps a teenager, standing next to his wife holding her in a warm embrace. The woman was dressed in a white mantle with gold trim and a sky-blue veil. Her gaze was totally focused on his agonizing wife, as if she was able to communicate with her and transmit an infinite amount of love and peace that radiated from her eyes, and also around and within her.

He knew his wife was dying, and a mixture of emptiness and peace enveloped his body. Emptiness because of the sudden and unexpected loss of his soulmate. Peace because he felt and knew his wife was now in a better place, away from the difficulties that surrounded their lives and in the hands of someone that had come to usher her to God. Someone who was all about peace and love. In and around her, the absolute absence of fear and desperation. Could it be that this was the Virgin that Christians prayed to?

Ghassan stared at the woman in awe. He realized he was witnessing something supernatural and extremely powerful. Her presence lit up the entire room in ways that not even the light of the sun could. There were no shadows, his eyes could remain wide open, yet the light was purer and more brilliant than anything he had experienced. It also created a feeling of peace that he did not want to end and much stronger than the empty feeling of seeing the earthly life of his young wife slowly vanish.

As his heart was bidding farewell to his wife with overwhelming emotion, Ghassan turned and saw Sister Lucia manipulating the infant out of the birth canal. The calm and blissful ambience was suddenly disrupted as the cry of a newborn punched through it like a spear. It was a beautiful baby girl! He looked at her as he was still kneeling on the floor and noticed the glow of a golden light on the baby's gorgeous face. It appeared to be a reflection, the source of which was coming from behind his shoulder.

As he started to get up from the floor to touch and hold his daughter, his knees could not hold his weight, and he slowly fell to the floor again due to emotional exhaustion and shock. As his consciousness faded, he heard a message from the Christian Virgin, "This is your home. Stay and raise your child here," and then one last thought crossed his mind. The prayer to the Virgin was not a prayer to her as the ultimate being that would grant his wishes. It was rather an intercession – *pray for us sinners, now and at the hour of our death...*

Contrary to what he had been taught, the Christian's Virgin was not considered by them a deity, but rather a very important and venerated agent of their God, who cared so much about humans, that she would intercede on their behalf regardless of faith. Even on behalf of a Muslim. With that final thought, Ghassan blacked out.

4

CHANCE ENCOUNTER

April 15, 2013, Fairmont Hotel, Washington D.C.

It was a little early for a drink, but after the presentation Nick made at the IDC e-Government luncheon at the hotel, several people came to the front of the room to chat with him. Some knew him and wanted to say hi, and some came for introductions and professional networking opportunities. After all, this was the primary motivation of the various agency CIOs that were present at the event. Lunch at a nice venue making contacts with key Information Technology influencers from the private sector is what would pave the way for their post-public sector careers. That is where money would be made, by leveraging their experience and contacts in government to land a senior role at one of the technology companies that, in turn, made a killing selling to the government.

Nick was well aware of this, and wasn't enamored with these interactions, but this was part of playing the game. His motivation for putting up with the superficiality of that world was to maintain a strong presence with key customers, in this case, at the largest potential client in his backyard – the U.S. Federal government.

On his way out of the luncheon, three Federal Agency CIOs walked along and conversed with him as he made his way to the hotel lobby. He stopped along the hallway, between the main entrance and the bar, and out of courtesy for the CIOs, invited them to a drink. There were two men already sitting at the bar, holdovers from a lunch meeting at the Blue Duck Tavern across the street. They were members of the faculty of the Georgetown Public Policy Institute, who went to the Fairmont in an effort to have a more private conversation about internal politics at the university, including the renaming of the GPPI to the McCourt School of Public Policy. They were both almost done having a beer when they noticed the breaking news on the bar's TV. There had been a bombing at the Boston Marathon a few minutes earlier, possibly multiple bombs, with several people dead!

Within seconds, Nick and the three CIOs had also noticed the news and turned their focus to the television. The CIOs quickly excused themselves, scrambling to get back to their offices and gain a better understanding of the situation and whether there was an implication to their respective agencies. Nick called his assistant to find out if anyone from his team or clients in Boston had been affected. Fortunately, none were anywhere near the route of the marathon. As he wrapped up that call, he remembered that two of his friends had actually qualified for the race and were most likely there, so he called and left voicemails for both. He stayed at the bar and sat down next to the only remaining patron, one of the Georgetown professors, who was glued to the TV, watching the updates.

Nick then said, "This is just sick! I know it's a different world now, that these things will happen, but this is just plain evil."

"Very sad," said the Georgetown professor, still in a trance and with his full attention on the news coverage.

"I just realized that two of my running buddies might have been there."

They kept going back and forth, commenting on the horrific events, while both continued to look at the TV. Then Nick turned toward the man and said, "By the way, my name is Nick Aday," and stretched his hand to introduce himself.

"Ewan Byrne, a pleasure to meet you," responded the professor. Ewan was a tall and slightly overweight man, with a full head of blondish-gray hair and poorly trimmed beard. He wore the standard college professor outfit of a tweed blazer, deck shoes, chinos, a checkered button-down shirt, and a tie that did not quite make it to within two inches of his belt and did not match the colors of anything he was wearing. "I teach nearby. Are you from out of town?"

"No, no. I just happened to be here at a technology event in the hotel, but I live across the river in Alexandria...Old Town, and work at Macro Insights in Tyson's Corner. The other gentlemen were Fed IT executives."

"So, Nick...right? What kind of technology?" asked Ewan, with a legitimate curiosity about Nick's profession, a refreshing change from the academics he surrounded himself with.

"What we sell is software that helps organizations analyze different types of data so they can make better decisions and improve their performance. It's called Business Intelligence. BI...and Analytics, in case you've heard the lingo."

Ewan opened his eyes wide in an expression that mixed total confusion with a hint of awe. "Makes perfect sense! And, no, never heard of that, but it sounds...expensive. Is it hard to sell?"

"Ha! Ha! It's probably no harder than selling parents on a sixty-thousand-dollar-a-year college education for their kids!" said Nick in jest and feeling more comfortable in the conversation. For him too, this was very refreshing. He could drop his guard and be himself. This was just a down-to-earth, fun conversation.

Ewan, looking again at the television, said, "I bet the police are going to wait until the very last minute to admit that this was a terrorist attack, and that radical Islamists are the ones responsible. The media will play along, not because of good reporting, but because they would prefer not to admit it. We will get inundated by bad information during the next few days."

Nick thought this was a little candid and direct for an initial conversation, and surprising coming from a university professor, but he was amused about the fact that he fully agreed with Ewan's comments. He said, "You can easily get in trouble for making comments like that, particularly in this town." He returned the smirk looking at Ewan in the eyes and added, "I'm with you, though. That is also what I expect," and then after a pause, asked, "Where do you teach? Georgetown?"

Ewan now turned to Nick, as if getting himself in a comfortable position before providing a complete response. "Yes, I teach Public Policy. I've been at Georgetown for almost twenty-three years now."

Nick responded, "Interesting. I guess you're in the right place for your field. There may not be a better place to study that than in D.C., and Georgetown is a great school."

"Agreed," said Ewan, "GW is also exceptional in the field, and there is no place I'd rather be than in this city. It is funny because my relationship with Georgetown is a bit of a love/hate story. I believe it is a great school, and I like the fact that it is affiliated with the Catholic Church, but I am not a big fan of my bosses. The guys from *the Company*, as they refer to themselves, are brilliant...but we don't always agree." He looked at Nick in the eye again to ensure Nick understood what he meant. Nick's expression and his light nod gave Ewan license to continue.

"Beyond family, I have two passions in life. The first one is my relationship with God. The second one is understanding the power structures that we have created as humans, how they interact with one another, and how balance is maintained...or not maintained. The forces of chaos are impressively strong, and yet, they don't always prevail. Actually, they fail much more often than they prevail. It is that impossible balance that I have always been interested in, and Public Policy is the closest thing I could find, maybe with Sociology as a distant second, which is why I also studied it. I find them to be a little weird though."

Nick was intrigued. "Oh, how so?"

"Well, there are different levels of weirdness in academia, and sociology ranks higher than what I do. They do a great job of studying and explaining social behavior but are light on what to do about those dynamics."

Nick had not spent much time with academics in his past, and while he respected them, was never impressed by that as a career choice. He thought for many it was a cop out, a way to avoid living and competing in the real world. Still, he found Ewan's response very interesting and wanted to understand more. "You said you're not always in agreement with the Jesuits, yet your main passion is God. That's interesting. If you don't mind me asking, why the conflict, then?"

Ewan initially felt that going deeper would probably be a bit too personal, but in fairness to Nick, he had opened that Pandora's Box, so he went on. "Well, how much time do you have?" he asked rhetorically. "I need to get ready for a 5:30 class, so it might be me that is on the shorter time fuse...especially given that you already did your good deed for the day meeting with all these customers." He smiled, then continued, "I was a Jesuit priest. Actually, still am. You never stop being one, even if you renounce your vows, which is what I did. It is complicated, but what happened to me is that I got frustrated with some of the internal issues of the church, but even beyond that, the leftist ideology of many Jesuits eventually made me feel like it wasn't my home. It's a long story, for another day, but the punch line is that I left and eventually met the love of my life, whom I married, and this is what I do now. I teach." He paused and looked at his watch.

"You have to go?" Nick asked.

"Yes, but it's been an absolute pleasure. I took an Uber to the restaurant but walking back to campus. Sort of a commitment I made to myself to create the illusion I am controlling my weight. Ha!"

Nick chuckled, then said, "I hope I did not spook you with all my questions." He got up and extended his hand again, saying, "It's been a true pleasure meeting you, Ewan. I hope our paths cross again."

Ewan reached for his wallet and handed Nick a business card. "Here, if you are ever in the Georgetown area, email or call me. I'll buy you coffee, but it would be your turn to tell me your story." And with that, he grabbed his backpack and umbrella and left.

Once Ewan left, Nick realized he had been at the bar for almost a full hour, so he checked his voice mail for messages. His phone was in *vibrate* mode, so he had not noticed the three calls that had come in. He was relieved to learn that his two friends had responded, and they were fine, having crossed the finish line an hour before the explosion, not quite breaking their goal of three hours for the race, but still at a pace that Nick could only dream of. There was also a message from his assistant reminding him that she had cleared his schedule that afternoon, but remining him of his early morning flight the next day. He thought, "No morning run tomorrow, but I can make it home in time for a quick run before it gets dark." He picked up his briefcase and umbrella and headed out the main entrance doors.

The walk to the train station took less than ten minutes. He started down 24th Street, across Washington Circle, and along the 23rd Street side of GW Hospital, where the Emergency room entrance is located. There, he went by two emergency vehicles parked along the street, which reminded him of the tragedy in Boston. The video in the news showed several people down several feet before the finish line on Boylston Street. His friends had run through the same spot only an hour earlier! Nick had also spent a lot of time on business trips at restaurants in that specific area. He recalled how the September 11th attacks had made a big impact on him and his worldview. The Twin Tower tragedy and the plane that was downed in Pennsylvania had been absolutely horrible, but he felt somewhat removed from them. They had taken place in locations that felt more remote, and he did not know any of the victims. By contrast, the crash on the Pentagon building, only five miles from their home, had been a traumatic event for him and Shannon. They knew one of the victims and several more that survived.

For many, including Shannon, the tragedy strengthened their faith. After all, faith in God also meant they believed there is evil acting in the world, and over time, a lot of good came out of the tragedy and suffering. For Nick, it had the opposite effect. He doubled down on his doubt and rejection of religion. How could people hate so much, to the point of committing an act of such evil, in the name of a god? How could they be so ignorant? And now, the Boston bombing brought back those thoughts, including a growing resentment of Islamic radicalism. It also sparked in Nick a newfound curiosity about the dynamics of the world where these radicals lived alongside more civilized people, so to speak, whose beliefs he was more familiar with. A place where this tension and conflict were an everyday occurrence – Israel.

Immediately after passing the hospital, Nick made a right turn to go under the signature glass canopy and down the massive escalators of the Foggy Bottom Metro station. He pulled his SmarTrip card and tapped the top of the faregate on his way to the Blue Line ramp to Franconia-Springfield. As he waited and during the short train ride to King Street station, he kept reflecting on the coincidental encounter he had just had at the Fairmont bar.

Ewan was someone who had probably conquered the faith issues Nick had always dealt with. He must have received a solid education in theology from the Jesuits, who are known for their academic rigor and focus on reason as a key pillar of faith. He was also very focused on his relationship with God, in spite of the conflict he had experienced with the Church and the Jesuit order. This also made Nick wonder about how these highly educated people would be willing to make that leap in belief and trust that there was a god. Nick's obsessive-compulsive nature would not allow him to think about anything else as he walked to his townhouse on Asaph Street. It dominated his thoughts during his run to Dangerfield Island and back. Upon his return home, his mind settled a little when he saw Shannon's car parked outside.

"Buonasera," said Nick as he entered the townhouse, happy to see Shannon. The greeting in Italian just a way to be playful. They had been married for more than sixteen years now, and while he was very much still in love with her, he had grown more distant due to his disproportionate focus on work. Even though their time together was limited, Shannon did everything possible to keep their relationship from becoming stale with little details that at first Nick appreciated, but over time, took for granted. She would insert love notes in his pants or suit pockets for him to find and also surprise him with special dinners at home on nights when she knew he would be stressed, extending the behavior that couples typically engage in when they start dating. At home, it was just the two of them;

they had not been able to have children and early on decided it was not a high priority for either one to consider adopting. Once Shannon started to regret that decision, she felt it was too risky as her biological clock was winding down.

She responded, "Salve, sera. I noticed your stuff was already here. What a pleasant surprise! How was your meeting in the city?" It was a very rare occasion that Nick would be in town working, and an added bonus for her that he would get home early.

"It was an interesting day, in many ways. By the way, it was not a meeting. It was a luncheon for a few IT executives from Fed agencies...I made a presentation about BI in Public Sector. It was good. How did it go with you?"

"Great. My meeting finished early, so I did research on computers. The new 27-inch iMac is amazing, but I wanted to ask what you thought before buying it," hoping that Nick would volunteer to go with her to the store that night and help her pick one out. Maybe a spontaneous dinner afterward?

Nick walked over, kissed Shannon, then said, "Sorry...a little sweaty. If you like it, go for it." He then paused, realizing he had missed the big story of the day. "By the way, I guess you've seen what happened in Boston, at the marathon..."

Shannon answered, "Oh my god, yes, so sad! Several deaths, including a little boy that was there to see his mom running. Just evil, horrible!"

"I cannot even imagine what it must feel like to the parents. I just hope we never find ourselves anywhere near monsters like those. I am tired of that whole situation with these radicals. Just frustrated that they can't be stopped. Anyway, I'm gonna shower, return a couple of phone calls, and catch up on email. It was good to have most of the afternoon off, but now I have to pay for that." With that, Nick left, and eventually disappeared into his home office.

To Shannon's disappointment, this was the third time in the

last two months that Nick had chosen to re-immerse himself in work on a rare weeknight that he was in town. The last time had been a few weeks earlier when he called from the office to say he would be late, and she had bought theater tickets for a surprise date that night.

5

THE SALEH FAMILY

June 17, 2014, al-Eizariyah

Ghassan was more than an hour late in arriving at his sister's apartment to pick up his daughter, Fatma. He was working on a construction project near the Old City of Jerusalem, and even with his permit, the barrier checkpoints had delayed his commute. Ghassan liked working on those projects because they paid well and on time, but they always translated into less time at home. They also piled on more stress on his sister Reema, who would take care of Fatma, now a teenager, after she came back from school in the afternoons.

Reema lived with her husband Omar, and Ali, their son, in a small apartment on the outskirts of al-Eizariyah, approximately a fifteen-minute walk from Ghassan's apartment. Omar was a tour bus driver and oftentimes would be gone for several days traveling the country. Ali was three years Fatma's junior and had grown up as a little brother to her. Their routine on weekdays after school was to do homework, and if there was enough time before Ghassan arrived, they would play in an empty field nearby, draw, or help Reema with house chores.

During the last year, Fatma's interests changed, so Reema could not rely as much on her to keep Ali busy and entertained. Fatma's focus was shifting, and she was starting to show a curiosity to understand the world at a different level than what she was being taught in school. Even though she had never traveled outside of Palestine, she was fascinated by what she read about Europe, and in particular, the birthplace of her parents and Aunt Reema – England. She was used to seeing the tourists visit the Tomb of Lazarus in her hometown, noticed how they dressed and looked different than the locals, and always wondered what it would be like where they lived.

"Afternoon, Ree. Sorry I'm late. The bloody checkpoint... ugh, it was bad today," said Ghassan as he walked in for a quick greeting before heading home with Fatma.

"Hi, Ghassan," said Reema, and getting closer to him so she would not be overheard, "We need to talk. It's not a bad thing, but you need to know. Fatma is growing and maturing...fast! She is asking tough questions now. Wants to know more about the rest of the world. How was it for us living in the UK? Women things," and looking at Ghassan with eyes wide open, "yes, that! She needs a mum, Ghassan!"

"Oh, brilliant!" Ghassan rolled his eyes and mildly shook his head. He then whispered, "It's too late for that, Ree. The time to do it was after Layla died, but...you know how my mind was back then." He shook his head again – a combination of frustration from having to explain and disappointment for having been so stubborn in the past. The stubbornness still carried on, as he was convinced that the window had already closed. "It is...what it is. How's Ali?" to quickly change the subject.

Ghassan and Reema, as well as his late wife Layla, were of Palestinian descent, but were born and raised in East London. After Ghassan and Layla married in 1994, they decided to follow several family members who had moved back to their home country as many did after the 1993 Oslo Accord. During that time programs were implemented to unify families in Gaza and the West Bank, and this provided a path for them to return. Many came with high expectations of living in peaceful coexistence with Israelis and contributing to building their homeland, but the peace and expectations were short lived, with the region spiraling down into a tenser and more segregated environment during the next few years.

Ghassan did not have strong opinions about the political situation, other than it was extremely inconvenient and unfortunate, and both sides were to blame. He generally conformed with the expected behaviors of a Muslim, though quiet and reserved about his faith. He was more open-minded about other beliefs than the average Palestinian. That worldview was shaped by his experience growing up, even though it was in ghettoish East London, but also from the mystical experience that he had the day Fatma was born and Layla died. There was a very specific command he had received from the Christian Virgin to raise Fatma in Palestine, and that was the primary reason he had decided not to go back to the UK. This was in spite of his belief that Fatma would have had much better opportunities in terms of education, and eventually work and being surrounded by a healthier environment. At least there, there were no barriers and checkpoints between East London and Mayfair!

Ghassan's time in the UK also exposed him to different opportunities and Western values, including individual responsibility and the importance of an education. For him it had paid off, as he went to a technical institute and became an electrician, a skill translated into a humble, yet stable life in Palestine. Ghassan had always wanted Fatma to have the same opportunity, but go farther than him, and that became an area of focus for her in her early years and up to this stage. She was smart and a great student who would devour books and anything she could get her hands on.

As they were about to leave, Fatma noticed the newspaper on the dining table. It was a printed copy of the prior day's issue of *The Guardian*, which Reema would occasionally get in the mornings if she happened to go shopping in Bethlehem. It was one way to stay connected to the place of her childhood.

"Aunt Reema, are you still reading the paper?"

"No, luv. You can take it with you. I was about to throw it away."

Ghassan then stepped in, "Fatma, there are better things to read than that garbage," and with that, they left.

Fatma had been particularly struck by one of the headlines, which read *The Terrifying Rise of Isis...*, and she had a solution to the problem of not being able to take the newspaper home. Ghassan had gifted her a smartphone for her thirteenth birthday, and all she needed to do was look it up online once she got home.

6

A TIME TO CELEBRATE?

J une 28, 2016, Tyson's Corner, Virginia
"Hey, Nick, have a minute?" said a highly energized Rich Bullock, as he peeked into Nick's office. Rich was in his early sixties, standing at a lanky six-foot-four. He had a growing bald spot, so his hairdo was a zero clipper throughout, which just left a shadow where hair was still grow-ing. Today he was wearing golf slacks and shirt, evidence that he had likely played a round earlier in the day as his tan was fresh. He was also about to retire as CEO of Macro Insights, planning to stay on as Executive Chairman of the Board. He did not wait for permission, or even an acknowledgment to enter Nick's office. Rich simply walked in, slid closed the glass door behind him, and sat down on one of the two chairs in front of Nick's desk. He leaned on the back rest and crossed his legs, a sign he was comfortable and in charge.

Nick was caught a little off-guard, as he was getting ready for the daily sales forecast conference call with his team, starting in a few minutes. They were two days away from the close of the second quarter, and this was always a time of high drama, as a big chunk of the quarterly sales historically closed during those last few days. It took Nick a split second to turn away his attention from the computer screen, then he spun to his left and responded, "Rich...sure. What's up?"

"Two things...shot a seventy-one at Westwood...thought you'd wanna know that. And two...I just wrapped up a quick call with the Board." He paused for effect and opened his eyes wide as he said, "I wanted you to be the first to know that the promotion has been approved. Everyone supported it enthusiastically...well, with the exception of Chip. He asked me to tell you that along with the promotion, I should deliver a bit of coaching. His words: 'Tell him not to be an asshole with Blake and Anand, now that they work for him.' Fair point. Be nice with your former peers, particularly those two. Anyway... Congratulations, Nick! You are our new CEO!"

Nick, who had been expecting this conversation might take place sometime in July, could not hide his excitement. "Wow! This moved fast!" After looking his boss in the eye, said, "Thank you, Rich! You went to bat for me, and I...wow, I really appreciate it. I won't let you down."

"It was well deserved, Nick," said Rich as he started to get up, "HR is working on the Ts and Cs of the offer letter and the exec agreement and should have something for you soon."

Nick also got up and went around his desk to shake Rick's hand. "Thank you. This means a lot." After they shook hands, he asked, "What's the latest with Project Napa?" This was the code name of the acquisition of one of Macro Insight's emerging competitors, a startup called Neural, based in San Francisco.

"I need to catch you up with that. I'd just been waiting until you were done with Q2, but real quick...due diligence is almost done, so moving fast, and nothing of consequence so far, so it looks like it'll happen. We'll probably be announcing it during the analyst call in three weeks. In an ideal world, you would not be having to deal with an integration as you step into the role, but that's our gig. You wanted to be CEO? You know what they say...be careful what you wish for!"

"Got it. I think this might be the one that finally gets me to move to the Bay Area. There will be a lot going on with the integration, and this is our chance to establish a strategic presence in the Valley. I'll need to be there."

"Think it through. You can also do it from here...with a fair amount of travel. Does Shannon even know you are considering this?"

Nick responded without hesitation, "Shannon will be fine with it."

"Cool," and with that, Rich patted Nick on the shoulder and turned toward the sliding door. On his way out, he said, "Good luck with the quarter. No pressure," and with that, he left.

Nick left the office a few minutes after the conference call, during which he paid very little attention, mostly thinking about this milestone in his career. His excitement was hard to contain, but he could not mention it to anyone other than Shannon. All that came across during the conference call was Nick in a very good mood, which surprised his team, given that he was famous for grilling people during the call, especially if they were delivering bad news.

The drive home took a long time, as beltway traffic was at its peak. This gave him time to think about changes he would make once he took over as CEO, and in his mind, confirmed the decision to move to the Bay Area. Shannon will get used to it, he thought, and establishing himself as a Silicon Valley player would be great for his career, for them.

Upon arrival at the townhouse, he found Shannon in the kitchen, still wearing her yoga outfit, researching online how to make a classic caponata, which was part of her dinner menu for tomorrow.

"Hey, you're early! Things must be going smoothly with the close."

Nick dropped his briefcase, walked over to her, and planted a kiss on her forehead before briefly hugging her. "I got the promotion!"

"Oh baby," and she hugged him back. Shannon was happy for him, but deep down was anxious about the potential for even less time at home and more stress. She thought there was no need for it from a financial perspective, and at this stage in their lives it was more important to her that they spend time together than to pad their already healthy reserves. "This is awesome! I thought this wasn't happening until... July?"

"Well, it's a done deal. Confidential for the next three weeks, but very real." He started walking toward the bar, and said, "I need a drink. Do you want something? White wine? Red? Any other color? Bubbles?" Nick was excited and wanted to celebrate this milestone with Shannon, but also trying to soften the message about moving. He needed to sell it to her in a way she would be as excited as he was.

"White. There's an open bottle of Rombauer in the fridge."

As he grabbed a tumbler glass for his scotch and a wine glass for her, he said, "There's something else I think you're going to be excited about. I know I am! You know that we are about to pull the trigger on Neural, and two of the execs in my new team are in Palo Alto anyway, so..."

"Nick," interrupted Shannon with a soft, yet assertive tone, and waiting for him to look at her in the eye, said, "does this promotion mean we have to relo–?"

"Babe, it's the Bay Area! We could move to San Francisco if you'd rather be in the city, or even Los Gatos. That's where the Kumars live..."

"So...I don't think you understand." Shannon cut him off again, this time her demeanor was more of disappointment and sadness. "Is it a done deal? Did you tell them, did you tell Rich that you would discuss with me?"

"Babe, you're processing this the wrong way. This is what's best for my career, for us..."

"Uhm, no...it isn't. It sucks for me, and in the long run, this will not be a good thing for you." She paused, slowly nodded as she closed her eyes. "I've been fearing this moment, but saw it coming. It's not so much about the move. You know I'll go anywhere with you. No...this is about how you have allowed all this that is happening at work pull you farther away from me. We don't do anything fun anymore, Nick. We live in DC where there's a ton of things to do and we don't do anything, not really. We seldom talk. You're rarely here, and when you are...physically...you're in your own world." Her eyes welled up with tears, then she had one last comment, "You don't see it. Do you?"

Nick remained quiet. In his selfishness, his initial reaction was actually one of disappointment in Shannon for not being more *supportive*. He thought it was her who was being selfish and ungrateful, after all the long hours and sacrifices he had made to get to this point.

Shannon broke the silence, "So, that's it? You have nothing to say?"

"I don't think there's anything I can say now to make you feel better. I came here with what I thought would be good news for you, and...ah, forget it. We'll pick this up when our heads are cooler."

"Fine, Nick. The problem isn't going away, but okay, we don't have to talk about it now." Shannon would have much rather had the conversation in that moment, but Nick's dodge made her give up. "I'm gonna take a shower, and...ugh, I'm not even hungry. Do you want something?"

"No, I'm good. I'll just reheat some leftover pizza later," and with that, he poured himself a glass of Balvenie, picked up his briefcase, and went into hiding in his home office. Nick and Shannon rarely fought, and while there was no screaming or high drama this time, both knew this was their first real fight in years and a there was not much clarity as to how this issue would get resolved.

After two hours of responding to emails and reviewing the daily sales stats, Nick's attention shifted back to what had just happened at home. He replayed some of the soundbites he had heard since that afternoon: Chip Selas, one of the Directors of the Board, sending him a message about *not being an asshole;* Rich telling him to *be nice*; Shannon venting her pent-up frustration about him being distant in the relationship. He also replayed recent interactions he had had with his team and how he had yelled at one of his VPs the prior day, doing it for effect in front of his staff. This had become customary for him. His downward progression had been gradual, but steady, and during the last few years he had become a person he didn't want to be. A guy other people didn't like, someone he didn't like! He had become someone that even his wife, the love of his life, felt uncomfortable opening up to, about the way she saw the relationship falling apart.

Reflecting on that, combined with the three glasses of scotch he had drank, opened the door to the tormenting thoughts he had so effectively blocked during most of his adult life, particularly when things were going well. All the questions about existence, time, and the eternal loss of consciousness were back and cycling at full speed through his mind! In a moment of despair, he got up from his desk chair and paced around the office to try to shake them off, and realizing he was starting to panic and needed more space, decided to go outside for a walk.

As Nick stepped down the entrance stairs of the townhouse, he was so self-consumed in his torment that he simply walked away without a plan or particular direction. He walked up Asaph Street, then turned right on Duke, walking at a brisk pace toward the river. It was just before nine o'clock and the sun had just set, still allowing the twilight coming from the west to shine on the buildings in front of him. Breathing the outside air gave him temporary relief, as he started to become more aware of his surroundings and the beauty of the Georgian and Victorian architecture styles in the Old Town, something he had never stopped to appreciate, yet was always around him. As he neared Royal Street, he saw the belfry towers of the Basilica of Saint Mary to his right, and for some reason kept staring at them and the façade as he continued walking. He started to cross the street, when at the last second, caught a glimpse of a black Suburban coming from his left. Nick reacted quickly and was able to stop before it hit him, but still lost his balance and fell, his head passing within a few inches of the rear tire of the moving car. The SUV kept going, the driver oblivious to the near miss. After the initial shock, Nick's reaction was anger. He kicked himself for allowing this episode to unfold, losing control to the point of missing a perfectly visible car moving in his direction. He was also furious at the distraction the Basilica introduced. He thought, "How ironic that focusing on a church building could have killed me! It is just an empty building! Why is it that people want to project their fantasies and imagination on something that is just not real, that isn't really holy or blessed? Damn! This is where Shannon spends all this time. For what?"

As he was fumed and recovered from the shock of almost being run over, and while still lying on the pavement, Nick took quick inventory of his body to ensure he had not been hurt. That is when he felt a presence behind him grabbing his right arm and sliding their hand around his left ribcage. Nick looked to his right and saw a man of olive complexion, Mediterranean features, likely in his early thirties, wearing a dirty dark gray long-sleeved shirt and black jeans with no shoes. His straight black hair was pulled back, tied on a ponytail, and looked like it had not been washed in weeks. As he pulled Nick up to a standing position, he said with a strong Middle Eastern accent,

"You good, sir? Gotta get outside that mind o' yours and see what's 'round you. Somebody got a second chance!"

Once Nick was on his feet and released from the man's hold, he turned around and responded, "Thank you, my friend! Man, this is embarrassing!" He then bent down to pat his slacks to remove the street dust and ensure he had not dropped anything on the street when he fell.

"Don't forget what the man said...*Go back to your roots. Let your curiosity guide you...*"

Nick couldn't believe what he was hearing! He stood back up, turning back toward the man, cutting him off, "How do you know...?" but quickly realized he was talking to himself. The stranger was gone!

7

FIGHTING BACK

Nick was back in the townhouse in what felt like ten seconds. On the way there, he felt fear and excitement. The entire experience of that night, including the tense conversation with Shannon and the fateful encounter outside the Basilica, had him wondering what the hell was going on in his life. His priorities and overall belief system had been turned upside down in just a few hours, and he returned home on a mission to find answers.

He rushed to his bedroom and quietly opened the door to find that the lights had been turned off and Shannon had fallen asleep. "Wow! That's early for her!" he thought. He wanted to apologize and tell her about the experience of the last hour. For a split second, he thought about waking her up, but decided it was best to catch her before going to work in the morning.

He walked back to his home office, fired up his notebook and opened his Chrome browser, not sure what to look for. The first words that crossed his mind were *fear* and *afraid*. Maybe there were methods to cope with his torment that either professionals or people having similar experiences would have shared online. To his initial disappointment, seven of the top ten results pointed to bible scripture, until one caught his eye. It was about the devil and talked about how the Virgin Mary is an incredibly powerful entity. Aside from God, the one that the devil hates and fears the most.

Nick thought, "I am about to immerse myself in the myth and superstition that I have been so critical of since my college years. How can there be so many people out there that really believe in this stuff, even smart and otherwise educated people, like Ewan?" Even with that initial reaction, he went on to read, and a thought started to emerge in his mind – *maybe there is indeed a spiritual world out there. Maybe someone has been trying to communicate with me, and that could hold the answer to regaining peace in my life.* He went straight to amazon.com and ordered five e-books: *How to Know God* by Deepak Chopra; *The Afterlife Experiments* by Gary Schwartz and William Simon; *Awareness* and *Sadhana – A Way to God*, both by Anthony De Mello; and *The Power of Now* by Eckhart Tolle.

Nick was reaching for anything he could learn, and ironically enough, did not pursue anything that was sourced by the Catholic Church of his childhood. The same church that Shannon was fully committed to and involved with. For reasons he did not even consider, he rejected those teachings and looked down upon them as if they were based on ignorance, superstition, and a scheme invented by powerful and rich people in the Vatican to continue enriching themselves at the expense of their blind followers.

In the quick research he did before ordering the books, he learned that De Mello, although a Jesuit priest and therefore Catholic, was heavily influenced by Eastern beliefs he learned in his birthplace, India. Nick found comfort in learning that someone from within had successfully challenged Catholic teachings and had developed quite a following. He found excerpts online from De Mello's retreat conferences and thought they included valid ideas that he could relate to and agree with. So, Nick undertook this research of spirituality concepts in hopes of defusing the fears and dark thoughts that had been following him and were now resurfacing. For now, he would have to put down the books from Geoffrey Moore, Thomas Friedman, and Jim Collins he had been devouring up until that point, and switch from professional growth to personal and spiritual growth. Growth he hoped would eventually end his fears.

He first downloaded *The Power of Now* and was done with it before 3:00 am. It presented many interesting concepts about the importance of living in the present and how the past and future are not *real*. These were basic ideas he had never stopped to think about. There were even references to bible scripture as examples of how Jesus based many of his teachings on living fully in the present. He thought that connection was interesting but was surprised with it in a book whose tagline mentions *Spiritual Enlightenment*. It was a good start, but Nick did not find it satisfying enough. He then moved to Chopra and was halfway done with the book when he noticed light coming from the hallway. Shannon had turned on the bedroom light, and he walked over and found her getting ready for her morning walk.

"Good morning, Cookie!" said Nick, reverting back to the nickname he used to call her during the first few years of their marriage.

Shannon, who thought the greeting was a little forced, considering how things had ended last night, turned her gaze toward him. She noticed he was wearing the same clothes as last night, had his sleeves rolled up, and scratches with dried blood on his left forearm. Approaching him, and with a tone of concern, she said, "Morning. You never came to bed last night. Are you OK?"

"Yes, I am. It was self-inflicted...the *not coming to bed* thing. I came to the room a little after nine, but you were already knocked out. Are you going for a walk?"

"Yep, a short one, while it's still cool outside."

"OK, I'll go. Let me change real quick," said Nick, as he quickly brushed his teeth and put on a T-shirt with running shorts and sneakers.

Shannon was mostly quiet as Nick got ready, and later, as they walked out of the townhouse at a steady pace. She pulled up her iPhone to check her calendar and confirmed that her first meeting was a Skype call at nine. When done, she put away the phone and asked, "So, apparently you had eventful night. What happened?"

"A lot. When I went to the room, it was to apologize, for last night...and I guess for the way I've been, which I guess has been a long time. I'm sorry!"

"OK, yes. Forgiven, but...what's really going on? I think, uhm...I think you've lost your focus. I get the career thing, but you are smart enough to strike a balance. There is no balance. I've been wanting to have this conversation for months, but I didn't sense you would be open to it...there has always been something else going on. It is true that we don't do much of anything anymore..."

Nick softly cut her off, "Shannon...you're right. I'm sorry. To me it has been more than the last few months. I have obsessed about the CEO thing for years now, and in the process, have drifted away from you, my friends at work, Ewan...I haven't talked to him since New Year's. There are things I have to work through, including being more transparent with you. Well, to start with, doing more of this. Just...talk."

"Uhum...I'm listening."

"The first thing I want to say is that I'll figure out a way to deal with the Bay Area situation. Let's stay here, and maybe you can come with me on some of the trips. We could make it a fun thing.

Maybe even get a condo in the city. But...I get that moving would not be a great idea. I'm good with that. I should've talked to you about it before. I guess the excitement got the best of me. I'm sorry."

"Thank you. I don't want to add stress or more travel. It's just that most of my life is here. My friends, clients, the church...and we are much closer to my parents in South Carolina. I only know people from your team on the West Coast, and you know I think they're all weird. Anyway, I'll sign up for the trips. Let's just start with hotel stays and we'll see how that goes."

"That sounds perfect." Nick gave his wife a genuine smile. "So, the other thing is... a little harder to talk about." He took a deep breath, swallowed hard, then said, "I envy your faith. I just...don't have it, not the same way. Since I was a child, I've had all kinds of weird thoughts and questions about life issues, about who we are and what we are doing here. I obsessed about things like the passage of time...still do. Anyway, all of that made me question what I learned about God and religion. By the time I was in college, my faith was gone. I kept going to church occasionally, but it was just out of habit, custom. It's hard to explain. I wanted to believe..." Nick tried to continue, opened his mouth, but then started to slowly shake his head, took another deep breath and remained pensive, as if the battle was brewing inside his mind and he felt trapped in it.

"Nick, I knew you were struggling with your faith. Trust me, I've been praying for that. But why didn't you tell me about this torment before? You have been battling with it from even before we met? And you've never asked for help. Oh my God!"

"It's complicated, Cookie. I've been able to push all that to the side, and most of the time it didn't bother me. I found a way to cope. I also didn't want to contaminate you with all that garbage...just saw it as a very negative thing, not worth talking about, especially with you. But now that I'm saying it out loud, I know I should have talked about it with you, so, again, I'm sorry. And now, I feel like I need to deal with it. I *will* deal with it, but I am convinced that is a big reason I've been such a jerk. I guess it happened so gradually that I didn't notice it, but last night I had this eureka moment where it felt like a mirror was put in front of me, and...I didn't like who I saw."

Nick felt short of mentioning anything about the stranger that helped him up near the Basilica, nor the episode from fifteen years ago on the flight from San Francisco. He needed to develop a better understanding and explanation for those before opening up. It was still too early to consider the real possibility that those events were anything more than coincidence, or a misfiring of neurons.

8

A NARROW SLIVER OF TRUTH

September 19, 2020 Chesapeake Bay, just East of Annapolis, MD

The wind blew from the northeast at twelve knots on a cool day with scattered clouds on Chesapeake Bay. Ewan had invited Nick sailing on his thirty-five-foot Catalina sloop, something that had become their getaway every few months, provided the weather cooperated.

"Nick, can you untangle the port-side jib sheet? It's stuck on the railings. It's keeping the jib from swinging all the way to starboard," yelled Ewan from the helm, as they went to a port tack, clearing Spa Creek Inlet and turning into beautiful Chesapeake Bay.

"Yes, capt'n!" responded Nick, who was an experienced sailor himself, and always found it amusing that Ewan invited him to go sailing so he could do all the work around the boat while he barked commands from his seat at the helm.

"Thank you. We can stay on this tack all the way to the southern tip of Kent Island, so I'm gonna leave it on autopilot. Can you keep an eye on the traffic? I'm grabbing a couple o' beers. Sam Adams?"

"That would be great," responded Nick as he crawled back to the helm area and sat on the port stern rail seat.

A few seconds later, Ewan surfaced from the cave-like saloon double-fisting the two beers and handing one to Nick. He then sat at the helm and said, "So, you are really going through with this retirement thing at the end of the year, eh?"

"Sabbatical. Don't want to call it retirement. That sounds too...permanent."

"And, why? Burnout?"

"I guess there's some element of that, yeah. Hmmm, but there's other things I'd like to do with my time. Travel, but on vacation, which is different than for work. The trip we made to Mexico City last year with you and Denise was the first time I visited for fun after being there more than twenty times in the last...whatever, ten years. The experience was totally different. I want to do more of that, spend more time with Shannon."

"I can see that...but Shannon may not be ready for all this time spent together. She'll need her space..."

"Yeah, yeah, but there's other reasons. For example, once I leave, it will create movement in the organization. You know, opportunity for people in my team to either be considered for CEO, or at least a different role in the leadership team. There will be a trickle effect in their own teams, and so on...The truth is I have been blessed with an amazing team, and..."

"Wow! That doesn't sound like the Nick from seven years ago! I mean, back then you were less about them and more about Nicolás, no? You were pretty driven."

"Ha! Still driven. Just not as selfish and foolish as back then. Well, still foolish. Ha, ha!" He took a sip of the beer, and then said while nodding, "Yes, I've grown."

"So, you went dark for about two years. I kept calling and leaving voice mails, and the few times you would call back, you seemed distant and for sure, too busy to talk. Then I read about your promotion to CEO, and it took at least a year before we had a real conversation. You had changed. I loved the old Nick, but this Nick 2.0 is more lovable." Ewan looked at Nick in the eye and smirked. "You haven't said much about what happened. Maybe Shannon's magic finally had an influence on you? She's special."

"Very!" said Nick while looking into the distance and taking in the miracle of being on a seven-ton boat gliding over the water. No engine noise, no diesel or gasoline smell, just Chesapeake Bay, blue sky, and a human invention collaborating with God's nature to make it move effortlessly. That is why he loved sailing so much. It was simply a spiritual experience. Then, in response to the question, "Shannon was definitely the catalyst. In a subtle way, and with lots of persistence, she helped make me aware of what I had become. She pointed me to the *what*, then I figured out the *why*...the root cause, and what to do about it. The *what* was clear – I had gradually become a selfish asshole."

"Hmmm. No bragging...please. What was the *why*?"

"The *why*. Well, to use a boating analogy, my compass was pointing in the wrong direction...and there was no GPS. Ha, ha!" Nick smiled at his own poor joke, likely a sign of nervousness as Ewan was pushing him into uncomfortable territory. After a couple of seconds organizing his thoughts, said, "It's interesting, but since I met you, I knew there had to be something wrong in where I was pointing. Someone with your level of schooling and smarts doesn't just believe in things unless there are good reasons for it. You probably thought I was hopeless...certainly stubborn as hell. But through those conversations, which sometimes turned contentious, you planted a seed."

Ewan started laughing out loud, and said, "If you think by being nice, I am going to stop trying to talk some sense into you, you're mistaken. But I do appreciate the kind words. It's hard for me to stay quiet about these things, or anything else, but it is good to hear that something good came out of it...eventually. So, back to the compass thing...pointing in the wrong direction."

"Ewan, I had pushed God out. I think it is as simple as that."

"Was God ever inside?" asked Ewan, emphasizing the last word and challenging him to go deeper.

"Hmmm...It was the God of Catholic elementary school and of practicing parents that were a great example, but I probably never allowed Him...never invited Him in."

"Yep, I think sometimes conversion is easier for non-believers than someone that grew up in it and then left. Funny how that works. So, would you say that you have fixed that? Still fixing?"

"Still fixing...for sure. But the process alone has made a huge difference."

"Well, we have at least an hour before our tack to return. I'd love to hear about the process. But first, can you get the beers this time?"

After Nick came back from fetching their second round, he sat at the port side cockpit bench facing the main sail, stretched his legs and leaned back, then started, "You know, I probably used the wrong words when I told you I had *pushed God out*. There's a difference between pushing God out and no longer believing there is a God. I did both...in sequence, by the time I got to college. But fast forwarding to five years ago, because during the time in between I had made zero progress along that journey...I didn't even know that was a journey I needed to be on."

"Gotcha."

Nick continued, "I had a bit of a collapse just as I was getting the promotion...funny, at a moment of celebration. But the consequence of this lack of belief and lack of willingness to embark on the *journey*, finally hit me...hard."

"So that was bottom for you? Probably the start of something important, no?" asked Ewan.

"Exactly. I had a moment of clarity. Shannon helped, but I also had a weird experience with this funny-talking homeless guy...a topic for the next time we sail. Anyway, that moment drove me to learn more. Initially I was a little scattershot in my approach, but eventually I converged on things that resonated with me as true."

Nick continued, "Sorry, it's hard to organize the thoughts in my mind and the progression I went through, but if I had to summarize it, it goes like this...first, I became convinced that there is a higher intelligence. I'd like to think it was *through reason*, as apologists say. Tons of scientific evidence points to that. Also, philosophical thought, theory, whatever you guys call it. I prefer the scientific stuff. There's a lot of good material," and listing several items by grabbing his fingers in sequence, Nick continued, "one: the concept of irreducible complexity; two: the DNA molecule; three: ordered evolution. Yes, evolution, in spite of the fact that this is used as an argument against God."

"Funny, I've always thought the same," said Ewan. "I find it to be much more evidence for God than Naturism or other theories explaining the forces behind evolution."

"Yeah. The Cambrian Explosion is another one. I've lost track of my counting...but, there is also the start of time, space and matter, Big Bang and so on. Have you even thought about the beauty and simplicity of the periodic table?"

"Not for a millisecond," said Ewan jokingly as he looked under the boom to ensure there were no boats to their starboard side. "What is beautiful about the periodic table? It's just a bunch of tiles with letters and numbers...and no one knows what they mean unless they are a geek like you."

"Indeed. I guess you have to be nerdy and into chemistry to understand the meaning of the different columns, the fact that elements as different as nitrogen and aluminum are made of the same building blocks, just a different number of them. Yet, they are as different as the air around us and the mast on this boat. There is a mathematical pattern to it that makes it seem... not random. What's the word I'm looking for? Uhm...*designed*. DNA is even more complicated, but a similar concept. Doesn't that blow your mind? There's just no way those two happened by chance."

"It does not blow my mind, but I get your point..."

"I mean, I could go on, but those are compelling examples... at least for people like me. OK, the philosophical stuff may be closer to your domain, but I did learn a few things in my readings. The concepts of meaning, the soul, and causation are also very compelling arguments. So, this concept of a higher intelligence, which now I believe is real, is what's otherwise called *God*."

Ewan said, "So, that was probably the biggest leap, no? To conclude there is a God. Everything hinges on the God question, doesn't it?"

"Yeah, for the mind, the intellect. But to me that was the foundation. There's so much more once you make the leap and land in that...*awareness*! Kind of like Super Mario. Have you ever played? Ugh, never mind..."

"Super Mario. Yes, big fan. I've slayed the real Bowser countless times..."

"Are you fucking kidding? That's my game! Wow, you are that good at it? I'd love some tips about getting to the eighth world and Bowser. Never made it that far..."

"Cool. This old guy will give you tips someday, don't worry. We have an excuse to go sailing at least two more times before the season ends. Keep going, but stay away from chemistry, or Mario, or Luigi..."

"So, the next step for me was to understand why, what was the motivation of this higher intelligence to create the physical world, leading up to life, eventually human life. That brought me back to the philosophy space...reluctantly. Science is good at answering *what* and *how* questions, but not *whys*. I read a lot about it, and all signs point to something as simple, but also as rich as...*love*. I don't think we can fully understand while here on Earth, but I am now convinced that there is a God that has been trying to communicate and establish a relationship with us. He wants that connection to be outside of time, or...eternal. We must play a part, though, and be willing to listen and learn. By the way, does any of this jive with what you learned in seminary, or am I off?"

"No, this is good. A lot of what I studied and what I teach today is about the *why*. What motivates people to do certain things, etc. So, yeah, yeah, you're spot on."

"Well, thanks. That's good validation! So, there was also a progression in my understanding of how God wants to relate to and communicate with us, and how we are wired for that, the embedded moral code, yada-yada-yada. Then, I got to the most difficult step I had to take...in my heart – to take all this knowledge that I am comfortable with and reconcile it with religion, with religious teachings that I am way less comfortable with. The historical evidence seems to point to Judaism and Christianity as having messages, teachings that resonate better with what our embedded code tells us. Christianity is a continuation and fulfillment of Judaism and also universal. Wherever it has been preached, the message resonates. It even resonates in places where you can be persecuted for being a believer."

"You went full circle, then? Back to your roots to being a Christian again?"

The *back to your roots* thing again, but Nick was not ready to get into that now. He responded, "Yeah, a different kind of Christian, though. I have a much better understanding now, a better foundation. By the way, faith is not for the lazy! I mean, it is there to be found, but it took that initial push, and then, a lot of effort and persistence to build that foundation of belief. I guess that was the case for me, but I recognize other people get there from a different angle. Along the way, I read a lot of weird stuff. Some of it pointed to the truth, some of it was just... strange. The last thing I'll say is that I am far from done, far from *fixed*, as you said. Most of the growth has been at an intellectual level. That is important to me, because that is how I'm wired – engineer, analytical, skeptical, whatever – but I don't have that inner relationship that you and Shannon have with God. I'm still looking for that, and it's not going to be found in a book. For now, I'm trying to let my actions and values reflect what I've learned, but I know I am missing that other component."

"Hmmm. Understood. Maybe the sabbatical will give you more time for that. It can be hard when you are going at a hundred miles an hour for that connection to be established. You need some quiet time for that. Who knows, maybe you have been invited, and for some reason, were not receptive to it. It happens a lot."

This last comment resulted in a bit of an epiphany for Nick. He immediately remembered his experience on the plane and church. "You know what, Ewan? I bet that has happened to me, and I didn't know how to respond. Actually, I didn't want to respond..."

"No worries. Keep seeking."

"I am, desperately, but I have to say I am much happier where I am today. When the time comes for that next step, I'll be ready."

9

DOUBT

September 27, 2021

"Medium latte, please." asked Fatma at the counter of the Rio Café on the campus of Al-Quds University.

Fatma had just arrived on campus for her two afternoon classes and stopped at the café to prepare for them. After paying, she moved to the end of the counter as she quickly scanned the room for any familiar faces.

As she waited, in came Jenny Campbell, a visiting professor in the Engineering Faculty, for a cup of coffee during her break before Statics and Dynamics class. At twenty-nine, Jenny was the youngest professor in the school. She had short brown hair, a fair complexion, and green eyes. Her features, combined with the business-like attire she wore in school, made her stand out as a nonlocal.

Fatma, who had never seen her before, noticed that she did not look like a local and focused on the small olive wood crucifix hanging from Jenny's necklace. "That's pretty." said Fatma in English, guessing that would be the most likely language the lady spoke.

"Oh, thank you. Very kind of you. It was made by a local

artist near Bethlehem." responded Jenny, who was distracted by trying to build a *to do* list in her mind to organize the limited time she had during the break. Jenny did not think much of the interaction, other than feel a little surprised about a local initiating a conversation with her, something she had not experienced very often in that area.

The Rio Café gave an element of normalcy to the college campus. Abu Dis, a village in Israel's West Bank is located within a few kilometers of the Old City of Jerusalem. While small in population, it was a place of significance in religious and political conflict dating back to the crusades. The opening of Al-Quds University in the mid-1980s started its more recent legacy as a center of culture, but also deep political tension. The University had become a breeding ground for Palestinian nationalism and radicalism, and these movements were palpable in the form of demonstrations and an increased presence of Israeli security forces. The combination resulted in detentions and arrests of students and other radical elements involved in them, as well as occasional class cancelations and even evacuations from campus. The school and small town were a microcosm of the tension that existed in the region, which were magnified with its proximity to Jerusalem.

In that setting, which would paralyze the typical college student in Western countries, there were still elements of college life that felt normal to the thousands of students that attended, most of which were commuters focused on getting an education with the hope of improving their lives.

Fatma was born and grew up in al-Eizariyah, the Arabic name of the biblical town of Bethany, located just north of Abu Dis, also on the West Bank. The West Bank comprised the historical regions of Judea and Samaria. Just as with its neighboring Abu Dis, al-Eizariyah was still a relatively chaotic place, with occasional flareups between different Palestinian factions as well as with Israeli forces. The main local factions were

Fatah, which had controlled the government of the Palestinian State for many years, and Hamas, a militant Islamic organization that had grown in power and size in its thirty years of existence. Both groups harbored resentment against what they considered the Israeli occupation of Palestine, and in the case of Hamas, a commitment to the destruction of Israel. This was the environment where Fatma grew up, and this was her *normal*.

And so it was that Fatma, who had turned twenty this year, was now a third-year student at Al-Quds. In addition to regular academic challenges, she faced doubts about her faith, particularly contradictions about a message of love and the lack of it found in the jihadist movement and some elements of Sharia Law. Her innermost voice was asking her to be honest and follow the truth where it led her, but the inertia of her upbringing and a sense of loyalty to her heritage kept her from pursuing that. In Fatma's world, any deviation from Islamic faith was met with absolute intolerance, leading to alienation from her family and friends, all the way to putting her life in danger. Even in the face of these risks, Fatma had developed a deep sense of curiosity about life and questions of faith that she felt compelled to pursue.

On that day, Jenny was lucky to find a table near the back of the café where she could have some privacy. She set her coffee on the table, sat down, and reached into her backpack to pull out a folder full of tests and her class journal. She did not realize that, along with the folder, she lifted her pocket-sized new testament bible from inside the bag and it slid along the side of the bag to the floor. She went on to record the grade for each of the thirty-four students that had taken the test, and as she was finishing, realized that she only had ten minutes to get back for the class. She swept the tests back in the folder and put it away along with the journal as she was already getting up.

Fatma, who had been sitting at the next table doing homework and preparing for her Microbiology class, noticed Jenny walking out of the café, and realized that she had left a black leather-bound book on the floor. She picked it up and read the cover: *Holy Bible, King James Version.* Her initial reaction was to drop it, but then realized that this may bring even more complications, as someone else would eventually see it there. She picked it up, making sure no one around her was looking, and put it in her bag.

That night, after Fatma had finished washing dishes, she went back to her room to study. The fact that the bible was in her bag was very present in her mind, to the point where she felt guilty about bringing such propaganda into her home. Fatma had been raised in a region, that while part of the State of Israel, was predominantly Muslim and in some cases extreme in the teachings that children received in school and church. In addition to Islamic religious doctrine, their leaders had always been very vocal about the evils in Judaism and Christianity, who were seen not only as different and false faiths, but also its people as inferior to Muslims. They were deemed lesser beings that could not be trusted, and the Judeo-Christian religion was seen as the work of Satan. The message Fatma had grown up with at home was more nuanced, with Ghassan and Aunt Reema being open to the possibility of goodness in Jews and Christians. Ghassan had worked for Jews in West Jerusalem and also worked part time for the local Franciscan Missionaries as a handy man and on small projects. Fatma saw in Ghassan someone who did not condemn Jews and Christians the way all their neighbors did – and were indoctrinated to do – and she followed her father's example in having a more open mind.

Fatma's curiosity about the bible had the best of her, and instead of starting with her homework assignments, she pulled out the book and opened it. There, on the first page, she saw a handwritten name and telephone number – *Jennifer Campbell, +1.512.471.9283*, so she thought it was early enough to call the woman so they could arrange for the book to be returned. She was able to get through and they agreed to meet the following day at the Rio Café at 14:00.

With that open issue out of the way, Fatma grabbed the bible and started to put it away at the bottom of her backpack. Then quickly pulled it out to take a quick look at the table of contents, at least. On she went turning the pages to see what was in it. She knew enough to realize that the Old Testament was basically the Jewish tradition, with some references and characters that were in the first two books of the Quran, and that the New Testament was written about Jesus' life and teachings, covered in the third book of the Quran, the *Injil of Isa*. The start of the New Testament included four gospel books, each labeled based on the author. Thinking that maybe the four were written as a chronological sequence, Fatma went straight to the Gospel according to John to see how things would end. Starting with the Prologue, she quickly realized that John was not focused only on the end of Jesus' life, but started at the very beginning. *In the beginning was the Word, and the Word was with God, and the Word was God.* The simplicity and fulness of this short verse captivated her. She kept on reading all thirty-two pages, realizing along the way that she had might have grown up with many misconceptions about the message of Christianity, but more importantly, she developed a heightened sense of curiosity to learn more. That would have to wait though, since she had a busy night of homework ahead of her.

The next day, Jenny arrived on time and saw no signs of Fatma, so she ordered a cup of coffee and sat while she waited. After ten minutes, she saw Fatma running to the entrance of the café. She came in and immediately walked over to Jenny's table.

"Ms. Campbell, sorry I am late. The bus I normally take at this time was late by almost thirty minutes," she said.

"No worries. I know how public transportation can be."

"Yes, terrible sometimes. But here ...here is your book," said Fatma as she handed Jenny the bible.

"Thank you so much, Fatma! I am kind of embarrassed that I dropped it here...but, thank you so much for going through all the trouble of returning it!"

"Oh, it was no trouble at all."

"THANK YOU, that's very sweet. I'm still learning the local customs, so forgive me if this sounds offensive, but I assume that being seen with a Christian bible is not..."

"No, you are not offending me at all. You are right. It might have been awkward to be seen with the book, but still, not that big of a deal." She paused, then asked, "Do you teach here?"

"Yes, I'm a visiting professor, and honestly, this is my first teaching experience. I have a Master's in Computer Engineering, but after graduating, I went to work designing circuit boards for a hardware manufacturer. My experience is in industry, but I thought it would not be a big stretch to teach, and Al-Quds was looking for help in the Engineering faculty. So, long story short, I decided to do this to force a change, do something interesting in a place where I could also learn, and... I guess, give back. I just started this semester. What about you?"

"I grew up in a town nearby, al-Eizariyah, and commute from there. I guess you would call it Bethany. It is where the Tomb of Lazarus is located. Anyway, I am a third-year nursing student here at the school," said Fatma, as she gave a soft nod and a smile, then continued, "...and, I am applying for an internship at a hospital next semester. You know, to get real-life experience. I am excited about that!"

"That's great! It's a wonderful career. Best of luck with that. I hope you can go to the hospital you like best."

"Thanks. Well, I hope you enjoy the experience here. Do you plan to stay for a while?"

"I'm on contract through the end of the school year, but not sure how long I'll stay. I just heard from fellow faculty members, that it is very likely we will not get paid for the fore-seeable future. I...I'm not doing this for the money, but I still needed to cover my expenses as a minimum, and if we don't get paid, I will not be able to do this for too long."

Apparently, going for months without pay was not unusual at Al-Quds or other Palestinian universities, and it stemmed from disputes between the Palestinian Authority and Israel. Jenny was also concerned about the tension and incidents that were so common on campus, which at least once had resulted in classes being cancelled, and she had heard that in the past there had been a few occasions where the entire student body had to be evacuated. Fatma was familiar with those events, having lived through some herself, but to her this was the norm. She had never lived in or traveled to another country, so she did not have an appreciation for what the student experi-ence was like in universities in America, Europe, or elsewhere.

Jenny looked at her watch and realized that, as much as she was enjoying the conversation, she needed to get going. "Well, Fatma, I need to go. Do you mind if I save your contact informa-tion so we can keep in touch? I would love to continue our conversation."

10

AN UNHOLY ALLIANCE

Novemeber 29, 2021 *Amman, Jordan*

Hassan was the first one to arrive at the Starbucks on Queen Rania Street, across from the sprawling campus of the University of Jordan. He was there following what he considered to be cryptic instructions from senior Hamas leadership. Hassan was the leader of a radical group within Hamas who called themselves the Sumaya Martyrs. Even though his permanent home base was in the West Bank, he was currently living in and directing the operations of his organization from Amman to avoid being tracked by Israeli authorities constantly. During the last few years, the Jordanian government had secretly started to establish ties with Hamas, and as a result, he was able to live there under an alias as a Jordanian national. Under normal circumstances, he would have been the one deciding where and when to meet.

As he approached the entrance of the coffee shop, he thought he would not have chosen a place like this in front of a university campus for a meeting. It made him uncomfortable not to be in control of the situation, and on top of that, to potentially be seen in a public space. Hassan opened the door and went inside to quickly survey the café and order a tall hot tea. He saw two students sitting at the low counter to his left, apparently collaborating on a class project. He slowly shifted his gaze to the right, where a dark, slender man, potentially a professor at the school, was sitting at a table immersed in whatever was being displayed on his laptop. Hassan ordered and got his tea, walked outside and grabbed one of two empty tables under the covered walkway. There was no one else outside, or within twenty meters of him.

A few minutes later, at exactly 14:15, a man in his mid-to-late thirties, wearing black workout attire, an AC Milan training cap and oversized Ray-Ban pilot sunglasses, walked up to the table casually and asked, "Hassan?"

So much for remaining secret in a public area, Hassan thought. He looked at the man, trying to make eye contact through the shades, and discretely nodded in agreement.

The man then extended his hand and said in English, "I am K. Thank you for being on time." He then sat down, and almost immediately, the college professor that was sitting inside grabbed the third chair and joined them. It seemed to Hassan that the other two men knew each other and were relaxed, with no concern over who might see the three of them together. Each pulled up their chair so they could be as close as possible to the table.

Hassan had heard of K through his network, which included senior Hamas contacts. The word about him was that he represented an alliance of external entities that was very powerful, well-funded, and connected with a network of countries and international organizations that gave them global reach and influence. Unfortunately for Hassan, he knew very little about their long-term motivation and whether it was aligned with the current mission of the local radicals in Palestine. That made K a somewhat mysterious, but important figure who had recently become more active in

Hamas' activities. For now, he was seen as an ally, his elders asked him to trust him on this project, giving Hassan some reassurance.

Hassan was unaware that their ideas and worldview were as radical as the most fanatical members of Hamas and the Sumaya Martyrs, but for different reasons that had little to do with religious differences. Their driving force was more about social engineering as a means to consolidate power.

The awkward silence of the first few seconds was broken by K, who said gesturing to the third man, "This is one of my lieutenants, Ahmed, who is in charge of the operation we are planning and will be your primary contact." He paused, looked around to see if there was anybody near, then said, "Have you been briefed on our plans?"

"I was not told much. Just to meet now at this location about a project you are planning with Hamas elders. They said you may need the help of my team...and not to be concerned about you being foreigners. They said I could trust you. I hope that holds true." Hassan paused and looked at both in the eye for emphasis, then continued, "So... just assume I don't have much context. Also, let's keep this as brief as possible. Here, the walls have eyes, and I have no idea whether you, or your lieu... uhm, Ahmed, have been followed," expressing a little frustration about the venue and trying to assert some level of control.

"They also told us we could trust you. I think we all better hope that is true," responded K, taking away any sense of control Hassan might have felt. It was important to K from the onset to convey that he was in charge, and Hassan and his organization were there to follow his direction. He continued, "So, let's get to the point. My organization is supporting Hamas on a coordinated, low-level attack in a few months. It will involve multiple cells in different parts of the country. This will be the first, but the intent is to establish a *rolling-thunder* sequence of attacks during the remainder of the year..."

Hassan interrupted, "Rolling thunder? Why...what's behind all this?"

K responded, "We need to do something that is disruptive, not just annoying." The slight did not go unnoticed by Hassan. K continued, "The goal is to break Israeli public safety and defense to the point where we undermine the confidence of tourists. Tourism has become a major part of the economy here, and its growth has been fueled by a heightened sense of confidence in Israeli authorities keeping them safe. We want to put an end to that and establish that we are at war, and it will continue until Palestinians get full control of their land. There are other long-term goals, but for now, this is the background you should be aware of." K then turned and made a hand gesture toward Ahmed, cueing him up, "Now, pay close attention to what Ahmed has to say."

Ahmed then took over, speaking directly to Hassan, "I am very familiar with your organization and appreciate your sacrifice and the progress you are making." Ahmed was well aware that the Sumaya Martyrs, and to a lesser extent, Hamas, had struggled in recent years to access to funding and tactical assets on a consistent basis to conduct their activities. Consistency was critical for them to establish the type of traction that would drive the policy and behavior changes they wanted in the region. He continued, "Through our organization, we are providing funding, equipment, and the tactical plans for this project, but require your commitment to follow our direction. The blueprint for this attack has already been developed, but we need your assets on the ground to execute it."

Hassan simply nodded as Ahmed continued, "We plan to launch a series of attacks, starting with the shooting of one or more Israeli Defense soldiers inside East Jerusalem, followed by rocket attacks from Gaza. The Gaza attacks will be similar, but with more intensity and better weapons than have been used in the past. However, in the case of East Jerusalem, we want to make a statement that they are vulnerable even inside their barrier."

Hassan smirked and said, "You plan to strike IDF in East Jerusalem, inside the barrier. Is it a suicide mission? Is that why you have come to me? We take on suicide missions all the time, but that is under our own initiative, not following someone else's agenda."

Ahmed was expecting this reaction, so he calmly responded, "Yes, we are asking you to take on that part of the project, but if you execute correctly, it does not have to be a suicide mission. Our plan is to extract the attackers, but if for whatever reason they are compromised, they need to be ready to become martyrs. You see, the value of an attack perpetuated in Israeli soil, not far from Jerusalem, showing the ineffectiveness of the barrier, and no casualties on our side, is beyond measure. You also need to understand that this will be a coordinated attack involving multiple Hamas radical cells, so senior Hamas leadership is directly involved and very interested in its success."

K then added, "Our organization is also very interested in its success. You don't know us, and for now, it is best that we remain anonymous. I will just say that during the last few months we have decided to make the anti-Israel initiative one of our top priorities, and that is good news to you and the rest of your organization."

After a thoughtful nod from Hassan, Ahmed continued, "So, let's talk about the attack. I have worked in collaboration with a small team that has deep knowledge of the East Jerusalem area on the initial planning, selection of targets, mode of the attack, and extraction back to the West Bank. The targets and location we have selected are intended to make a bold statement about our tactical capabilities. We have identified a location where there is a gap of approximately thirty meters in the surveillance cameras, and as long as we operate within that range, it will be very difficult for the attackers to be identified. We prefer this not to be a suicide attack...and it doesn't have to be if your people execute our plan."

Hassan was skeptical, particularly about the local knowledge that these two *masterminds* had about local conditions. "So, you have a plan, and all we have to do is execute it? How familiar are you and your local contacts with this area?"

"Did your elders say you could trust us?" asked K.

"Yes, they did," answered Hassan.

"Then you should trust them," said Ahmed in a calm, soft voice. "We were told that you are tech-savvy. Is that right?"

"I am not a developer, but still above average. Why do you ask?"

"Because the next part requires that. Pay attention closely to all the technical rules we *must* follow. Take this phone," as Ahmed pulled an iPhone from his pocket and placed it on the table. "It has location services and cellular data disabled. Keep it that way. You should only connect via WIFI. There is a messaging app and a browser that use a VPN that will tunnel all communications." He looked at Hassan in the eye waiting for a reaction.

"Yes, I follow," acknowledged Hassan.

"Good. This is how we'll communicate. During the next few days, you will receive an encrypted message with a URL, along with a passcode. Do not navigate to that link outside of this phone. It has secure browsing and is the only way for you to access that web page."

"What's on the web page?" asked Hassan.

"Instructions. But they will look like garbage. You'll need to decode them with the key in the Notes app on the phone. It is a static note. Always there. No need to connect to view it," and to illustrate, Ahmed opened the application and showed it to Hassan. "See? There is a different decoding key for each day of the week. The instructions each day will be relatively short, so you will not spend much time decoding. Follow?"

"Yes. Why all these layers of complication? What's the big mystery?"

"One...we don't want to fail. Two...there will be details about location, weapons, and other elements of the attack that we don't want our friends in IDF or Mossad to know about. Three...this will be good practice for you. If it works, we'll keep communicating this way...and there will be more to do. If you have questions, send me an encrypted message. No more than one a day and be smart about how you word them. Assume they will be intercepted. And do not...I repeat, do not try to contact me through another device. I'll monitor this one closely. Twenty-four-seven."

Before they parted ways, Ahmed said, "The attack will require two men with the potential to carry an attack successfully, but who are also expendable. Do you have anyone in mind?"

"Yes, I do. My cousin Abdul leads a Hamas radical cell that goes from Jericho to al-Eizariyah. He is not part of my Sumaya group, but we work together, and he is a very smart and hardened tactical person. Abdul knows that area better than anyone. He will be able to train two of his people for this attack, and I trust he will find the right ones for it."

11

BUCKET LIST ITEM

*D*ecember 9, 2021, Café Milano Restaurant, Georgetown, Washington D.C.

Nick arrived a few minutes late to a standing lunch date he had established with Ewan at the end of each semester as a chance for them to get caught up. It was half psychotherapy, and half, a way to stay connected. That day Ewan asked for a larger table and was already sitting with someone Nick had not met before.

As Nick approached the table, he said, "Hi, y'all. Sorry I'm late..."

"Good afternoon, Nick, please allow me to introduce a colleague, Youssef Khoury. Youssef, this is my good friend, Nick Aday." Youssef looked more like a GQ model than the average college professor, particularly based on his attire of designer jeans, pink Peter Millar button-down shirt, and casual Bally loafers. He had a dark complexion, big hazel eyes, closely trimmed curly black hair, an athletic build, and did not appear to be anywhere near forty.

After Nick and Youssef shook hands, exchanged pleasantries and sat at the table, Ewan continued, "Youssef probably knows more about getting around in Israel than anyone I know. I thought it would be a great idea to have him join us for lunch so we can get some recommendations for our trip."

Nick and Ewan, along with Shannon and Ewan's wife Denise, had recently been talking about their common bucket list goal of traveling to the Holy Land. None of them had been there before and were overwhelmed with the diverse opinions they had been exposed to about the region. Most of what they had heard about modern-day Israel was delivered through news stories as well as content on the web, which unfortunately included an element of alarmism that was overdone. Ewan's main concern had been about safety, mostly out of a lack of knowledge and experience about the region. Nick had less of a concern, in part because he had traveled to places that were not known for great safety. He also had several colleagues that worked in or had traveled extensively to Israel, as Tel Aviv had become an important technology hub. All of them were impressed with Tel Aviv as a beautiful cosmopolitan city on the Mediterranean with incredible cultural heritage and had never experienced any safety issues.

Youssef then followed Ewan's cue and proceeded to introduce himself. "Well, I hope I meet your expectations, guys. I have mostly spent time in Israel on work-related matters and not as a tourist." He paused, and then turned to Nick, "Ewan speaks very highly of you, and to give you a little context, I work here at Georgetown too. That's where I met the Big E, Professor Byrne," he said playfully while turning to Ewan for a reaction. "I work in the Center for Contemporary Arab Studies and am also involved in a couple other organizations that study that area."

Nick said, "Interesting. It would be great to get your thoughts on what to do, places we shouldn't miss, and so on." He had been expecting an accent on the part of Youssef, because based on his name, his strong Middle Eastern features, and the credentials of being an expert in that region, he thought Youssef would have been raised in the Middle East. Instead, Youssef had perfect mid-Atlantic prep-school English. His demeanor and style were reflective of, not only a high level of education and refinement, but also experience interacting with people in diplomatic circles, people of power and influence. Youssef was not just an academic. He had a presence that reminded him of senior executives in his industry, which in many ways was a positive, but also alerted Nick to raise his shield and be alert, something he had been conditioned to do during his years in the corporate world.

Nick then asked, "At the risk of sounding naïve, do you have a personal connection to the area?"

"Yes, I do. My area of focus is Christians in the Middle East. Mostly, Palestine, where I am now spending a good amount of time. I am of Palestinian Christian descent myself but grew up near Baltimore. I went to St Casimir for elementary, high school at Georgetown Prep, and here I am teaching at a Jesuit college."

"Interesting. I guess that makes you a minority when you travel there. Doesn't it?" asked Nick.

"Yes and no. If I lived there, it would. As a visitor, I am in the mainstream."

Ewan then asked, "Youssef, any words of wisdom? My biggest hang-up is this whole political environment that you read about in the news. Do you...?"

Youssef interrupted, anticipating the questions he was always asked, "It's safe. Yes, there is tension, but the bigger issues are near Gaza, and there's no reason for you to go near it. Israel is fine. Tel Aviv, a great city on the Mediterranean with marinas and beaches. Pretty. Modern...there's a Ritz Carlton there. Most of the West Bank is fine too, and there's lots of religious sites there. You'll be fine. I'll connect you to a local guide if you're interested."

"Group tour or private guide? Which do you think is best?" asked Nick as they continued going back and forth extracting some local knowledge from Youssef.

After a few minutes of that exchange, Youssef changed the topic, "So, Nick. I'd love to hear about you. There's an accent there I am trying to figure out, somewhere in the South? Would also love to hear what you do for a living. Ewan has said you were in tech, but I suspect that he's pretty clueless about it."

"Ha! True. It reminds me of my father-in-law, who would tell his friends that I did something with *stocks and Wall Street*. I guess that having an MBA, wearing a suit, and sometimes a tie, to work, put me in that bucket." He turned to Ewan, who was less amused than him and Youssef about the slight, then continued, "Ewan, pay attention this time."

Nick then complied with Youssef's request, "Let's see. I guess the *y'all* gave me away. That's Louisiana. But rewinding a bit...Son of Cuban immigrants. They were one generation removed from Spain, so I grew up eating Spanish food at home, and not so much black beans and rice." He grinned, and continued, "I grew up all over the place. My parents moved a few times after leaving Cuba in the early sixties... you know, after Castro took over. So, I was actually born in Spain, but spent my early years in Louisiana, then South Florida."

"I guess we have a bit of a comparable background in that sense. Parents running away from a bad system," commented Youssef as he leaned forward and rested his forearms on the table. "What about school?"

"Tulane. New Orleans. Double-E, uhm...Electrical Engineering...when they still had a School of Engineering at Tulane, and then MBA at Georgia Tech. I don't want to bore you with all the in-between, but I am now the CEO at Macro Insights across the river in Tyson's Corner. It's software in the BI/Analytics space...at least for a few more weeks."

"The guy's not even sixty...and is about to go on a long vacation," said Ewan.

"Hmmm. Retiring?" asked Youssef.

"I prefer to say sabbatical, but, uhm...yeah, stepping into the unknown," answered Nick.

"Out of curiosity, have you had any interest in teaching?" asked Youssef. "Many of the professors at the B-School fall into that category of having a corporate job and teaching part time. Some go full-time when they retire."

"Oh yeah, I thought about it," responded Nick, "May do it one day, but for now, I'd rather not commit to a schedule. One of the main reasons I am retiring is to have more control of my time." He paused, considering that the next thing he was about to say could trigger a reaction, then continued. "Besides, and please do not take this the wrong way, but I don't think I could deal with the politics and ideology that you guys are surrounded with. I am not political but having to be so careful about expressing your opinion is not that appealing...just not a great fit for me."

Ewan joined in with an even more charged comment, "Well, this has been my life for almost a quarter century, and sometimes I wonder if it is a good fit even for me! The lack of tolerance for different views is ironic and frustrating. Many of my peers and a good majority of administrators are angry activists. When you express any disagreement with their beliefs around hot-button topics, the conversation ends. At that point, the shield goes up, they know something is wrong with you, outrage and anger take over, and the personal attacks begin. And this is a Jesuit school...well, maybe that's part of the problem." Ewan chuckled, reflecting on the irony. "Imagine what would happen if us Christians tried to impose our beliefs that way."

Youssef responded, "Well, it is true that the left acts with more zeal these days, and that makes them look like religious fanatics, but the Church has gone through periods in which their beliefs were imposed as well."

Ewan responded, "I'll give you that, but would qualify it. True – Church leaders have done some bad things during the last two thousand years, and still do – but I cannot think of a religious organization that has taken more responsibility for mistakes of the past. There have also been many lies and exaggerations that, over time, have been debunked. That includes the classic ones, like the role of the Church in colonizing the New World, the Crusades and the Inquisition. The truth is much more nuanced than people think, and you have to invest time to get to the truth. Anyway, there have been many mistakes. Many. But that has more to do with flawed humans, not so much Church doctrine."

Nick, reflecting on how he had opened a can of worms, said, "Woops! Sorry for starting this. I guess that's an example of what I was talking about."

Youssef then said, "No, no, we actually enjoy this. At least I do. Ewan gets all red and agitated, but I love to see that passion. It's good debate," then turning to Ewan, said, "I still love you, big guy."

The conversation continued along the same topic, and before they knew it, they had spent nearly two hours on topics that had little to do with their upcoming trip to Israel, the original purpose Ewan for the lunch meeting. Nick found the mini debate refreshing and really enjoyed meeting Youssef.

As they walked out, Nick said, "I'll buy both of you lunch before the start of the semester as long as you promise to debate some more. There's a lot of material out there."

"I'm up for that," said Youssef. "Let's make it about something really controversial. I'd say Nationals baseball...or Ravens football, or maybe even why Ewan has never taken me sailing."

"Youssef, that's not fair!" responded Ewan. "I keep inviting, but you're never here. You were gone for most of this semester and are probably doing the same in the Spring."

"Yep, true that. I'll be gone again right around the time sailing season starts. Anyway, it's been a pleasure, Nick. Hope to see you guys soon!"

12

HAMAS IN AL-EIZARIYAH

*D*ecember 11, 2021, al-Eizariyah
It was mid-morning, and Nabil and Fathi Awad rushed to arrive at the place they called the *safe house* on time. They had just gotten off a bus near the center of the town of al-Eizariyah and started walking east along Jericho Road. After less than a hundred meters, they turned left on a narrow street and walked for a short block before turning again to their right where the rear entrance to the safe house was located. The street was deserted, with all traffic and pedestrian activity taking place along the main road one block away.

Fathi walked up to the back door, looking around to ensure they were not being seen, and punched a security code on the keypad. When the door lock snapped to the open position, he pulled on the door and they walked in. The safe house was a small industrial building originally built to house a machine shop that had now been turned into what looked like a very rudimentary office. Its front entrance door was covered in rust and faced Jericho Road. It was closed shut permanently, so the backdoor was used as the main access. The overall space was approximately one hundred square meters and had no inside walls. It was used mostly to store weapons and ammunition, hold small group meetings, and serve as a temporary place to hide and rest. Inside, there was a small, spartan meeting table pushed against the wall on the left. It had four small chairs around it. Along all four walls there were several metal storage cabinets, one bookshelf, and a small refrigerator. There was also a toilet and a sink in the far-right hand corner, also with no partitions. The space in the center of the room was open. There were no windows, but there were cameras mounted outside to have a full view of the two streets and two alleyways that formed the perimeter of the building.

Fathi sat on one of the chairs, then said to Nabil, "I have no idea why Abdul wants to meet with us so early in the day and risk being seen in the middle of town. I hope we are not in trouble. Just in case we are, do not say a word, and let me do the talking."

Nabil was twenty years old, the younger and better looking of the two Awad brothers, who were born in the Jericho area and then moved to al-Eizariyah as young children. He had shown great athletic ability growing up, but because of the difficult economic situation he grew up in, was never able to play organized soccer, his favorite sport. Instead, he played pick-up games and competed in foot races with friends, oftentimes on the street or a deserted field where they had enough space to kick the ball. Nabil was also smart and had done well in school, even though his discipline was inconsistent, particularly if the topic was not of interest to him.

Fathi, twenty-five, had been involved with a Hamas cell inside the West Bank since he was a teenager. He was a bitter young man with a strong hatred for Jews and Christians. From an early age, he was taught that the Jewish people did not belong in Palestine and had been allowed to settle there by the Britons, French, and Americans, all of which were evil and satanic societies seeking the destruction of Muslims there and around the world. In the mind of most Palestinians, the Jews were occupying land that belonged to them and all the countries of Christian heritage that supported them were evil and hated Muslims.

Hamas had a solid footing in the Gaza strip, but not the same level of influence on the West Bank, where the Palestinian Authority ruled. During the last few years, the relationship between the Palestinian Authority and Hamas had deteriorated. The leadership of the Palestinian Authority recognized the existence of Israel, and their main goal was to establish an independent secular nation. They had engaged in negotiations with Israel's government and at least on the surface, appeared to favor a diplomatic approach to resolve the Palestinian State situation. Hamas was a militant Islamic group who saw no value in pursuing diplomacy, did not recognize Israel, and favored a two-pronged approach of violence and strict adherence to Islamic law, not too different from the approach of the Taliban in Afghanistan.

This Hamas cell Fathi and Nabil belonged to started to gain notoriety during the last few years based on attacks on Israelis and foreigners. They were small, but intensely loyal to their cause, and growing in membership. Fathi's involvement with Hamas had become almost a career, as he decided not to pursue an education beyond the ninth grade and over time became one of the lieutenants of Abdul Al-Nashar.

Abdul was a high-ranking Hamas member in the West Bank and first cousin of one of the main Hamas leaders, Hassan Al-Nashar, of the Hamas underground militant group called Sumaya Martyrs. Abdul relied on Fathi for minor attacks and general disruption of Jews and Christians within the territory they controlled, which included the Palestinian towns within five miles of the Israeli-Palestinian border just East of Jerusalem. Abdul also had an intense hatred for Jews, but also found a target in Arab Christians living in the West Bank. Arab

Christians were a small minority in Israel and the West Bank, many of whom were descendants of early Christians from that area. Conversions from Islam to Christianity were practically non-existent, at least not in the open, so most Christians in that area had been born into it. Ironically, as difficult as it was for them to practice the faith in that environment, their fervor and loyalty to Jesus was unmatched in comparison to Christians living in other countries that practiced freedom of faith. Abdul had moved up in the organization with a reputation of being ruthless, not only with his enemies but also with his subordinates. He completely bought into the cause, but now, he rarely got his hands dirty.

The door lock snapped again, and the door swung open, allowing daylight to come in and they saw Abdul at the door surveying the room to ensure it was just the two brothers. He walked in, and both brothers stood up to greet him. Then, Abdul gestured for both to sit down by the table, as he pulled up a chair, turned it around and sat on it with the backrest to his chest.

Abdul was a burly man of medium height, who appeared to be in his late forties. He had a hard expression on his round face, and intense black eyes that would pierce through you. His hands were thick and rough. Even with this rough appearance, once he started speaking, he came across as thoughtful and calm. That was, unless he became frustrated, when his ruthless second persona would emerge.

"Allah shines on you today. I have good news," said Abdul, calming down a very nervous Fathi, allowing him to breathe normally again. "Before I say anything else, let it be clear that you are not to mention any of this to anyone. The only three people that know this are the three of us. If I learn that it has leaked beyond that, I will personally execute you. That will be an example to the rest of our team that you must remain obedient and be smart about what you are doing. Is that clear?"

Any relief that Fathi had felt a second earlier had been quickly replaced with anxiety. He knew himself, and among many other things, was well aware of his lack of maturity and self-control. This would be a test, one that he would better pass successfully, or otherwise face fatal consequences for him as well as his younger brother. He swallowed hard, then said, "Yes, Abdul. Clear," and turning toward his brother, "I will make sure Nabil remains quiet as well."

"Good, good. We are planning a coordinated attack with our brothers from Gaza. Our cell will strike first to catch the IDF by surprise. Gaza will then unleash a series of missile attacks to Sderot and other areas to their North and East. In addition to the disruption we want to cause, we want to send a message to the infidels that hostilities in the West Bank are now going to extend into East Jerusalem...and it is going to happen constantly. We want the Jews and the visitors in Jerusalem to start fearing for their lives. That will disrupt tourism and put pressure again on the Israeli government and international community. It is embarrassing that tourists from countries that we detest and are friends of the Jews can come and walk around Palestine like everything is normal. This also means that our cell will become much more active in months to come and will play a bigger role in pushing away the occupiers from our land." Abdul stopped, made eye contact with Fathi first, then Nabil, as a way of reinforcing the seriousness and magnitude of what they were about to take part in. He continued, "Our attack will be more surgical and targeted," then proceeded to lay out the details of the attack and the way they would train for it.

When he was done with the preliminary outline of the plans, he said, "I must tell you that this is not designed to be a suicide attack. You execute well, then you get out alive and without being identified. You will learn new skills, which will be needed to continue our fight. But if something happens, you cannot be captured alive or traced back to this Hamas cell. That would make us have to retreat back to Jericho or Ramallah and set us back several years."

Then, to reinforce the importance of the mission, Abdul concluded with, "You should know that this assignment was given to me directly by my cousin Hassan. He is entrusting the success of this mission on us, but he will also be here with us as we prepare for it. There are some very powerful forces behind this. The mastermind of the plan is working closely with Hassan and top Hamas leaders. He is also the right-hand person of the mysterious K that we keep hearing about. We better get this right!"

Fathi had difficulty hiding his enthusiasm but remained surprisingly quiet and paid close attention to the details. He saw this as a tremendous vote of confidence on the part of Abdul and his superiors. A great opportunity for him and Nabil, and one where there was no room for failure. If they were caught by Israeli authorities, they would surely die, and if they failed and were not caught, it would be even worse. They would face the unmerciful wrath of their leaders, a much more painful and shameful death.

13

FATE

Since they met for the first time earlier that semester, Fatma had met Jenny on several occasions. Initially, their motivation was that of learning about each other's culture. To Jenny, getting to know a young local student was fascinating. She had not been able to establish that connection with any of her students or even with the local professors. The only person Jenny had established a friendship with was another member of the visiting faculty, an older female professor from Canada.

In the case of Fatma, Jenny represented someone that she was intrigued with and looked up to. First, she was an American, but there was also something different about a person that had chosen to teach abroad, particularly in Palestine. During the course of these interactions, they developed a friendship, and over time, Fatma started to open up a little about her personal life.

The last time they had met was toward the end of the Fall semester, when Jenny decided to probe a little bit about Fatma's spiritual life and beliefs. She had asked, "How much would you say religion is as a part of your life?"

"What do you mean?" answered Fatma.

"Well, is it at the center of how you view the world and live your life, or is it more like, uhm...like something cultural, a custom?"

"I guess I have never thought about it that way," and after a few seconds, Fatma continued, "there are some things that I find...inconsistent. Really, it has more to do with the attitude that I sometimes see with some of the people I grew up with or in school. As I meet more foreigners, I realize they are not as bad as I had been led to believe."

"Is that also the way your parents taught you, or do you see that perception more outside of your home?"

Fatma was surprised that Jenny would be probing so much, but thought her intentions were pure, and answered, "My father, no. He is probably the most open-minded person I have met regarding outsiders. And...my mother died when I was born...during delivery..."

"Oh my gosh! That is so sad. I'm so sorry. It must've been hard for you growing up."

"I grew up not knowing her, at least not in person, so I guess less difficult than for other people. My father and Aunt Reema have told me so much that I feel I know her, but... it's just a different situation. In any event, things I thought were true in the past are now in question. I do have some doubts..."

Jenny sensed that Fatma was receptive to remove some of the mystery that surrounded the *Westerners* that she had grown so weary about, and said, "There's nothing evil in Christianity, contrary to what many people say. Have some Christians done bad things? Of course. You could say that about people from any religious group. I would be happy to tell you more about it if you are interested."

Fatma now felt that the probing was about to turn in preaching, so she did her best to deflect the subject, "I know,

Jenny. Please don't misunderstand me when I speak about doubt. I am still a Muslim."

While it had been an uncomfortable moment, it left Fatma with an even higher sense of curiosity and excitement and a reason to spend some time trying to discern how she was feeling about that entire situation. So much so, that she was now looking for the opportunity to reengage in that conversation but did not know how to do it and thought it might be uncomfortable. It was a tricky internal struggle, since her practical side was very clear on how unrealistic it would be to explore Christian teachings, but since this process started, she had developed a sense of anxiety and unease that could only be satisfied by learning more. With this internal tension, Fatma was hesitant to pursue the next step, so for now, avoiding Jenny would be best.

Several weeks later, during the third week of the Spring semester, Fatma saw Jenny at a distance as she walked across campus on her way to class. She did not have the time and was not in the state of mind to re-visit their last conversation. Fatma looked away and pretended to be answering a call on her cell phone to avoid being approached by Jenny. No such luck. As Fatma put up the phone to her ear, she heard Jenny calling behind her. Jenny was no more than ten steps away, and it was obvious Fatma could hear her, so she turned around and said, "Hi" without slowing down her stride.

"Morning, Jenny," said Fatma.

"Hi, Fatma! How have you been?"

Fatma kept on walking and quickly responded, "I've been super busy working on a project. Going now to deliver my presentation in class. It is due in less than fifteen minutes."

"Can you chat after class?" replied Jenny. She had her pinned down with no excuse or way of getting out. She could only try to minimize the time they met, but could not come up with an excuse to say no. So, they agreed to get together at the student lounge after her 10:00 am class.

Fatma got through her presentation just fine, even with the added anxiety of knowing that a potentially challenging conversation would immediately follow. She walked over to the lounge, where Jenny was already sitting at a table with a cup of hot tea reviewing her schedule for the remainder of the week.

"Hello," said Fatma with a tone of assertiveness as she approached and sat down. She was now prepared for this moment.

"Hi, Fatma, do you want anything to drink?"

She simply shook her head while keeping her gaze fixed on Jenny. She was ready to go straight to the topic of discussion, so she sat quietly waiting for Jenny to break the ice.

"There are a couple of things I've been wanting to chat with you about. The first is to let you know that I am moving back home. I'm still waiting to get paid for last semester and so... because of that, I'm not teaching this semester. I went home for the Christmas holidays, gave it a lot of thought, and realized I could not afford to stay here."

"Jenny, that's too bad!"

"I just flew back to pack my belongings and return. I leave tomorrow, so the timing here was great. The other thing I wanted to talk to you about is our last conversation." She paused, took a sip of her tea, then said, "I want to apologize for coming on so strong. I probably offended you, and that was not my intention." Not what Fatma expected, as she thought that Jenny would want to launch into recruiting mode from the onset. Jenny went on to say, "This is such a big part of my life and such a source of meaning, comfort, fulness...that I want to share it with everyone I care about."

Fatma remained quiet. She wanted to hear more, but her silence and facial expression did not reveal that. Jenny was not sure how to interpret Fatma's silence but could only project into the situation her perception of how Muslims must feel about attempts from Christians to preach or evangelize. "So, I hope you forgive me, Fatma. I did not intend to insult you." She looked her in the eyes to demonstrate the sincerity of her apology.

The next few seconds seemed like an eternity, as Fatma dropped her eyes, not wanting to make eye contact. She finally broke the silence. "What you did was done in an effort to share something that you think is good. There is no need to apologize." This made Jenny feel relieved, but also gave her a sense that there was more for Fatma to share. And there was.

"I am confused...and afraid. My reaction to your comments were out of fear, not because I disagree with what you said. I was certainly not offended...I just felt very uncomfortable because...I am afraid to be even consider this, and in you I see someone that can increase my doubts. I don't know if I am ready for that now."

"I understand," said Jenny.

"We come from very different cultures. I think that people that live in America have a level of freedom to decide what religion they pursue. Here, we are born into our religion, and are raised with the understanding that it is not to be questioned. There is no *shopping around* for the church or message you like better. We are also taught that our religion is the only truth and that the rest of the world is wrong. I guess all religions have that absolute view, but at least others seem to have some openness toward others, because of tolerance, or because of humility. No such thing here. Crossing to the other side is seen as a tragic failure, a loss, and what happens after is not good for the person that converts. Being honest with yourself and converting has to be so important that you would choose to give up the life you had before."

Jenny slowly nodded in understanding but did not interrupt her.

Fatma continued, "I have been resisting even thinking about it because I don't want to go through all that. I love my father, my aunt, my family, and don't want to break their hearts." Fatma's eyes were starting to well up, and she needed to pause and take a break. After a couple of short breaths, she went on, "I have resisted it, but I am also restless about understanding things better. There are many things about Islam I don't understand and am afraid to ask. I don't want it to be interpreted as doubt...but that is exactly what it is. I don't know what to do, and now that I have met you, I am afraid that this will lead me to do something crazy." She paused. "Anyway, that is why I left so abruptly the last time. I didn't know how else to deal with the conversation. But, since that happened, I have not been able to stop thinking about it, and I think I want to understand more."

Jenny was not expecting this. "I am not sure what to say, Fatma. Can you describe a little bit the restlessness?"

"There is a voice inside of me that tells me the truth lies elsewhere, that I need to question what I have learned and be open to a different teaching. I hear it in quiet times, when I am about to go to bed. It is an unusual experience, because it doesn't feel like my consciousness. It is from the outside..."

"Does it make you scared?" asked Jenny.

"No, not at all! Whatever its source, it makes me feel comfortable, it's even...*familiar*." Fatma shook her head and said, "I know. This sounds crazy. There is one thing I never told you. The night that I had your bible with me...well, I read some of it. The Gospel of John. The beauty of the writing style and the message had an impact on me. I also felt a certain...how do you say? Resonance? It hit a chord in my heart that said *this is true*. Ever since that moment, I have been sensing that presence, that voice."

"Wow, Fatma. I am envious. Not because you feel conflict,

but because I also think it is unusual. I think you are being called."

"Yes, it is a call. What shall I do? I am sure that, if I lived... like you, in Texas, it would be much simpler. Wouldn't it?"

Jenny looked at her with compassion, trying to understand Fatma's world a little better. She then said, "These are not easy conversations to have, even where I come from. As a technical professional, I am supposed to base my beliefs and understanding of the world on science. Particularly now in an academic setting, I have also felt the need to keep this to myself. The consequences are not as dire as they are for you in this environment, but even back home, you can certainly be alienated by your peers and even risk losing your job if you are not careful about what you say. And it is getting worse...even in Texas," she said with a chuckle, reflecting on the irony.

"So, what do you think I should do? Have you ever experienced anything like this?"

"I also went through a journey to get to where I am spiritually. I still feel that the journey continues and have unanswered questions as well. For example, I grew up in a Catholic family, went through a period of challenging everything I learned at that church, and am now Baptist..."

"Wait, so there are different Christian groups?"

"Yes, there are. They all point in the same general direction, which is Jesus Christ and His teachings. But...mainly Jesus Christ, Himself. It's not only about understanding a set of rules. It's more about establishing a relationship. Different Christian denominations may have different interpretations and rules, but all converge on Jesus."

After letting it sink in, Fatma said, "And so, you changed. Why?"

"My path to the Baptist church was paved by Brian. I haven't told you, but I am a widow. Brian was my husband, and he passed last year. He was only twenty-nine...topic for another conversation..."

"I am very sorry to hear! You are so young!" said Fatma, with a look of authentic concern for Jenny.

"Oh, it's starting to become more...normal? It gets easier with time. Anyway, Brian grew up Baptist and asked me to go with him to a service. This was during a time when I saw things in the Catholic Church that broke my heart, and I wasn't super involved. Not as devoted as I should have been. So, I went with Brian, and the Baptist community felt like home. I met people whose faith appeared to be burning within them. They lived it and it appeared to be a more important part of their lives, much more than what I had experienced. But..." she paused and looked at Fatma in the eye to emphasize what she was about to say, "I don't agree with all the teachings of the Baptist church, particularly things that they reject in Catholic teaching."

"For example?" asked Fatma.

"There are Catholic teachings that I still agree with, like the role we have to play in our own salvation, the presence of Christ in the Eucharist...I mean, the bread of communion, if you have heard of that."

"Nope, this is all going over my head. Give me another example."

"Well, also, what Catholics believe about the Virgin Mary and her role. As a Baptist, I am not supposed to believe in the virginity of Mary, or even in the dogma of her being the Mother of God. Heck, I am supposed to reject the entire concept of praying to her, even if all it entails is asking for her to intercede before her son." Jenny paused, realizing that she was starting to preach, then went back the original point, "People of other religions may perceive us as being a happy and unified Christian family, but the truth is that we haven't been like that for more than five hundred years. Actually, it has been like this since Jesus lived, for two thousand years!"

"Hmmm, interesting. We have some of that in Islam as well...to the point it becomes the source of violence and persecution. But it sounds like there are still things that all Christians agree on, and maybe that is a place for me to start. Can you help me sort through that? For example, that Gospel that I read. Is that common across all Christian groups? I really want to understand," said Fatma.

"Yes, it is common. We mostly agree on the texts. Well, not a hundred percent, but the four main Gospels, yes."

"You mentioned the Virgin Mary, and there is one thing about me that you might find ironic, maybe even funny. I was given this name not because it is a variant of what is a popular Palestinian girl's name, Fatima. I guess that is one reason for it, or at least that makes it blend more with our culture. My name actually comes from what Catholic Christians celebrate on my birthday. I was born on May 13th, the day of the first apparition of Virgin Mary in Fatima, and was delivered by a nun who informed my father of this. He has never told me, but my aunt Reema did. She said that is where my name comes from."

Jenny found that intriguing. "That is interesting and may be more than just a coincidental factor that over time has driven you to explore the Christian faith. This is not because of the name alone, but maybe the role that Mary might have played or is playing in your life."

And so, their conversation began, only to be interrupted by Fatma's next class, which was starting in a few minutes. They hugged and said goodbye, not knowing if and when they would see each other again. They had each other's contact information, so they would be able to stay in touch until that time.

Before Fatma left, Jenny gave her some homework, "Please read the four Gospels and Acts of the Apostles. If you are concerned about being found with a Bible, just look them up online."

During the next few weeks, Fatma devoured everything she

could read about the New Testament, and when she had questions, she would text or email Jenny, who was always responsive
and excited to offer guidance. In addition to the biblical and
historical topics they covered, Jenny told Fatma about her life,
losing her young husband Brian to leukemia, and how in the
middle of all that suffering, her faith in God grew stronger.

The topic of suffering kept coming up and was a concern
for Fatma, which she wrote to Jenny about. Sensing that trepidation and knowing how it was one of the major objections of
agnostics and atheists, Jenny responded in her most recent
email:

*I hear some people talk about how they have lost their faith
because of suffering, and the belief that suffering is not compatible
with the concept of an all good and all-powerful God. However, if
you examine this concept deeper, you will realize that you must
struggle to find meaning and fulfillment. You can have all things you
want, never hearing the word no, with everything coming to you
easily. That just leads to wanting more and more, and eventually
emptiness, anxiety and despair. Suffering has a very important role
in our spiritual growth, and we should embrace it. Jesus himself was
not spared of suffering. He lost loved ones, experienced similar issues
others went through, and before His resurrection, was tortured and
killed. His experience on Earth includes a fair amount of physical, as
well as emotional suffering, and God had good reasons for things to
unfold the way they did. Why would we think we should deserve
better?*

*Another interesting example of suffering is the experience that
Palestinian Christians go through during their entire lives. They are
considered a minority and are persecuted, in some cases risking their
lives. Yet, they demonstrate a deeper faith and are more fulfilled in
their relationship with God than people in Western countries who
can practice freely. Even in a country like Israel and Palestine they
are persecuted. Just ask the Christians that live near you, like those in*

Bethlehem. If their suffering brings them closer to God, maybe we should accept that good came from it.

Through these exchanges, Jenny helped Fatma overcome her initial fears and moved her along in her understanding of Jesus and his teachings. Fatma was answering the call, and the more she learned, the more she felt that mysterious sensation that truth resonated in her. The seed had been planted.

14

FINAL PLANNING

5:07 am Wednesday Feb 16, 2022

Nabil was the first one to get through the narrow tunnel that had been carved under the barrier just west of alZa'im, a Palestinian settlement approximately three kilometers from the Old City in Jerusalem and adjacent to East Jerusalem. Once he cleared and got to the other side, he turned around to grab the duffel bag he had been pulling as he crawled the twenty meters to get across. The duffel bag was filled with seven one-gallon water bottles to make it as heavy as possible, to simulate the weight of the weapons and ammunition they would need to bring the day of the mission. A few seconds later, Fathi came through the end of the tunnel as well. Both were wearing disposable white coveralls, which they immediately removed, folded, and rolled up neatly to store in their backpacks. The coveralls were meant to protect the clothes they were wearing underneath, so as they walked around, there would be no sign they had been crawling on the sandy soil of the tunnel.

Abdul had picked the alZa'im area rather than the Gush Etzion barrier gap for a few reasons. Gush Etzion had gained too much notoriety during the last ten years, so it was under much more vigilance. However, just as important was the proximity of alZa'im to al-Eizariyah and the area where they planned to conduct the attack. Both factors would contribute to a safer return back to Palestinian territory.

The brothers had rehearsed the crossing at least ten times under Abdul's supervision inside an old warehouse near Jericho, going through checklists of the various steps and precautions they needed to take. Today's crossing was the third time they had actually gone into the Israeli side since they began their training two weeks earlier. The first two crossings had just been to learn how to navigate the tunnel, and as soon as they made it through, they turned around and came back to the Palestinian side. They were now able to crawl across in less than ten minutes, and were used to doing it in total darkness, knowing where to anticipate different bumps and narrow spots throughout the rudimentary route that had been carved by members of their cell. The repetitiveness of the training had been effective making their pre and post crossing routine almost routinary. Among the many steps they had to take, the most important one was to ensure both mobile phones were fully charged but turned off. They kept them only in case of an emergency, knowing that Israeli authorities would detect and locate them as soon as they were turned on. They had also discarded the idea of using non-GPS mobile phones, as those could still be located through triangulation of cell towers, something that two of their former colleagues had learned in a painful way a few years earlier.

This morning, the training would be riskier, as they had to make their way into the street where they would conduct the attack. They needed to find the most efficient way to get in and out, review the traffic in the area at the time they were planning to execute it, as well as any patterns that would show the level of presence of local police or IDF, which performed an important security role in the Area C of the West Bank, as well as in the adjacent East Jerusalem.

The landscape around Jerusalem has beautiful rolling hills, so there was some level of hiking involved, and that made carrying the duffel bag and backpacks a bit of a challenge. They hiked for half a kilometer uphill on a dirt path until they arrived near their rendezvous point along al-Hardub Street. Their local contact was supposed to be meeting them before 5:30 am on that street just a few meters from the dirt path. The only car they saw parked along the side of the street was a gray Toyota, approximately fifty meters away to their left, that fit the description they had been given. They stopped at the end of the dirt path and both took a knee to assess the situation and ensure they were not about to make a mistake. Everything so far had worked out as they expected, but establishing contact with their driver, Mendel, was a riskier endeavor. This is someone that not even Abdul had personally met. All they knew was his name, the make and color of his car, the general location where he would meet them, the protocol for establishing contact, and the fact that Abdul's superiors had compensated him very well.

Mendel was a Russian Jew who had migrated to Israel six years earlier and was now a local taxi and Uber driver. He had struggled financially since arriving in Israel and had resorted to participating in a local network of low-level drug dealers. Through that group he had also met several Palestinians that eventually led him to Hamas contacts. These, in turn, would occasionally hire him for tactical errands inside Israeli territory, mostly transportation. He was already used to operating underground, so the additional risk of working with the radicals was something he was willing to undertake, particularly given the compensation. Mendel did not feel a strong loyalty for Israel or his Jewish heritage, a product of being born and living the first few years of his life in the communist system that was the

Soviet Union and having to worry more about survival than tradition.

This morning he had been hired to pick up two Hamas members and drive them around East Jerusalem. All he was told was that they would walk past his car, the one on the left would light a cigarette, and that would be a sign that they were there, making contact. He was then supposed to start the engine, drive up to them, and let them in the car, one on the passenger seat and the other one in the back.

As planned, Fathi and Nabil walked over in the direction of the car, as soon as they passed it, Fathi lit up a cigarette and both kept on walking. They heard the engine of the Toyota Corolla start, followed by a slow roll of the tires as it approached them. The protocol had worked. They were able now to proceed with their reconnaissance mission, gathering as much information as they could about their target. The brothers spent the entire day with Mendel, communicating in a rudimentary mixture of Arabic and English, but through that, getting to know one another fairly well. Out of caution, in order to avoid establishing a pattern that could be detected by local authorities, this was going to be their only opportunity to review the area before the day of the attack.

When night came upon them and it was now safe to make their way back, Mendel drove to the rendezvous point and waited for any local traffic to clear before dropping them off. The brothers headed back through the tunnel without incident. It was even more important for them to be able to execute the crossing on the way back on a timely manner, and they were able to execute that flawlessly in less than eight minutes. They were starting to feel confident in their ability to conduct the attack and quickly get back to the safe house.

During the next three weeks, they focused their preparation on the actual shooting. Hamas had provided them two new Russian Chuvakin semi-automatic sniper rifles with silencers and had arranged for the logistical support inside the Israeli side. This included Mendel, as well as a vehicle that had been secured for them to conduct the actual attack. Fathi and Nabil had alternated training in the role of the shooter, with the other focused on the driving. Both needed to be prepared to play either role.

Nabil had demonstrated to be the more accurate shooter, but Fathi was still better than the average Hamas operative. This attack was a test, and the first time that Abdul had entrusted Fathi and Nabil with a mission of this importance, but also one where they would have to kill someone. Fathi was the leader of the mission because he was older and more tenured at Hamas, as well as for the skills and reputation he had developed as a relatively accurate sniper, but Nabil started to emerge as the raw talent that Abdul wanted to develop.

15

SHANNON

Tuesday Feb 22, 2022

Nick had exchanged text messages with Ewan the night before with a last moment request to meet for lunch at The Tombs in Georgetown. Given the late notice, he did not want to inconvenience Ewan too much, and chose a place that was next to the main campus. He knew that Ewan was not teaching during the Spring semester this year, since he was working on completing two research projects for which he needed to publish something, so his schedule was much more flexible. Still, giving him such short notice was a bit unusual. Considering that both respected each other's schedules enough to plan their meetings with more anticipation, Ewan was a little concerned about what may have prompted the urgency to meet. (law, 2019)

Ewan walked in a few minutes past noon. As he started removing his scarf and overcoat heading toward the bar, he found Nick already sitting on a stool with a glass of ice water in front of him. "Good afternoon Mr. Aday, it is great to see you on this off-cycle lunch meeting," he said playfully as he walked up to Nick, who stood up and gave him the customary handshake and hug.

"Thank you so much for coming on such short notice. How are you?" said Nick, with a tone of anxiety and darkness that Ewan had not seen in him.

"I'm great," responded Ewan. "Had a relaxing President's weekend holed up in my townhouse, given the gloomy weather, but it was a good opportunity to do a little reading and even some writing. All is good. Very excited with the countdown to our Holy Land trip. How about yourself?"

"I'm well," said Nick almost mechanically and looking down, not really meaning it. "I am...good, I guess," and upon further thought, "Well, I'm actually a bit of a mess right now." He then turned to Ewan, making eye contact for the first time, and said, "That's why I wanted to talk. We just learned that Shannon has advanced pancreatic cancer. It is stage four, which means it has already spread to other organs. It's pretty advanced. Not good. Terrible, actually."

Ewan's initial reaction was one of denial, assuming that someone, somewhere must have made a mistake. "What are you saying? I saw Shannon less than a month ago and she looked great. Is it possible that she has been misdiagnosed, or maybe is dealing with pancreatitis or some other issue instead?"

Nick just looked at Ewan, clenching his jaws. There was nothing else for him to say at the moment. Ewan needed time to let the news sink in, but there was no escaping the truth. After a few seconds, Nick said, "She is also trying to decide whether to fight it or not. It is very advanced. The prognosis, even with aggressive treatment, is not good. The main pancreatic specialist she is seeing doesn't think the tradeoff is worth it. Her quality of life would be terrible, and it would just extend the agony. 'Better to manage the pain' is what he said."

By now Ewan understood and began to accept this was real. "I wish I had words of comfort or wisdom for you, but I've got nothing." He paused, took a deep breath, then added, "I guess this is the type of situation that tests our faith. It is impossible to understand or draw any meaning from it in our lowly and unintelligent state, but we do have the option to pray for strength. Heck, we can also pray for a miracle while we're at it, but the likelihood of God granting that is miniscule. Let me guess, Shannon is pretty calm about it?"

"Surprisingly, yes. How'd you know?"

"Well, I guessed based on how I see her behaving when things are fine. I've always seen Shannon show this inner peace that, in my humble opinion, must come from a strong spiritual connection with God. I think she simply...trusts Him. Don't you think?"

"I mean, the shock of the news initially was not easy for her, and she asked a lot of questions. You know, trying to figure out how to fight this thing. But it didn't take long for her to realize that this is it, her time is finite...and that is the reality she has to deal with. Since then, she's been the one calming me down."

Ewan's eyes sparkled as a small tear started to drop from his right eye. Even in these circumstances, it was a tear of happiness. He was happy that, in the middle of this inevitable tragedy, Shannon was already tapping into a source of peace that could only come from God. He said, "Wow. She is such a good, blessed person! I am so lucky and happy to have met her and benefit from the light she emanates. You too, Nick. God has allowed you to borrow her as a gift for all these years, and He is not taking her back as we always seem to think. He is just allowing you to realize how much you love and need her, so that when you see her again, your love will be greater. You will see her after she leaves. This is just a matter of time for us now, but He will be with her in eternity, and so will you. What am I saying? He *is* with both of you in eternity already. We are subject to time, but God is not." With that Ewan started to cry and extended his right arm over to Nick to give him a big hug. The two men started crying like small children, which made for an interesting scene at the bar of The Tombs.

16

SUSPENDED

M*arch 8, 2022 Makassed Hospital Main Entry, Rub'a el-Adawiya Street, East Jerusalem*

Fatma was starting to grow anxious about not making her 13:00 Basic Nursing class on time, as she waited at the bus station for the bus to the Abu Dis campus. Public transportation between East Jerusalem and the West Bank was run by private bus operators who had small fleets and had to battle the traffic and checkpoints that exists in and around the Jerusalem region. There was no set schedule for the pickup right outside Makassed Hospital, where she was working part-time in her internship, but a bus would typically go by between 11:00 and 11:30 in the morning, and that was Fatma's only alternative.

The crowd at the relatively quiet bus stop was small and scattered, with a few students, a handful of hospital employees, and a few locals who relied on public transportation to get back to the West Bank. Some were standing next to the snack shack right outside the Emergency entrance gate. The hospital and most buildings along that street sat behind robust granite and steel fences, and the two-lane street was lined with parallel parked cars on both sides, making the path for traffic narrow and slow. There were also two uniformed soldiers of the IDF at the bus station for added security. During the last few months, there had been a few incidents involving radicals sneaking across from the West Bank, and since then IDF had been on heightened security around critical infrastructure areas and soft targets, like hospitals and schools. The side of the road was the usual chaotic scene, with heavy local traffic that included several large coach buses with tourists, vendors opening their stores mixed with a little bit of hammer and metal-to-metal banging from small construction projects in the area.

Fatma looked at her watch again. 11:22 and no sign of the bus. She was not sure if the growing feeling of anxiety was because of the increased risk of being late to class, or if there was something else bothering her that morning. She noticed a drop of sweat starting to trickle down her forehead and her sense of unease was now starting to take over with cramping in her stomach and a mild shaking of her hands and jaws. What was going on? Did she overdo her morning coffee? She then saw a white van coming from her left. It was disappointing that it was not the bus, and given where they were standing, it was likely an ambulance about to pull into the Emergency parking area. She moved toward the snack shack to avoid being in the way of the ambulance and hoped the bus would arrive soon.

The anxiety made her turn her focus inwardly, and she almost missed the commotion around her as the group of people to her left ducked to the ground upon hearing the thumping sound of what appeared to be gunshots through a silenced weapon. There were three in quick succession, followed by a fourth one, less than a second later. Fatma turned around to her left and watched, in what seemed like slow motion, as one of the IDF soldiers had been hit and was twisting his body, spraying blood on the people near him. Almost simultaneously, the woman standing next to him was hit and fell as if being pushed down to the ground. The fourth shot hit the other IDF soldier on the side of the neck as he was turning to the right.

Fatma might have been the only person on the sidewalk that stayed on her feet, focusing on the IDF soldiers. The first one to fall had been shot on his right temple and back of the shoulder. He fell to the ground and laid motionless. The other one was shot in the neck below his left ear. He began to stumble as he reached for his X95 riffle. Moshe Bitton, father of two young kids, living in East Jerusalem, grabbed the handle of his rifle and switched off the safety lock. He then reached for his radio and hailed the nearest squad to report they had been hit, asking for help. He was losing strength and acting out of instinct and following what he had learned in training but could not muster the strength to continue. He looked at his partner, Jacob Dahan, who had apparently died on impact. This would be their last day on Earth.

Through it all Fatma remained standing, and a sense of calm fell on her. Everything was happening so slowly that she felt that life was frozen in time and her consciousness was entering a different realm. She saw three people on the street in front of her that she had not noticed before. They were also standing and were not wearing regular street clothes, but rather what appeared to be military attire from ancient times. The color of their clothes was a radiant white and gold that appeared to have a moving light source within it. There was a glow to them, and a sense of peace in their gaze, which was shocking considering the circumstances. She made eye contact with the one closest to her, and he signaled in the direction of a white van not more than twenty meters from her, moving along the street away from her. She looked and realized this was not an ambulance. She glanced over and, focusing on the area around the passenger window, saw two men. One had his head partially out the open window, and she saw the other one through the reflection on the side-view mirror. Fatma saw their faces clearly as if she was able to zoom in from a distance of what was now almost thirty meters. With the first one, she just saw a profile as he was turning his head back into the car. The one in the mirror was actually looking at her! She detected a mixture of fear and sadness in his gaze, and his young face appeared familiar. Maybe someone that she saw in town, or at school? She felt sorry for him, and the thought that came to her mind was, *I am so sorry you are trapped in that misery. I hope God forgives you...*

Next to them, two more of the glowing warriors, and behind them, a third, very disturbing and dark presence. All three were suspended on air next to the van. The glowing warriors appeared to be trying to fend off the dark one from approaching the shooter and his driver companion, and neither one of the three appeared to be subject to the slow-down in time as they noticed Fatma in the distance. The disturbing looking individual was not armed and was wearing a similar attire to that of the three *warriors* standing by her side. However, his was of a different color and style, and around him an aura of darkness. There was no glow. His behavior was also unexpected, as he appeared to be grinning when Fatma first locked eyes with him, but he quickly changed his expression to one of concern, even fear, from seeing her there. Before she could observe more details about his appearance, he vanished. The look of absolute horror in his face was the main thing that struck her about their quick interaction.

Fatma was surprisingly calm considering what had just happened to the men standing next to her, and the situation that she was still experiencing in this time freeze. She also felt a deep sense of sadness, not only because of the dead men, but also for what she could perceive of the two men in the van, particularly the driver. While she appeared to be in a different dimension than the driver at the time, she softly whispered, "Why did you do this?"

Focusing again on the entities immediately next to her, Fatma realized that the only movement she could detect now was hers as well as the glowing warriors. Two of the three had knelt by the side of each of the IDF soldiers, while the third one, closest to her said, "Demons thrive when they operate in darkness and cannot be seen but are fearful of being seen and exposed. Fear motivates most of their actions." He paused, looked in the direction of the van, and then asked, "Had you seen him before?"

The entire situation was absolutely bizarre, and yet felt *normal* to Fatma. It was as if she had stepped out of time-bound existence and her only company were these entities that she could not fully comprehend or identify, and all the while, her anxiety attack had disappeared. The warrior at her side asked again, and Fatma answered, "Yes, I have seen him before, but I don't recognize where or who he is. Who are you, and who are your companions?"

The warrior explained, "We are messengers from God. Angels. I have been by your side since God gave you life, and my mission is to protect and guide you in your quest for salvation. The dark presence is a very powerful demon that has cursed the two attackers with his presence for a long time. They do not realize it, but in worshipping what they think is good, they are allowing that evil influence to control their lives. His name is Agares, and he followed the same tactics of deception, lying, and accusation as his leader Satan. There is a reason why you recognized him, not based on your human senses, but a more elevated sense in the spiritual realm."

This demonic presence had tried to instill fear in Fatma since she could remember, whether in dreams, when she was alone, or even when she recently went through the transforma-tion of her faith. She knew he had been there to plant seeds of doubt, discouragement, and despair.

The angel went on, "My name is Barachiel, and these are two of my army of angels. They were assigned to Moshe and Jacob, the Israeli soldiers, and will now accompany them in their next journey, as the one on Earth has just concluded." Barachiel went on to explain that God had imparted graces on her that she would gradually become aware of and understand, only to be used to help others get closer to Him by having a clearer understanding of the truth. It was very important that she understood that angels could communicate with her and engage in many activities in the spiritual realm, but it was up to her and other humans to be the ones acting on the physical realm. This is something that would be more important now, as the battle between good and evil was intensifying, and the time had come for her to play an important role in that battle on Earth. He concluded by saying, "There is more that I need to tell you, but at the right time. For now, pray to God, to Jesus Christ His Son, and to the Holy Spirit that flows between Them. Also, pray to the Blessed Virgin Mary, so she can inter- cede for you. They are always at your side and have selected me to look after you."

Fatma felt a sense of excitement and also validation about the fact that her instincts, and the help of Jenny, not to mention the grace of God, had led her to the truth. At that moment she felt a closeness and love to the humanity around her that was overwhelming. She felt awful for what had happened to Moshe and Jacob, but knew that they would be well, not in this world, but in a better much more meaningful realm that was full of true life. She continued to think about the attackers, sensing that their actions were based on hatred, which was rooted in fear. She sensed that in the shooter's eyes, but mostly the driver.

With that, Fatma suddenly felt a mild stomach cramp, and that sense of anxiety slowly building up again as she realized that time was rolling again in the physical world around her and she was in the middle of a chaotic situation at the bus stop.

Two young men that had been walking on the opposite sidewalk came rushing in and started to pump their fists and yell *Allahu Akbar* as they approached the bodies of the dead IDF soldiers. Even though they were in Israeli controlled territory, other rioters started to join in the chanting and rushed to the bus stop where some of the people were still slowly getting up. Bystanders pulled out their mobile phones and to record the commotion on video. The mob that started to form approached the bodies, not in an attempt to check on their condition or help, but rather to grab them and parade their bodies as a sign of victory against the hated Israelis.

The first one reached for Moshe's right arm, and at that point, Fatma launched herself on top of the two soldiers to block the angry mob from touching them. This infuriated one of the first two rioters, who grabbed her by the arms from behind and lifted her to a standing position. Before Fatma could say anything, he violently struck her in the face with the palm of his right hand and she fell to the ground. As they were starting to grab the soldiers again, the sound of an approaching siren made the mob dissipate. The scene was chaotic, with people running away in all directions. Left behind on the sidewalk, three dead bodies and an unconscious Fatma Saleh, the victims of a senseless act of cowardice and violence.

Meanwhile, Fathi and Nabil took advantage of the chaos. They quickly stashed the rifle inside the duffel bag and abandoned the van on the side of the street. Even with the traffic along Rub'a el-Adawiya Street, the oncoming vehicles had not witnessed the shooting, so no one paid any special attention to the white van driving up on the sidewalk and parking there. To most bystanders, the van must've looked like an ambulance or a commercial vehicle, and when they got out of it wearing scrubs, they were dismissed as being health workers with some connection to the hospital. The brothers blended in with the mob walking in the direction of the downed IDF soldiers but kept moving up the road toward the north, where, after a few more steps, they got inside Mendel's car. They had counted on the normal chaos of the street and the hospital entrance, as well as their swift and deliberate ditching of the van to minimize suspicion from any possible witnesses but were even more pleasantly surprised with the unexpected distraction the mob created.

Mendel was parked in front of the Princess Basma Center, across from the hospital. Once the two passengers came onboard, he immediately took off in the direction of his apartment in Bnei Ayish, near the upscale Jewish-Russian enclave of Ashdod, approximately a one-hour drive. The three men would remain there in hiding until nightfall, when it was finally safe to go to the rendezvous point near alZa'im.

Ahmed, who was able to move freely between Israeli and Palestinian territory, had been watching from the opposite sidewalk. He was confused and frustrated about seeing the van take a second go-around before taking the shots. He did not realize that the brothers had switched roles but knew there was something that made them hesitate the first time. He watched amusingly, and from a distance, as the mob started to congregate after the attack, waiting for it to defuse before slowly starting to walk toward the scene of the shooting pretending to be a curious bystander. While Ahmed walked, his gaze followed Fathi and Nabil as they went past the mob, approached Mendel's car and smoothly got in and departed. The deception worked, there were no signs of witnesses pointing in their direction, and he congratulated himself for the brilliance and simplicity of that part of the escape plan.

Ahmed continued to make his way to within twenty meters of the crime scene, surprised to see that most people were walking in the opposite direction, even though a few curious bystanders still converged around the police, and an IDF armored vehicle had also arrived at the site. Within seconds, Israeli police drew a perimeter around the scene. It was done to protect any evidence and as a safety measure. There was no way to predict if a volatile situation would emerge, and particularly the IDF contingent was very aware of the horrific episode that had taken place in Ramallah in 2000, where two IDF soldiers had been lynched by an angry crowd as the indifferent Palestinian police stood by. This time they were inside East Jerusalem, which would be much safer, but they chose not to take any chances.

As Ahmed reached the edge of the perimeter, he saw four people lying on the sidewalk, three of them on top of pools of blood. Both uniformed IDF soldiers were motionless and pale, no doubt dead from the bullet wounds. Two women lay on the ground near them, both unconscious and breathing, but the older one appeared to be gasping for air, and her breaths became weaker and farther apart. Emergency hospital personnel rushed outside and started to tend to both women. They moved them onto stretchers and rushed them inside. Ahmed thought, collateral damage. Totally acceptable given the jackpot of killing two IDF soldiers in plain daylight. A small victory for Hamas, but forward progress in his organization's plans to destabilize Israel, he thought, in his twisted way of justifying the carnage and horror that had resulted from their attack.

The dead IDF men were loaded into an ambulance that arrived a few minutes later, which took off in the direction of the HaKirya IDF base in Tel Aviv. Four Israeli police officers stayed behind surveying the crime scene, while the other two and the IDF officials followed the injured women into the hospital. Ahmed had seen what he needed, so he turned around, sent a couple of text messages from his phone, and left.

17

CONFLICT

2 *2:15 March 8, 2022*

After being dropped off at the rendezvous point by Mendel, Fathi and Nabil walked down the dirt path toward the tunnel at a brisk pace, hoping there would be no witnesses, particularly after the shooting and the expected mobilization of IDF and Israeli police in all areas within a five km radius from Makassed Hospital. The two had been extremely quiet during the drive from Bnei Ayish, some of it planned, as they were not to divulge any information in front of Mendel unnecessarily. However, some of it was because their mood had changed significantly given the amount of time that had elapsed and the fact that they were about to enter the riskiest part of the mission – crossing the barrier.

Aside from those, Nabil was also dealing with other concerns. The excitement and euphoria he had felt immediately after Fathi took the shots and their successful escape had been abruptly squashed when he experienced two things he had not expected.

As soon as Fathi fired and saw the IDF officers collapsing to the ground, he had seen a young woman standing next to them turn around and look in the van's direction. She was the only person to remain standing and did not appear to be fazed by the commotion. While he had only seen her through the side-view mirror, he felt her eyes piercing through and looking into his soul. Then, he heard the voice. There was no judgment or hatred in it, just compassion and an innocent disappointment at what a human being would be driven to do for the wrong reasons. The voice simply asked, "Why did you do this?" and that sucked away any feelings of victory or accomplishment that might have fleetingly overtaken Nabil at that time. This was not a subliminal experience. It was absolutely real, and he could not file it away as a byproduct of the anticipation and rush of emotions that he was experiencing. He also knew this was not going away, and he needed to pursue a better under-standing of what happened. His mood started to shift based on that unusual experience, but also because he started to ques-tion the justification for what they had just done. While he had performed petty crimes targeting Jews and felt resentment toward them, he had never been involved in a direct attack that would result in taking people's lives. He was regretting being a part of it and became upset at his brother for getting him involved in the mission.

Fathi's concerns were different. During the drive back to East Jerusalem he had seen much more police presence than earlier in the day when they left the crime scene. He was fearful they would come upon a roadblock that would trigger a part of the plan neither of them wanted to go through – they would have to kill Mendel, take out as many Israelis as possi-ble, then kill themselves. He was also replaying the attack in his mind, and while he felt it had been a great accomplishment, he was concerned about mistakes they made in the last few minutes. Mistakes which would undoubtedly provide the Israeli police more information to track them down. One specific concern was the last-minute change they decided to make about who would shoot. It wasn't until they were within two hundred meters of the hospital entrance that Nabil froze with second thoughts about pulling the trigger, so Fathi decided to continue driving past the hospital, switching places, and driving back Rub'a el-Adawiya Street one more time before making a U-turn to set up for the attack. There were no other roads around the hospital that would allow them to go around quickly, so they had to go back and forth on the same street four times instead of the single pass the plan called for. This would provide investigators more images of the vehicle as they reviewed footage from the many security cameras near the hospital.

The brothers cleared the tunnel and successfully got back to Palestinian territory without incident. Now, close to midnight, they walked along Jericho Road at a brisk pace. They entered the alleyway that led to the back door of the safehouse. There was no one on the street, so they punched in the code of the electric lock and entered. As planned, Abdul was there. He greeted them with, "Allahu Akbar!" and hugged and kissed them both. They paused for a few seconds for a brief prayer in the darkness of the room, and after that, Abdul asked for their full report and whether they had encountered any problems at the crime scene, in hiding with Mendel, or when sneaking back under the barrier wall. By then Abdul had seen plenty of coverage about the coordinated attacks in the news and heard from Hassan about Ahmed's assessment.

"I am sure both are dead, and we sent the right message to the infidels that we will not sit idle while they occupy more of our land," said Fathi, unable to hide his excitement. "I told you we could do this. Nabil and I are ready for this kind of mission and want to eliminate these worshipers of Satan from the face of Palestine...all the way to the Mediterranean."

"Your work is not done. I know you are excited, but for now, the first thing you need to do is calm down and debrief the details of what you saw," interrupted Abdul. "Did anyone see you at the shooting or at any point after you dumped the van?"

"No one," answered Fathi without hesitation.

Nabil had been standing quietly behind Fathi and lowly whispered, "There was a girl, a young woman...the only one in the crowd to remain standing. She was calm and acted as if she felt she could not be hurt by the bullets or anything else and turned and looked in our direction. I don't know how, but I am sure she saw us and what we did." He paused, and then to emphasize, said, "She saw our faces. I think she would be able to recognize us."

Fathi looked at Nabil in the eye. His expression was one of confusion, but also of anger, as he felt betrayed. "How could she see our faces and recognize us from that distance in a moving car? How could she see your face while driving if she was on the opposite side of the car? We have a better chance of being captured by the surveillance cameras outside the hospital than by some girl who was probably in shock! What kind of nonsense is this?"

Abdul, who up until this point was overcome with excitement and a feeling of victory, started to get anxious. He thought it was hard to believe, and Fathi had made some valid arguments, but he trusted Nabil's judgment and instincts as well. Nabil, while younger and less experienced, always led with the truth, even in situations that would get him in trouble. He was normally quiet, but when he spoke, he was direct and said what he thought and felt.

Abdul turned to Fathi, trying to maintain his composure, "The cameras are not going to be a problem. What could be is that you drove the van twice through the area before finally taking the shots. You have said nothing about that. Did you think I would not find out? Maybe you were lucky that the security cameras have a blind spot in that area. The stone fence and the pine trees that line up the hospital perimeter block the view of the area you were supposed to shoot from. The people that work for K scouted that area for weeks, and that was one of the reasons they selected that spot." He paused, then went back to learn more about the concern Nabil had brought up. Addressing Fathi again, he said, "Did you debrief with Nabil about what both of you saw before, during, and after the attack?"

Fathi became defensive. He knew he had missed an important step because his euphoria took over as soon as he realized he had effectively killed the two IDF soldiers. He had gone from anxiety, to anger over having to switch roles with Nabil, to an uncontrolled heartrate as the van approached their target, to exhilaration once he saw the two soldiers collapse. Too much emotion for him to step back and act more analytically, more surgically. This mission was not the end-all, just one small step of progress against a formidable and hated enemy. But in his small mind, there was no capacity to view things that way. He responded to Abdul, "I saw enough. I saw more than Nabil, who was sitting in the driver's side of the van, away from the target. He speaks nonsense."

Abdul did his best to remain calm, although he did not appreciate the lack of control that Fathi was demonstrating. He said, "The mission was successful, and that is the most important thing. The only concern I have about the girl, or woman, is that she may be the only witness that we can think of at this stage, and if she is able to identify either one of you, that would be one step removed from me and our cell. Our next step would be to find her, ideally before she tells anything to Israeli authorities."

Then, out of nowhere, Abdul swung his right arm and slapped Fathi on the side of the head a few times, and asked, "Why did you not know about this before? Why did you not shoot the woman too, if she was right next the soldiers?" He stepped back and started pacing around the room. "No witnesses! If Nabil saw her standing, you should have seen her as well. What were you doing? Celebrating on your own while your brother was still driving and surveying the surroundings?" The realization that they could have been spotted and traced to the area was a big concern for Abdul. Any little piece of information could be a problem, and Israeli authorities had very strong investigative capabilities. A sense of fear started to grow in Abdul's mind, some of it because of the threat of losing what he had worked so hard for, but also because he knew the consequence of making a mistake.

Fathi felt he was cornered and turned his fear and anger onto Nabil for being so paranoid and for betraying him. He yelled at him, "How could she *see* us? If she did, why did you wait until now to say anything?" The situation escalated and became chaotic, with Abdul and Fathi screaming at the top of their lungs and Abdul grabbing the rifle and hitting Fathi in the stomach with the butt end. Fathi, in turn, started crying and yelled at Nabil, calling him an ingrate.

"Stop blaming your brother!" uttered Abdul as he forced Fathi to his knees and pulled out a knife. "You had plenty of time to debrief on the way over. Did you ask him what he saw, or did you just talk about how great you are and how famous you will become after this little mission? He spoke now because I asked him. You were the senior person on this mission and could have done the same thing, you idiot! You have no one to blame but yourself and your childishness."

All Nabil could do was sit on the floor with his back against the wall and his head between his knees, praying that this would end soon. Abdul pulling out a knife in the middle of this agitation was a terrible sign. There were stories about Abdul getting so enraged with one of his top lieutenants that he cut off one of his pinky fingers after a failed attack. There was also a myth about a low-level member of his cell being castrated by Abdul, dying a few days later. It was Nabil's brother and he felt a certain responsibility to defend him, but he froze when he saw such raw rage in Abdul. His energy was dark, violent, and extremely volatile.

After a few seconds, Abdul calmed down as if a switch had been turned off, then turned to Nabil. "How can you be so sure that the woman saw you?" He went from extreme volatility to absolute calm in a split second. "I want the two of you to stay here for now. No one is to see you in al-Eizariyah, or anywhere else for that matter, at least for the next twenty-four hours." Then, as if nothing had happened, he turned around and left.

Fathi and Nabil stayed in the house. Fathi kept on crying and cursing after the realization that Abdul perceived the mission had not been as cleanly executed as it should have been and that this could set him back significantly in his quest to become a more prominent and trusted member of Hamas. Considering all that had gone well, mainly that they killed their targets and were able to escape, it was hard to believe that Abdul would be so obsessed about a single witness. The threat from Abdul made Fathi forget about his anger against Nabil. At this stage he was still in shock, but content to be alive with all extremities intact. Nabil remained in the same pose praying, and both were quiet until they succumbed to exhaustion and fell asleep.

18

FATMA RECOVERS

A s Fatma slowly regained consciousness, the first thing she noticed was pain and swelling on the side of her face. She opened her eyes and found herself in a place where she recognized the sounds, smells and the little she could see initially. She was in a hallway inside the Emergency area of Makassed Hospital. She could discern the shapes of three people standing next to her stretcher. Her vision came into focus, and she noticed two people wearing green scrubs behind the group that was immediately next to her stretcher, one with a white robe walking with a sense of purpose and urgency as they were taking care of the woman who had been wounded during the attack, now in critical care. She had been brought inside to Makassed Hospital.

As she scanned the room and her immediate surroundings, she noticed Ghassan standing next to her. Standing at his side was a uniformed Israeli Police officer, and at the foot of the stretcher another man dressed in civilian clothes.

"Hello, Father," Fatma whispered as she started to feel more alert. She was not totally surprised to see him in the restricted

East Jerusalem area. Ghassan's current project took him to that side of the country, so he had a valid work permit.

"How are you feeling, little one?" he said as he grabbed her hand in an expression of affection that was uncommon for him. This was a terrifying experience. His daughter had been right next to the line of fire and was incredibly fortunate to not have been shot, even though she had obvious signs of trauma to her face and head from the brief attack of the Palestinian mob. In addition to that, she was now surrounded by Israeli Police and IDF, whom he did not fully trust. But that was likely the least of her problems, as he thought there might be a chance that the radicals would recognize her. If they could identify her and knew she was a likely witness, God only knew what could happen.

The two Israeli men looked at Ghassan and Fatma with a bit of surprise after hearing the exchange in English, their accent appearing to be straight out of the UK. The vast majority of Palestinians communicated in Arabic, and this was some-what unusual to hear. Maybe that explained his general demeanor toward them, and the fact that she was allowed to attend college, which based on her books, appeared to be on a science or health care topic. Isaac, the Israeli police agent, had already performed a thorough inspection of all her belongings, which is how he found her identification card, and through it, a way to contact Ghassan. Even though she appeared to be an innocent bystander, no precaution could be too excessive when dealing with some of these young Palestinians, particularly college students.

Ghassan then said, "These men were kind enough to contact me after the shooting to inform me you were here and gave me a ride. I also called Reema to let her know you are fine. She and Ali are worried about you." He paused, then commented on the situation, "I am so relieved you were not shot. It looks like some coward struck you in the face, but the doctor says you will be fine in a few days."

Isaac then interjected, "Hello, Fatma, my name is Isaac Levy. I am with the Israeli Police here in Jerusalem." His tone was dry and efficient, and interestingly enough, he did not acknowledge nor say a word about his companion. "I would like to ask you some questions about what happened this morning. I am sorry about your injury. I hope you recover soon." He then started with a warm-up question to get her to focus on her most recent memory. He would then work his way back to the core of what he was interested in knowing. "Do you remember what happened *after* the shooting? Did you see the group of people that started to form around the bodies?"

Fatma took a couple of deep breaths as she tried to recall that last thing that happened to her before being knocked unconscious. "I don't know where these people came from, but a group of six or seven men came running in my direction, I think to take away the bodies of the soldiers. All I remember after that is trying to prevent them from pulling one of the soldiers by the arm, a lot of yelling, and then I must have blacked out. Their rage was so bad that they were willing to injure me for getting in the way of their hatred." She paused, holding back tears and taking another deep breath as she relived the horrific moment. "It all happened very fast, and I don't think I remember any of their faces. I just saw them as a crowd, not each individual. I am sorry I cannot be of more help."

Isaac, undeterred by the obvious emotional shock that Fatma was going through, continued the interrogation, "What about before that? Did you notice something before, during, or right after the men were shot? All indications are that the shots came from a passing car. You were there, I presume, waiting for the bus, so you must have been looking at the passing cars. Did you see anything unusual?"

Fatma took more time to think about this question, as she replayed the memory. "The last car I remember seeing was a white van that I thought was an ambulance. I think it drove by...at least twice, not sure why. Maybe it was looking for a place to park." She kept trying to hone in on any other detail she might recall, when the memory of looking at the driver in the eyes came to mind. She closed her eyes so she could picture it more clearly. As horrible as it was, she felt a certain connection to the young radical behind the steering wheel. She then opened her eyes, looked at Isaac, and shook her head and said, "That's it. I don't remember anything else."

"Alright," said Isaac, "If anything else comes to mind, please let us know. The Emergency Room doctor wants to keep you here overnight under observation. We will be back in the morning to give you a ride back home, just to be safe." Isaac did not want to pressure Fatma because he thought it would be counterproductive, but he at least wanted to maintain the communication lines open, since at this stage, she was the only potential witness.

Isaac and his team had already reviewed the recorded footage from the surveillance cameras of the hospital, as well as the Princess Basma Center across the street. They had seen the white van that was left abandoned in front of the hospital drive by twice, but those video segments did not show the actual shooting. The short footage they were able to aggregate across all cameras did not show a person in the passenger seat, and the face of the driver was not identifiable given the angle and reflection on the window glass. Surveillance footage from cameras on the ground was not going to be much help. Satellite imagery was an option, but that was not up to Isaac. It was the domain of the Ministry of Defense as they investigated the death of two of their troops.

19

IN PURSUIT

Abdul came back to the safehouse the following morning. He brought them fruit, bread, yogurt, as well as some hummus. There was bottled water in the refrigerator, so they had something to drink. Fathi and Nabil were already awake and a little surprised by the unexpected early visit, as well as the shockingly nice gesture on behalf of Abdul to bring them breakfast.

Adbul appeared to be in a more positive mood, but also a bit anxious. Instead of a good morning greeting, he led off with, "You killed the two IDF pigs, a bystander, and might have hit a fourth person that seemed to be in relatively good condition." He went on, "She was young and wearing jeans. Your typical, disgusting, western wannabe. Probably a student at Abu Dis. That is what Hassan has heard from the person on the ground, Ahmed. He is the mysterious planner of the attack, was there and got close to the crime scene, staying for a few minutes after you escaped."

Fathi responded without giving it much thought, "I hit the two IDF pigs and one woman. I am certain it was just three people."

Nabil came out of his trance, realizing that the woman who spotted them might be the same one that Abdul was talking about as one of the injured. "Were they black jeans, and was she wearing a green sweater?"

Abdul looked at him and immediately understood the connection. "I am not sure what she could have seen, and why you are so concerned, but if we want to be sure, we need to try to find her. She was taken inside the hospital, and the police has most likely already questioned her. As a minimum we need to find out what she has told them, then eliminate her." He then rushed them to finish eating, or even take the bread with them, and to get in Abdul's car.

Abdul's excitement and paranoia had clouded his mind. His impulse was to rush to the hospital expecting to get in, interrogate, and then take out the potential witness. However, as he calmed down, he realized he needed to evaluate the situation before just walking in. That was, assuming that he would be able to get that far. He had not gone inside Makassed in years but was fairly certain they would have metal detectors and security at the entrance. He also figured there would be heavier than normal police and IDF presence after what had happened. The first big hurdle, however, would be the checkpoint into East Jerusalem. Sneaking in through the tunnel near alZa'im would take too long and arranging for transportation locally, even with Mendel, was not as easy as calling an Uber. He knew the odds were low, but felt the need to try, so they left in the direction of the hospital. One step at a time.

The car ride to the hospital was eerily quiet. Nabil was still rattled after the sequence of events in the last day, and in addition to the immediate crisis, was dealing with a more profound internal conflict. Nabil considered himself a faithful Muslim who followed the teachings of the Quran, but there was a sense of rebellion in his mind that did not allow him to blindly follow all that was expected. He could not reconcile the Quran's message of love with the calls to violence that were embedded within its text. He also did not fully understand how their prophet could have resorted to violence and forced people to follow his faith and teachings through the use of the sword. It stood against the concept of free will, one of the rules in the relationship between an all loving God and humans. If God did not consider it right to force us to follow him, why would it be right for humans to force that choice? This, he felt, was a very important concept that weakened the foundation of his faith and made him question whether his path to God was the correct one in the Muslim faith, or whether he should be open to and learn more about other faiths, such as Hinduism or Buddhism. Certainly not Judaism or Christianity. Not after all those religions had done to his people, which was so evident in their marginalization in Palestine. There was a long history of persecution and violence associated with those religions, and that made them no better than the faith that he had followed since birth. The emotional impact of the events in the last twenty-four hours jolted him to the point of questioning everything, so this topic was at the forefront of his concerns as he quietly rode in Abdul's car to the scene of the fateful incident.

FATMA WAS a bit paranoid as Isaac and the IDF officer in civilian clothes gave her and Ghassan a ride back to their apartment in a black SUV, easily identifiable by locals as an Israeli police vehicle. She knew there were radicals in al-Eizariyah, possibly connected to those that executed the attack, and they would immediately spot them. She rearranged her headscarf to cover most of her face to avoid being recognized inside a police vehicle. She also knew that at least one of the attackers, the driver, had seen her at the scene of the crime.

She felt calm only because of how real and peaceful the experience with Barachiel had been, but she had been through a lot during the last twenty-four hours and was still trying to take it all in. Her newfound awareness about the spiritual realm also made her more sensitive to everything in her surroundings, so during the drive back home she carefully examined the details of what she saw. As they were making their way to the barrier checkpoint, she scanned every car around them to look for the people inside and see if there was anything suspicious. There were commercial vehicles and large coach buses filled with tourists on religious pilgrimages, as well as the multitude of compact personal cars with local commuters, typical traffic for a weekday afternoon in the settlements and neighborhoods adjacent to East Jerusalem.

THE DRIVE, and slowdowns in traffic, gave Abdul time to think through what he wanted to accomplish once arriving at the hospital. For one, he would not be able to get his pistol through the metal detectors at the entrance, and the injured would likely be surrounded by armed police. The mission for now had to involve the best possible way of finding out if the woman was still at the hospital and find out her identity. Israeli police moved swiftly and would not be wasting any time as they investigated the killing. This morning's mission also made him acknowledge that he needed more help. Perhaps an insider at the hospital, someone who could obtain information about her location, and could also provide cover for them to go inside. He thought about making a phone call to one of his contacts, but then he would have to explain why they needed to get into Makassed. He had not told anyone in his command chain about the possibility of a witness and was not ready to admit that yet.

He turned his focus to the more immediate step of getting through the checkpoint into East Jerusalem, which was challenging given that his car had a green Palestinian license plate and those were not allowed to cross the checkpoint unless they had special permission, something he lacked. Abdul's hastily devised plan was to make a plea that Nabil was feeling ill and needed to get to the hospital urgently. He decided to try the a-Zaitun/Ras Abu Sbitan checkpoint, which was closest to al-Eizariyah, just North of town. They might not be able to cross with the car, but if they found a private company crossing guard, might be able to convince them this was a medical emergency and be allowed to walk through, then take a taxi for the three-kilometer ride to Makassed. One thing they might have going for them was that an official checkpoint would be the last point of entry that would be expected of the attackers.

As they approached the checkpoint, there was a long line of buses and a few cars to get through into East Jerusalem. Two crossing guards screened cars before the checkpoint booth in an effort to triage and screen out anyone trying to enter Israeli territory without the necessary credentials. The agents spotted the green license plate and walked over to the Kia to defuse any potential situation way before they got closer. There was no greeting, just a quick question and a statement in Arabic from the female checkpoint guard, "What is your business today in East Jerusalem? Your car cannot go inside." She must have been no older than twenty-five, still with signs of acne around her chin. The young appearance did not take anything away from her assertiveness and aggressive tone. Extensive training and more than two years working the border compensated for her lack of combat experience. Her uniform was relatively plain, olive colored with a bulletproof vest, and no name tag. She stood close to the driver's window, her index finger on the trigger and thumb on the safety selector of a Tavor X95 submachine gun pointed strategically just below the window. Her partner stood to her right in a similar pose watching the passengers – Fathi in the front passenger seat, Nabil in the back. There had been many of these highly tense interactions at these Israeli-Palestinian checkpoints, particularly in Gaza, but now starting to become more common in the West Bank. The crossing guards approached each of them expecting an imminent threat.

Abdul was not intimidated. "My friend in the back has a bad pain in the stomach, maybe his appendix, and needs us to take him to the hospital. It is urgent! We need to take him to Makassed as soon as possible. Even if we cannot bring the car through, we'll take a taxi or the bus once we are on the other side." Abdul tried to appeal to agent's mercy, hoping she would be open to an exception for humanitarian reasons.

"We can't," she responded without giving it a millisecond of thought, and after some weak pushback from Abdul, she said, "These are not my rules. They exist to protect the people of Israel from possible hostility. You have probably heard about what happened yesterday at Makassed, and I am sure you know there have been enough incidents at the checkpoints to warrant the heightened security."

Abdul responded in obvious frustration at realizing that there was no way to persuade her, "That is not true. The reason for the security is that people like you see us as second-class citizens and want to keep us locked behind these barriers."

The agent, who had likely heard that line hundreds of times, responded, "Doesn't Palestine have checkpoints? Have you ever crossed the Allenby Bridge checkpoint? They have hundreds of arrests there every week. The difference is that everything we do here is under a bright spotlight, but what happens in Palestinian checkpoints is a big mystery. Why don't you complain about those? Turn around now. There is a long line of cars and buses behind you and we are taking too long."

Reluctantly, Abdul performed a U-turn in the middle of the chaotic traffic, then started to head back to al-Eizariyah. He could not contain his anger and frustration and began to yell in the car and bang the steering wheel. "How can we accomplish our mission if we cannot get around the stupid country? They keep us locked like animals inside our own territory! Do you see, Nabil, why we must carry on with our mission to destroy these satanic infidels?" He knew Nabil was not as fanatical about their mission as Fathi, so in a way, this was a test.

Nabil would not bite. He remained quiet during the entire rampage and assumed the question was rhetorical, with no answer expected. He was more focused on his surroundings, worried about the woman at the attack scene pointing him out to the police. His eyes were on the cars around them on the road. He noticed an unmarked Israeli police car behind them, moving above the speed limit, so he looked in the opposite direction when it passed them. When the police car was a few feet ahead, he slowly turned and looked at it again from behind. There seemed to two men in the front and a man and a woman in the back. The woman was wearing a headscarf of the same fabric as the student in front of Makassed, but this one covered her entire face with a small sliver of an opening for her eyes. Could it be the student? Or was the memory of her making him imagine things?

As he debated whether to mention this to Abdul, Nabil caught a glimpse of the woman slowly turning her head around to look inside their car. That simple motion reminded Nabil of the moment immediately following the shooting, when he saw the female student and heard a voice in what at the time felt like a whisper, which he was not sure was necessarily directed at him. He started wondering whether there was indeed a connection there, as if the woman was trying to communicate with him. He replayed it in his mind, "Why did you do this?"

THE POLICE CAR had been moving faster than the surrounding traffic, and Fatma noticed a car on the right lane with two men sitting in the front and one in the back. As they were about to pass, the two men in the front turned around to see who was in the police car, while strangely the one in the back looked in the opposite direction, as if he did not want his face to be seen. She saw enough without turning her head as they were passing, but her curiosity eventually had her turn slightly to see if she could see the man in the back. Fatma was able to get a quick glimpse of his face. It was the driver at the shooting!

After the initial reactions of shock and fear, she again felt a certain empathy and concern for him. He looked younger than the other two, just about her age, and she did not detect the same look of anger prevalent in local radicals, some of which she had seen in town and at the university. Fatma also felt a strange sense of connection to him, as if somehow there was a role for him to play in her life or at least this new reality she had entered in the last twenty-four hours.

As they got closer to the center of town in al-Eizariyah, traffic started to back up, and that forced the police car to slow down. They were only four cars between the two once they hit the traffic congestion, and there was no room for the police car to move ahead. The tension that both Fatma and Nabil felt started to grow. Her human instincts suggested she was at risk, that it was very likely he had recognized her and had told the others. Her newfound spiritual reality gave her a feeling that she had the strength to deal with whatever challenge was in front of her, that this was intended for her to fulfill the purpose she was starting to discover in her life.

Barachiel had emitted an incredible sense of peace but was not indifferent to the suffering that had taken place that morning. He made it clear that there is an absolute right and wrong, good and evil, and that whatever mission they were undertaking was not for the fulfillment of her individually, but rather to align with the will of God. Because of that, she also sensed that this might not be free of pain and suffering but was willing and committed to pursue it if it moved her closer to the truth, and ultimately to her Creator.

Nabil was equally as anxious, particularly for the risk of being exposed, which would likely cost him his life, either at the hands of the Israelis or within Hamas. The stakes were as high as they could be, yet he chose to stay quiet. It did not seem completely rational at the time, but it was not normal either that he felt that strange connection to the woman. He started to seriously consider the possibility that it was her who had asked the question, that somehow, she recognized him after the attack and knew it was him in the car. There is no way that she would under normal circumstances. There was no way she could have seen his face with any kind of detail at that distance and through his reflection in a mirror when they made eye contact. So how else would she know it was him? He still sensed that she knew, but that she was not going to let this be settled by the authorities. She would not turn him in.

Fatma whispered to Ghassan, "Father, I do not think it's a good idea from them to take us all the way to the apartment. Please ask them drop us off at the bus stop." Ghassan thought about it for less than a second and said yes. He looked at her with concern after realizing that whoever did this might connect them with the Israelis. His mind had been occupied by concerns about Fatma, and he knew this would leave emotional scars. While she had experienced her share of violence in the town and school while growing up, it never involved an attack on human life of people standing right next to her. She was too young for that.

Ghassan asked Isaac for them to be dropped off at the bus stop. Isaac immediately understood and offered to take them a few blocks away from the main road and drop them off at a place where they would not been seen by as many people. Ghassan agreed and thanked Isaac. Isaac turned left from E-Sheikh Street on to Route 417, or Jericho Road in that part of the country. They proceeded for a half a kilometer, then made a right turn onto a narrow city street.

Fatma had been able to follow the Kia behind them through one of the side-view mirrors and was relieved to see that it had made a left turn a few blocks earlier. Once Isaac got far enough from Jericho Road for them not be seen, he stopped the car and turned around.

Isaac said as he reached back with his business card, "I am sure that this episode will not be easy to forget, and you may have concerns about your safety. This is my card. Call, text, or email me should anything unusual happen that requires our help. I hope you feel better."

They thanked him, got out of the car, and walked toward the apartment, which was only a few hundred feet away. On the way, Fatma recorded Isaac's contact information on her smart phone. She was sure she would need his help if the radicals found her.

20

LIFE GOES ON

Week of March 21, 2022

After only six weeks from the original diagnosis, Shannon finally succumbed to pancreatic cancer. By the time she was diagnosed, the cancer had already progressed and spread too far. The cause of death was kidney failure, but this was just the final step in a quickly deteriorating situation where most major organs in her body were consumed. She died peacefully, although heavily medicated to manage the intense pain in her abdomen. The six-week process was the single most painful event in Nick's life, leaving him emotionally devastated. The sense of loss, guilt, and general sadness were disorienting.

Nick worked almost unconsciously through all the arrangements and questions about what to do next, from deciding whether to hold a wake for an extended time, to determining if she should be cremated or buried. He had Ewan and Denise helping him through all that was happening. Denise and Shannon's younger sister took over that process, dealing with the funeral home, the cemetery, and their church. While Ewan was not very helpful with those details, he provided Nick company during a time in which he felt abandoned. The couple had arrived at the house within an hour of Nick's call the morning Shannon passed. Shannon had been under the care of an amazing hospice nurse during her last three weeks at their townhouse. Nick had decided to keep her at home since there was nothing to be done at a hospital. At that point, hospice had taken over, focusing on pain management and tending to her basic needs.

Three days after all the arrangements were completed, Ewan invited Nick to lunch in the Georgetown area. He thought that restarting their routine would give Nick some sense of normalcy. He also knew it was very early, and at this stage it was unlikely that anything would feel normal to him, though he had to start somewhere. This time he recommended the Peacock Café, since it had an atmosphere that was a little livelier than some of the pubs and more traditional eateries in the area.

This time it was Ewan who arrived early and asked for a table for two, specifying that he would like a location that was as private as possible. The hostess walked him to a four-top table in the far corner, where she said she did not expect to have too many people seated nearby. Ewan walked up to it and hung his umbrella on the backrest of one of the extra seats before sitting down. He was not a big smart phone user, so while he waited, he simply used that time to anticipate and prepare for what could be a difficult conversation.

During his years as a priest, he had dealt with parishioners who grieved the death of loved ones. There had been difficult and tragic situations, where the loss of a working parent had derailed the entire financial situation of the surviving spouse and young children. He had also dealt with parents who lost children, which were the absolute most horrible situations he had witnessed. Even with that, he had not had the experience of a close friend dying and providing support to the surviving spouse, also a close friend. Ewan was personally affected by and involved in this one, making things tougher for him.

Ewan kept looking at the front entrance. Even though the hostess knew to bring Nick to the table, Ewan wanted to make himself visible to him when he entered. A few minutes later, Nick came in and quickly spotted Ewan. As he walked over to the table, Ewan noticed that he was moving with a good sense of positive energy and appeared generally upbeat. When he was within five meters of the table, he jokingly said, "I guess this is a first. The busy college professor got here ahead of the retired guy!" With that, he stretched his hand and shook Ewan's, followed by a hug that lasted a few seconds, during which Nick whispered, "Thank you for making the time. I needed this."

"Happy to make the time, my friend. You look great!" Then, he signaled to Nick to please take a seat, and as he was sitting down, said, "You surprise me. I am very happy to see you with this pep. You need it and deserve it. How are things?"

Nick sat down, picked up the menu in order to retrieve the cloth napkin, and as he went through his ritual of re-arranging the location of the silverware, bread plate, and water glass, said, "Oh, it's all a façade. I am still struggling but choosing to stay afloat. The four walls of my home office are collapsing on me. But I have to say that getting out of the house and getting together is something I was looking forward to and needed badly. Thank you so much, seriously. How's Denise?"

"She is fine," responded Ewan. "Thank you for asking. She sends her love, and asked me to tell you she has been praying for you."

Nick smiled. "Please tell her that I really appreciate it. When she asks about me, please tell her that I am OK, that you were surprised to see how well I am adapting." He paused, looked at Ewan in the eye, and in a softer tone, opened up, "I don't want you to lie to her, but I also don't want her or anybody else to worry more than necessary. This is a natural process and it will take time, but I am gradually feeling better. I'm actually able to breathe normally now, and yesterday I ran again for the first time in five weeks, so no need for drama. I will do a little better in a week, then a lot better in a month, and so on. Oh, as a final point, I will continue to pray as well."

The waiter came by the table, and they ordered after quickly scanning the menu. Once he was gone, Nick got to the topic he really wanted to talk about. "So, on the point about prayer, that is probably the area that worries me the most. Maybe you can help me with that."

Ewan jumped in, "OK, I'll try my best, but I didn't think that praying was something you were challenged with."

"Well, it is the overall topic of faith. Prayer is just one part of it. During the last few weeks, I have experienced a gradual erosion of my faith that is untimely and concerning. It has been a spiritual storm, and I am now realizing that my faith was not as strong as I thought. I guess when all is fine, it's easy to believe, be thankful...you know what I mean." He paused, and with both elbows on the table, started to massage his forehead with his left hand. "I think I expected to feel differently and be more accepting of the end, since her suffering was so...horrible!" He paused, holding back tears, then continued, "In the big scheme of things, that is where we are all headed. It's just a matter of time, and I guess we are supposed to be better off once we cross..."

After a couple of awkward silent seconds, Ewan said, "Nick, this is normal–"

Nick cut him off, "When my father died...roughly ten years ago, I experienced some of the same feeling of emptiness. Abandonment, maybe. But just as he was agonizing, a school friend of his, who was a priest, came by to visit and anointed him. He had no idea Dad was in his final hours, so the timing of the visit was interesting, and we all saw it as a blessing. The priest said something that, at that moment, resonated with me in a big way. He was talking about suffering, and why God would put us through it. Then he mentioned something I had read or heard in mass hundreds of times, but never internalized to grasp its true meaning. He said, 'Whether it was following the death of his friend Lazarus, or during His passion, Jesus suffered to the point where he cried.' To emphasize he looked at us and said again, 'God cried!' That was not only very deep and hard to understand, but just reflecting on it made me feel like we were connected at that moment. Actually, it made me realize he had been there all along. I left the room, walked outside, and broke down, crying like a child. I will never forget how that crying felt. It was not sadness. I don't think it was even happiness. It was more about fulfillment, about clarity, about a sense of optimism and ultimately peace." He paused, thought about it some more, then said, "I guess that is happiness. Just not that *happy* happiness the way we are so conditioned to define it."

Ewan asked, "And even now that you have that awareness, and can recall that experience, you are not experiencing the same thing, right?" After a nod from Nick, he added, "Hard to understand, the inconsistency and almost randomness of God's approach. We have these expectations about His behavior, and when they are not met, we get frustrated, sometimes to the point of losing faith. But...the randomness has existed in the past. There were several instances during Jesus' life where he tested his friends, not being there when they expected it. He fell asleep on the boat in the middle of a tempest. He also appeared to ignore the cry for help from Lazarus' sisters when their brother was dying. If you explore what that priest said at your father's deathbed, we don't know if Jesus got that spiritual embrace from His Father before dying. And this is someone who was in constant prayer and communion with the Father, but as he was nearing death, he even asked why he had been abandoned. That distance from God is what can be the source of the worst suffering, more so than the physical one."

"Yes, that distance has been tough. I guess I am going through one of those painful phases of spiritual growth. Not fun."

Ewan then asked, "Are you having thoughts that you know are downright lies? For example, are you thinking that you did not do enough to save her, that you allowed the cancer to take over without putting up a fight? Are you also hearing in your mind that she is just gone, no more Shannon? Are you also hearing the classic *what if there is no god* question?" He looked at Nick, who had his eyes wide open looking at him, an indication that he was amazed at Ewan's insight.

The expression amused Ewan, who kept going, "Not a big surprise. Those are all lies, and in a time like this, the typical ones that the devil and his followers would be whispering in your ears. They love to do it when you get up at 3:00 am for the conveniently scheduled bathroom trip we have every night once we pass our fiftieth birthday."

"OK. Yes, to all of that. So, what do I do?"

"In the Jesuit tradition...actually, based on teachings that were developed by St Ignatius himself, there is a process called *Discernment of Spirits*. I am not going to try and explain the entire thing, since there is a lot, but one of the foundational concepts in it is that we go through up and down cycles during our entire life. The upswings are periods in which we feel what he calls *Consolation*, and in the downswings, *Desolation*. Based on what you are telling me, your experience when your father died was an episode of Consolation, and the opposite is happening now."

"Yeah, that seems accurate." Nick said.

"There are a lot of negative things that happen during an episode of Desolation, and one of them is this bombardment of lies that start circulating in your mind. There are several factors that can bring about Desolation, like your own weaknesses, but there can also be external influences, like Spirits. Demons. Being aware of that is a big step in itself, but also realizing there are things you can do while in Desolation that can help you manage it. Read up on it. There are many books on the subject, and many of them explain it in a way that is not high theology." After a brief pause, he finished with, "For now, I would continue praying. Pray with faith that you will soon be consoled...because you will."

"I am so jealous of your faith. I so wish that mine was half as strong. In a moment like this, which is a test, I fail miserably."

They continued the conversation, with Nick doing most of the talking while Ewan listened. It was great therapy for Nick, reflecting on and confronting what was causing his pain. The loss of Shannon was devastating, but it had exposed a weakness in Nick he thought he had fully conquered years ago. It made him realize that, just like staying in running condition, his effort to grow spiritually would have to continue...always.

"And, changing the subject, if you don't mind," said Ewan, "I know it is early, but have you considered powering through with the plans to go on the Holy Land trip?"

21

NABIL AWAD

Wednesday March 23, 2022

Ever since the shooting took place, Nabil had grown more obsessed with being identified and caught. This time he had committed a very serious crime, and the Israeli authorities would likely find him, and once caught, would show no tolerance. His life as a student had changed, as he now felt out of place at the school among his peers, most of which were in it to improve their situation and hopefully start a career. There were many that had been radicalized, but their focus was on demonstrations and being disruptive, the kind of thing that Nabil had been involved with earlier.

Now, he had elevated his role to another level, and the murder of the two IDF officers had become a rite of passage into becoming a core member of Hamas. While their execution had seen its flaws, Nabil was seen as the more level-headed and talented team member who did his part well. Everyone knew that Fathi was sloppy, impulsive, not as smart, and when confronted with a difficult situation, could resort to unnecessary violence. There was a role for people like that in Hamas, but that was normally relegated to the grunts in their ranks, who ended up being disposable.

Nabil had two afternoon classes that day and was out by 15:00 and on his way to the bus station. Since the start of the semester, he had stayed on after Statistics to meet with the team that he had been working with on a group project. He had missed the meeting and the entire day of class two weeks earlier, so he could not afford to skip another meeting until the project was completed. The meetings would typically last until 16:00, but today's meeting had been shortened by the absence of two members. No one knew for sure, but the word was that they had been detained by IDF for acts of vandalism after a demonstration on campus last Friday.

So, with his meeting ending earlier, Nabil rushed to the bus stop, hoping to catch an earlier bus. As he approached, he noticed a long line of students already in queue. This guaranteed that, if he was lucky enough to get on the bus, he would be standing for most of the ride to the shack where he and Fathi lived, just east of al-Eizariyah, near Jahalin. He would still be better off, arriving home an hour early.

Unbeknownst to Nabil, Fatma was about ten people ahead of him, standing in line. She was wearing her earphones listening to a replay of her Sociology class and doing a bit of multi-tasking by writing down a few items she would have to work on once she got home. She was used to spending so much time waiting at the bus stops or in slow-moving traffic, that she was conditioned to making it as productive as possible. While Nabil was listening to reggaeton and rap, Fatma was getting things done. That was a great example of the contrast between the level of maturity and sense of purpose between the two. Fatma did not know exactly her destination, but she knew elements of it. She wanted to be independent, fulfilled personally and professionally, and more importantly, living elsewhere. She was fine living with her father, but not depending financially on him. Nabil had ambitions too, wanted to eventually be successful. He just didn't know in what. There were also many influences acting on him, particularly the organization of radicals that he was a part of, and that clouded his vision.

The bus finally arrived just before 15:30, and the students started to get in. Fatma was fortunate to find a seat at the back row of the bus. She sat down and surveyed the people around her. There were several familiar faces that took that bus on Wednesdays, but none that she personally knew. The bus filled up to the point where a few of the students in line could not get on, a typical occurrence at that stop. These private buses also operated on a highly unstructured schedule, and the one after this one, having to deal with heavier traffic, could be as much as an hour late. There was a little bit of banging from the ones left behind on the side of the bus as the door closed, and then they started making headway.

Nabil was lucky enough to be among the last three people to get on board. Boarding a packed bus increased his level of anxiety, but this was better than walking four kilometers in the hilly area around Abu Dis. As soon as the door closed behind him, he looked around to assess the crowd inside. He started with the rows of seats immediately next to him, and slowly moved into the rows toward the back. He was wearing sunglasses with reflective lenses, which gave him some comfort about his gaze not being detected. There were a few workers from the villages south of Abu Dis, but it was mostly college students commuting back home.

The bus came upon the Jericho Road intersection and stopped to unload some passengers, most of which had been riding before the Al-Quds stop. The movement of people standing up and exiting opened up a clear line of sight to the last few rows of the bus, so Nabil, with his head slightly tilted to his right, scanned the back of the bus as well. He quickly jumped from face to face, particularly looking for anyone that might have been staring in his direction. His routine was suddenly disrupted when he detected something unusual just before the crowd of newcomers started to push him and those around him to the back. That push made him get closer to everyone in front of him, blocking his view. The same move-ment took place a few minutes later when they stopped near the Church of Saint Lazarus, but this time, there was not enough clearance for him to look at the back row again.

The next stop was right before the roundabout, and this is where a larger group of twelve students got off the bus. Nabil thought this could be an opportunity to refocus on what had caught his attention in the back row. At first, there were too many people blocking his view for him to discern any of the individuals coming from the back as they exited and walked down the steps. Perhaps there was no reason for concern, he thought. As the bus moved again, he noticed something that alarms in his mind. A student who had just exited and was walking in the opposite direction of the bus, away from the roundabout, was wearing the same veil color-pattern as the female witness! Looking at the back of her head offered no chance to identify her facial features, but her build and height were consistent with the witness. The sight flashed back the memory of the question, *why did you do this?* and triggered a light cramp-like sensation in his upper abdominal area, imme-diately followed by a rapid heartbeat. He could clearly hear the thumping following that rush of adrenaline, the body's not-so-subtle reaction to suddenly facing a threat. His mind also started to race. What now? Should he ask the driver to stop so he could follow her? Should he just stay on the bus and flee, as confronting her could be even more dangerous? He paused for a second to take inventory of how he felt, realizing that this was not the time to make a rash decision. His heart rate started to slow down, and he took a couple of deep breaths, which helped him calm down and clear his mind.

In less than ten minutes, Nabil got off and began walking home, still in shock over the somewhat subliminal, yet powerful, encounter. He was still preoccupied but started to feel that this was likely going to work in his favor. As long as she did not see him, which he thought was the most likely scenario, he had an advantage. He knew the stop where she got off, and if he was lucky, her Wednesday schedule as well. He pulled up the calendar in his smart phone and confirmed that there were team project meetings scheduled all the way through April 20th. As anxious as he was to reach closure with the threat of her as a potential witness, he also thought that with each passing day the risk of being caught by Israeli authorities would be reduced. He would deal with the witness when the time was right.

22

NATHANAEL'S HOMETOWN

After giving it a lot of thought, Nick decided to push ahead with the Holy Land trip as originally scheduled. This was a trip that he and Shannon had always wanted to do, and now had finally gotten to the point of finding a travel group they liked and making all the required travel arrangements. They, along with Ewan and Denise, had opted to sign up for a pilgrimage being led by the local Franciscan Missionaries. It was their first time in Israel, and they were more interested in the trip serving a spiritual purpose as opposed to a cultural, touristy one. The format of the pilgrimage included daily masses and reflections at each holy site about the bible events that took place there. They figured they could always return if they wanted a more cultural experience, as long as they liked the country, found it to be safe, and just as importantly, if they liked the food.

After Shannon's death, Nick's initial reaction was to cancel and let Ewan and Denise do the trip on their own. He thought he would probably not be the funnest person to travel with and was afraid that being in all these places that he and Shannon had anticipated traveling to would only extend his grief. He felt his state of mind was too negative to go and get any enjoyment or fulfillment from the trip.

As time passed, and with a lot of convincing from Ewan, Nick opened up to the idea. He began to see how it could be a way to break the cycle he was in by changing the scenery, occupying his thoughts with something that he was interested in and possibly take advantage of an opportunity to enhance his ongoing spiritual *training* and growth. He was unsure about the last one, as lately he had regressed significantly in his faith and overall attitude toward God...if there was one.

With less than a week before departure, Nick got up early one morning and went for a five-mile run on a path along the Potomac. The weather was perfect for running, which put him in a good mood, the best he had felt in more than three weeks, since Shannon's death. As he came back, he stopped at the Starbucks on King Street, just a few blocks from his townhouse, to grab a bottle of Smart Water and a tall dark roast. He sat down at a table on the sidewalk, and dialed Ewan's mobile.

"Good morning. To what do I owe this call on a Thursday morning?" asked Ewan cheerfully, happy to hear from his friend.

"Good morning Professor. I realize you are a lot busier than me, but I wanted to let you know I am in for the trip." And after a quick pause, "Maybe it is the mix of endorphins and caffeine. Not sure, but before I change my mind, I wanted to let you know I plan to join you and your lovely wife at Dulles next week."

TEN DAYS LATER, *Saturday April 23, 2022*

The second day of the pilgrimage started with a trip to Cana, where married couples in the group would go to the Wedding Church to renew their vows. It was a relatively short bus ride from Tiberias, where they stayed the night before. The bus dropped them off along the main street in Kafar Kanna, near the intersection of a wide alleyway that was part of the old town. One big difference that Nick noticed from day one was the much larger number of tour buses and pilgrims at this site.

With the increased volume of people, there was another dynamic he found interesting. There were groups of people from different parts of the United States, several Latin American, Asia-Pacific Rim, African and European countries. Many of the groups carried flags from their country of origin, and even those that did not, could be easily identified because of their overall look, attire, and speech. It was a tremendously diverse group of pilgrims, which made Nick reflect on how all of them had at least one thing in common – they had freely chosen their Christian faith. For some, it could be the legacy of colonialism, but those forces had not been present in the last two hundred years, and in some of those countries, practicing the Christian religion involved personal risk. He was particularly impressed with the devotion that was on display from people that came from countries were Christianity was not mainstream, particularly India and many of the African countries. He thought to himself, "Whether it is Catholic, Orthodox or Protestant Christians, they see truth in the message regardless of cultural or geographic upbringing!" This was one of the biggest surprises he had on this trip. The historical and Biblical sites were expected, and visiting them was special, but the faith that he witnessed in those around him was overwhelming. This was certainly a sign of a living and vibrant faith, much more meaningful than the physical and archeological evidence in front of him. It was also then that he started to make the connection about the role that each of us plays in keeping that faith alive and sharing it. God is willing to intervene, but He would rather allow us to be His agents in this world.

Right before approaching the Nathaniel Bartholomew Church, their group stopped for the Gospel reading of relevance at that landmark. All had their headsets on, and Father Daulton picked a volunteer from the group to read John 1:47-51:

When Jesus saw Nathanael approaching, he said of him, "Here truly is an Israelite in whom there is no deceit."

"How do you know me?" Nathanael asked.

Jesus answered, "I saw you while you were still under the fig tree before Philip called you."

Then Nathanael declared, "Rabbi, you are the Son of God; you are the king of Israel."

Jesus said, "You believe because I told you I saw you under the fig tree. You will see greater things than that." He then added, "Very truly I tell you, you will see 'heaven open, and the angels of God ascending and descending on' the Son of Man."

EVERYONE TOOK a few seconds to reflect on the reading before moving on. Nick wondered what Nathanael was doing under the fig tree. It must have been something meaningful to the story, since Jesus' mention of it was enough to make him believe. Nick also felt a sense of envy of those that were witnesses of Jesus on Earth and had direct contact with him. He thought it made it much harder for us now, being two thousand years removed from those events.

The group started walking up the alleyway, and as they passed by the Franciscan School on their left, Nick heard a voice from his right call his name. When he turned, he was almost blinded by a brilliant flash of light, and then his surroundings completely changed. The busy alleyway with the hundreds of tourists were no longer there, and as he started to scan the space around him, he realized that the buildings were gone. He was standing on a rocky area with patches of grass. This was the surface of the hilly landscape as far as he could see, with the exception of the medium-sized tree with a wide canopy of large leaves that provided shade to a young man sitting underneath no more than twenty yards away from him. He was dressed in a simple tan tunic with sandals.

Nick was startled with this abrupt transition, which just as the vision on the plane, seemed supernatural. Yet, he remained calm and felt a great sense of peace. Deep down, he knew it was right for him to be there. His focus turned to the young man under the tree, who now Nick realized was crying unconsolably, in deep despair. He was screaming, repeating the same word, which sounded like "Al-Moh-Ah." Even though Nick did not know which language it was, he somehow knew that it meant *why*. He felt an urge to walk to the man and see how he could help, but quickly realized he could not move. He was there to be a witness, not to interfere.

A second person under the tree was then revealed. Its image started as a dark haze directly behind the crying man, and eventually it came into focus, but still remaining in shades of darkness, almost as in sepia. He towered above the crying man, almost as tall as the bottom of the canopy. While it had a human-like appearance, it made jerky movements with his arms and head, with an expression of deep hatred in his angular face. As unusual and otherworldly as it appeared, Nick felt a sense of familiarity with it. It continued moving and interacting with the youth in a way that made it obvious it was a live entity. The interaction was difficult to watch, as it appeared the young man was not aware of its presence, yet it was inflicting some sort of torment on him, most likely the reason he was crying and yelling in such despair.

During the entire episode until now, Nick could see a dim white glow just under the canopy and around the trunk of the tree, as if the tree was a light source. Suddenly, the youth went from sitting to kneeling, lifting his arms and yelling in desperation, "Ah-Lah-Hee," which Nick somehow knew meant *My God*. Almost instantly, the white light lit up the entire space under the tree and two warriors in gold appeared next to him. The first warrior confronted the dark presence, only needing the light that emanated from his body, which interestingly, appeared to draw energy from the white bright light under the tree. After a brief struggle, the dark presence collapsed in space and was no more. The young man fell to the ground crying, totally unaware of what had just happened around him. It appeared as if he could not see the warriors nor the light. Then, the white light and the first warrior disappeared. The second warrior started walking in Nick's direction, and as he drew closer, Nick remembered him. It was the same man from the vision on the plane!

The warrior said, "Do not be afraid, Nick. Do you remember me?"

"Yes! I saw you on the plane that night! Who are you? What's happening? How did I get transported to this place, and where are we?"

"*When* is it, you meant to say?" said the warrior, emphasizing the first word.

"When?" said Nick, trying to process the meaning of what appeared to be a clarification. "You mean, we are in Cana, but... at a different time?"

It would have been redundant for the warrior to confirm, so he went on, "What did your eyes just see revealed?"

After a deep breath thinking about the unusual circumstance, Nick said, "So, this is some sort of mystical experience, a revelation from a different realm? From God? If that's it, then... did I just watch Nathanael under the fig tree?"

"It was. Did you see his torment? Did you notice the lack of awareness of the powerful presences around him?"

"Yes...he looked to be unaware. The figure in sepia was some sort of evil spirit, a demon. I saw the two of you that came once he implored God, so I presume you are angels...of some sort?" Nick paused, reflecting on his crazy question, then said, "and the white light?"

"What do you think it was?"

Nick knew the light was the ultimate power, not only what fueled the warriors, but ironically what had created the demon and allowed it to live. "The white light was always there, waiting for an invitation to come. Yes," and slowly shaking his head, Nick said, "the light is God...Jesus, isn't it? May I ask, who are you?"

"I am Zaphkiel, an angel of God, assigned to you as a guardian. Just as God is always that light waiting to be invited, I am with you as well. Always have..."

Nick was in absolute awe! The dots that had been floating around in his mind all his life were converging, connecting.

Zaphkiel continued, "You remember seeing me on the plane, but do you remember what I revealed? Where you open to it?"

Hearing this, Nick broke down crying and said, "I am sorry. I was blessed enough for God to punch a hole into this world to tell me something...and I blew it. I am so sorry! Is it too late? Can I make it up to you, to Him?"

"Nick, I did not come to judge or punish you. Eventually you started to find your way and worked very hard to get where you are. But...there is so much more! The revelation you received that night was like a seed planted. At that time, you were not ready to understand it. That is why you suppressed it from your memory. Do you think you are prepared now, not only to see what was being revealed, but also to be closer to understand what it means?"

With that, Nick started to feel like he was transitioning to yet another point in time. He began to discern shapes in front of him that gradually came into focus. He found himself standing in the hallway of the business class cabin on that flight from San Francisco. He was transported to and reliving that moment from more than twenty years ago in vivid detail, as if it was happening now. He was the same person, the same witness. Only, this time, he had better context for what he was experiencing, and it was not about to be rejected by his consciousness and memory. A second chance!

He noticed a very pleasant smell that felt like a combination between the salty fresh ocean air and a bouquet of roses. Nick instinctively knelt and knew he was in the presence of an entity that was not from this world, but more importantly, radiated love and an incredible sense of peace. He found himself in a space that was full of light, energy, even colors he could not identify or describe. There was no voice coming from Zaphkiel, but rather an unusual sensation where he could understand what was being communicated. It was a much fuller way of understanding. Deep down, he knew it was raw, unfiltered truth. It started with what he understood to be a greeting, the same one he had just heard; "Do not be afraid, Nick." He found himself thinking that this was highly unusual, but did not feel afraid, uncomfortable, or even unfamiliar with this incredible environment. The entire situation felt *normal*, nothing to be worried about. He also had a sense that this was someone he knew, felt at that moment that he was there to listen, so he patiently waited for the messenger to take the lead.

Zaphkiel then said, "I am with you always. I know that many questions are troubling you and you are hungry for answers. Today I will start to help you understand why you don't need to be troubled."

He proceeded to show Nick three situations that he had lived through, the first one as a boy not quite ten, the other two later in his teenage years. All three were episodes that were so intense and traumatic, that they were forever imprinted in his outlook. All three were also very sad memories, the type he wanted to run away from and preferably forget. His story was told in more than just words, and he could see himself at the place where each one took place.

The first episode happened when Nick was a boy and at a

bowling alley playing with a group of older teens. He was brought by his cousin and excited about being allowed to play with the cool, big-kid crowd. Something as simple as arriving at the end of the ten bowling frames made him realize that everything ends. There was this inevitability of the passage of time – every future event that you have been anticipating eventually arrives in the present, and then it moves into the past at the same speed – which crushed him as a nine-year-old, with the realization that he, and everybody around him, had no control. You could not freeze the present! Everything in time eventually arrives and ends, and if you extend it long enough, includes our last breath. It was not only his first encounter of the reality and finality of death, as he had just recently lost his grandfather, but that felt more distant since at the time he felt his grandfather was infinitely older than him. How the present *burns* the future as it becomes the past without ever stopping is something he had just become aware of and gave him an intense sense of fear.

As the nine-year-old he was at the time, Nick reflected on how there were many truths he had learned and understood until that point. He felt that as he grew older, he would develop the capacity to also understand the deeper and more complicated ones, so there was no need to obsess over those...yet. The God that was taking care of him would eventually answer them when the time was right.

After witnessing the first episode, Nick felt the ground below him collapse into a void, then he was pulled from below through a stream of light, until the light started to fade and he saw himself and his mother in a room he recognized as the family room of the house where he grew up. Nick must have been in his early teens, sitting down watching TV, while his mother read a book. This was happening several hours after dinner on a Friday night. He had stayed downstairs to be with her, as she waited with anxiety for her husband to arrive from work. During the entire time he had gone back to be with her, neither one had said a word about the reason they were there. Words were not necessary for him to let her know he was there to give her company, support. She did not need to explain why she was so stressed. They both knew.

At around midnight, Nick saw the reflection of a car's head-lights through the windows. The car made an abrupt right turn into the driveway, stopped, and the driver's door swung open. Nick's father, who had been fighting bouts of depression since he was a child, did not do well when combining stressful times with alcohol. So, after a night of drinks with his friends from work, he finally got home, intoxicated, and at the edge of a nervous breakdown.

Nick and his mother got up and rushed to the kitchen, the closest entrance from the driveway. After seeing her go through the anguish of not knowing his dad's whereabouts, he was heartbroken that she did not even have a chance to ask him a question upon arrival. The scene immediately turned into chaos as he got out of the car and broke down into an anxiety attack, yelling and punching the car's hood. His father's yelling appeared to be the continuation of a dialogue that had started while he was driving in, and where he was asking to be relieved of this torment. Was he talking with his conscience? Was he addressing God in what would be an unusual way of praying? Was he yelling at some other entity? His father then slid down from the hood of the car and unto the driveway, staying on his knees while now slapping the ground repeatedly and contin-uing to yell.

As a teenager, Nick had never experienced this before and his first reaction was to try to wake up, since this must have obviously been a nightmare. He then realized that this was really happening and jumped in to help his mom, who while suffering through the episode, acted as if she had dealt with similar instances in the past and knew what to do. She ran to the kitchen, filled a plastic pitcher with water, walked outside, and dumped the water on his head. After the splashing, Nick's father started to slow down his tantrum, and the yelling turned into sobbing. He dropped to the ground and laid there crying for the next ten minutes. Mom and Nick stood by his side. She calmly told Nick, "It will be OK. This is not the first time your father has had one of these. He will be fine. Please go to your room and get some sleep. I can take it from here."

Nick was crushed for many reasons. The image of his father as the righteous, loving person who was always *in control* took a severe smearing. Realizing for the first time the suffering that his mother must have lived through in their marriage broke his heart. But the most difficult thing to accept was that, for the first time, Nick realized that God does not provide a safety net to prevent suffering. He was directly in contact with raw suffering, and there was no supernatural intervention to make it go away. Suffering was real, would happen again, and he had to learn to deal with it on his own. At the time he was too young to understand that suffering had a purpose. Developing that understanding would take effort and time, something that would happen later.

The third episode took place on the night of Nick's high school graduation, when after all the excitement, partying, and being surrounded by friends and people he loved, he found himself alone in bed in the darkness of his room, confronted with many life questions and thoughts that had been accumulating over the years. The most difficult thought was one that had kept growing in intensity during the last few years, and he did everything possible to block it – *what if there is no God?* He recalled his thought process at the time; his curiosity as a little kid could be satisfied with simple answers and by being smothered with a message of a god, that he took at face value and was enough at the time. It provided hope and made him feel there was meaning, and that there was someone keeping track of him as part of a much bigger plan. Over time, being exposed to additional information made him challenge those beliefs and introduced doubt. As the distance from that childhood innocence increased, and difficult events further shook his foundation, so did his doubt. The possibility, even if remote, that he, and the rest of humanity were here by accident, with no purpose or meaning, and that individual consciousness would eventually cease to exist, was excruciatingly painful for Nick to think about.

The thoughts were not going away that night, and Nick felt he was falling into an abyss of despair. He had experienced life events that introduced this anxiety, but at that time had the faith of a child and *knew* that someday God would provide an explanation that would satisfy him and give him peace. The hope of an explanation by a god was now erased, as the existence of that entity was in question. No God. No explanation. No peace. That night he had a full emotional collapse, and that started a long journey into questioning and eventually rejecting his faith.

Within this re-playing of the plane vision, Nick could actually see and feel what was going on in each of the three episodes, almost like re-playing the memory across all his senses, consciousness, and elapsed time. This was a very bizarre situation, but his *present* had moved to 2001, then earlier, to the day of each of those events. Each one was happening again. Two of the episodes involved no external drama, and that made him realize how events that have had a profound effect on him did not always involve much fanfare. Rather, they were events of the mind, taking place in an entirely personal and lonely setting.

Reliving them this time, in the expanded awareness he was experiencing, he had also noticed three people present by his side in each episode. The first one was always next to him, sharing in and embracing him through the suffering. His presence was overwhelming, but at the same time peaceful, unassuming, and...familiar! It was the presence of a loving older brother, not a concept or a symbol. It was not an esoteric spiritual entity, but a person, and he knew who it was – Jesus.

The second person felt like a childhood friend that you know can be trusted, makes you feel at ease, and is interconnected with your conscience. Nick looked at him, and felt this amazing sense of warmth when he realized this was the same person he encountered on that redeye flight from San Francisco and was with him now. The experience had somehow been suppressed from Nick's memory, with the exception of the message he continued to hear occasionally during the years that followed – *Go back to your roots. Let your curiosity guide you. Will you let God act through you?*

The last person was also a familiar presence from his early childhood years. One that he associated with a deep sense of sadness, emptiness, and darkness. One that had infiltrated his thoughts and dreams in the most unpleasant ways, and whom he knew but could not identify. That presence was there in each of those life events, and Nick was not sure what his role was or why he had picked on him.

Zaphkiel then told him, "His name is Agares, and he is an extremely powerful fallen angel that commands multiple legions of demons. He developed a particular interest in you ever since you were born. He has been behind the lies and distortions that led you to fall from your faith. He operates in stealth...as long as you have no awareness of his existence. As hard as it may be for you to believe, Agares lives in fear. He is afraid to be exposed. You need to know this, as he will hide his fear behind rage and intimidation, but as it relates to influencing you, he knows that you have access to forces that are more powerful."

"So, he is not going away?" asked Nick, with a tone of concern and disappointment.

"Not as long as you are in this world. He is wise enough to know that you will deal with more episodes of suffering and will be there to seize the opportunity. He is also trying to block you from fulfilling your potential, from making a difference in the life of others..."

"But Zaphkiel," Nick cut him off, "I'm almost sixty, hardly the young person with a full life ahead of them that can make that big of a difference. I don't understand."

Zaphkiel answered, "There is nothing to understand in human terms. These are mysteries that can only be reconciled in a much more powerful and encompassing mind. Besides, you would not be the first person that is recruited after being a mature adult to carry out an important mission in the name of God. You have read the Old Testament, and there are numerous examples dating back to the book of Genesis. Many of those stories are now discounted as metaphorical, but there is more truth there than people realize. Do not be afraid, you are in good company."

With that, Zaphkiel and the intense light slowly faded, and gradually Nick noticed that time was back in gear around him. He was back to Cana and the Nathaniel Bartholomew Church, with the group of pilgrims around him as if no time had elapsed and nothing had happened. No one else in the group noticed this pause in time and Nick's encounter, so he would keep it to himself.

The lessons in the revelation were overwhelming in the amount of knowledge that was imparted, but also a tremendous gift. It connected key moments in Nick's life with a parallel spiritual side that was always there and active around him. It confirmed one theory that Nick had developed as he learned more, which was that suffering was an integral part of life's journey. The purpose of being here is not to be *happy*. Rather, it is to get close to God, and just as importantly, to help others do the same. That requires growth. Suffering plays a big role in any type of growth, and it provides a great point of reference without which there would be no appreciation for moments of joy.

There was also an incredibly direct message and call to action for him – *you have seen just a sliver of the Glory of God. It is an amazing and undeserved gift. Let it be your clarity and your inspiration. Put that to use.* The message had finally landed, even after all the barriers that Nick had built around him to deny it or not let it get through. God was certainly more patient and persistent than he could ever be!

23

AMBUSH

1 *5:54, Wednesday April 27, 2022*
Nabil's Wednesday schedule had now changed as they were nearing the end of the semester and start of final exams. He was now able to test whether the female student witness was on a consistent routine on Wednesdays, and if so, learn more about her, particularly where she lived. This time, instead of risking being seen inside the bus, he waited near the roundabout on Jericho Road, where she had gotten off a few weeks ago. He had arrived shortly before 15:00 and waited for an hour for the bus. He patiently waited as he watched the heavy traffic slowly pass. The explosion in religious pilgrimages from virtually every country, combined with very limited infrastructure, resulted in traffic congestion throughout the entire day.

Nabil had not told anyone about his plans since he still was not sure what he was going to do once he learned more about the woman. While she posed a threat to him, he was also intrigued about what had happened and the message he thought he had heard.

Finally, just after 16:15, the first bus made a stop and ten people disembarked. Seven of the ten were women, and of those, five turned to their right and started walking away from the roundabout. With their backs to him, Nabil was able to follow them without being seen. Three of them appeared to be together, while the other two were on their own and moving faster. None of the three that were together fit his recollection of the woman. They were all slightly overweight, and were wearing more traditional Muslim attire, with long abaya outer garments. The two in the front were similar in build and height, wearing thigh-high jilbabs with jeans underneath and sneakers. He picked up his pace to get closer, and as he did that, he passed the slower moving group of three.

Suddenly, the one directly in front of him, now less than twenty meters away, turned to her right to cross the street. As she looked at traffic on both sides of the road, Nabil could clearly see her profile. It was the woman from Makassed! His patience had paid off. He had found her!

After crossing the street, she headed toward the town market at a pace that showed purpose. He gave her a lead of a few meters, crossed the street, and continued following as she walked up to the market to buy vegetables. This was followed shortly by a stop at the town's oven to buy bread. Packed with all the necessary items to cook dinner, she set off for her apartment, only three blocks away. Nabil now extended his distance from her as she turned into a street that was much quieter, not wanting to raise suspicion. He saw her open the door to an apartment and walk inside.

Nabil could hear his heart beating faster as he had a decision to make and thought, *Do I force my way in? If I do, what next? Is she married? Who else lives with her? Would she even recognize me?* He still did not have a plan and forcing his way in would have increased the risk of getting in trouble with the local authorities. Still, he was obsessed with knowing more about this woman, and more importantly, what she knew about him. After considering how unprepared he was, Nabil decided to go back to the safe house, only a few blocks away. He needed to think things through and determine what to do next. At least he knew where she lived.

Fatma got into the apartment at 17:10 and was quickly greeted by Ghassan from a distance. The door to his room, which connected directly to the main living area of the apartment, was open. He was sitting working on an old VHF radio from his construction site that needed to be repaired. He acknowledged Fatma, but barely lifted his head to look in her direction, engrossed in troubleshooting the radio issue he had in front of him, which held his focus at the time. Fatma dropped her backpack on the dining table and after getting a glass of water sat down to study. After spending just over ninety minutes working on her Anatomy and Basic Nursing assignments, she showered and began to prepare dinner. Ghassan had now moved on to his next project, which was to change the brake pads of his bicycle and clean it up. This was his main mode of transportation around town, and he tinkered with it almost every night to ensure it was in good condition. This was how Ghassan spent his time at home, using his hands to fix things. He was not much of a reader, and a long time ago he had decided not to have a television in the apartment. He would occasionally watch football games at a local business with his friends, but that was the extent of his interest on it. Through Fatma's insistence and coaching, he had learned how to use a smart phone to communicate and check on news, and that is how he stayed informed about world and local happenings.

That night they would have a fairly typical salad with tomatoes, olives, and cucumbers, and maqlooba for the main dish. She started to cut the tomato wedges and cucumber when she heard the start of the Maghrib call to prayer coming from outside of the apartment. She paused and offered a quiet prayer to the Virgin Mary. It was her way to reconcile her cultural and religious upbringing with the faith she had now embraced and was such an important part of her life. She was open to the possibility that the Allah that her people prayed to was the same God that she now knew and loved, but she was also convinced that the way to that One God was through Jesus Christ, and His Mother Mary played a crucial role in showing the way.

As she finished her prayer and continued to work on the salad, she felt a very strong, horrible smell surrounding her. The hairs on the back of her neck stood up as if charged with static electricity, and she felt an intense feeling of emptiness, then sadness mixed with fear. The small lamp in the kitchen flickered and then died, and in the twilight of the late afternoon, the room became filled with shadows in fast and random motion. Suddenly, the door to Ghassan's room violently swung shut. He got up to try to open it, to no avail.

Fatma put down the knife and stopped preparing the food, focusing on what was going on around her, taking inventory of the overall situation. Her heart was beating normally, her breathing was under control, and she was still serene. She then turned her attention to the shadows floating around the room. She could see the outline of some of the individual entities, could identify a face and a body in each. They appeared to be uncomfortable, in pain, and in a state of fear and paranoia. They all had a dark aura around them, as if sucking the little light that was in the room. Most had a similar appearance and floated around her as if being stung by insects or chased by wild animals. She heard what sounded like a variety of animals barking, shrieking, laughing like hyenas. Adding to the disorder, voices grew in volume and number. It sounded as if fifteen or so people were also in the room, some speaking Arabic, others speaking English and Yiddish, both of which she recognized, as well as what sounded like Greek or Latin, or maybe both. They chanted something that sounded like, "I bear witness that Mohammed is the messenger of..." but the ending of the verse was not *God*, but rather it sounded like *Agar* or *Agar-es*. It was a perversion of one of the verses of the adhan, the call to prayer. The chanting and the animal sounds, combined with the constant banging on the door by Ghassan, created an environment of chaos and confusion.

There was also a second type of entity, maybe a handful of them smaller in size. These were not moving with the same energy but also participated in the chanting and chaos. Fatma did not understand the roles or difference in identities, and her general sense toward the group was of feeling sorry for them. They appeared to be trapped in a situation that they did not want to be in but had no choice. Something that should have brought her to her knees in fear had no effect on her. She was initially startled by their abrupt and loud arrival, of course, but remained calm and simply asked out loud, "Why are you here, and what do you want from me?"

At that point the chanting stopped as they yielded to a new presence that entered the room. Standing at the threshold of the kitchen entrance was a man dressed as a Muslim cleric with a black turban that covered most of his face. Fatma could see through the constantly moving shadows in the room that his eyes were fixed on hers. She felt and understood that this was indeed a very powerful presence. Most likely a demon, a fallen angel. She knew this visit was connected to her choice to secretly convert to Christianity, as well as to her witnessing the murder of the IDF soldiers and the deep spiritual experience she had at that time. What she did not realize was that this demon wasn't there for anything she had done up until that day, even though those recent steps were the early part of a larger progression. He was there to stop her from fulfilling her destiny, something he was terrified about.

He then spoke in a deep voice that reverberated in echoes of many voices together, "Fatma Saleh. I see you are a little anxious about these annoying creatures. Do not worry, I will not allow them to harm you. I have decided to come to you today because I have seen how you are turning your back on the faith of your ancestors. It is a tragedy that you have chosen to follow that cult of Islam-haters called Christianity."

"I don't know who you are, but you are not welcome here. Please leave."

He slightly tilted his head and gave her a look of disappointment. "Is this how you welcome the angel that is coming to save you?" and after a brief pause said, "And who were you praying to just now? You did not even stop to get on the floor to pray to Allah, instead stopped and said a meaningless prayer to that whore! Don't you know that she works against you?"

Fatma said, "If you were truly an angel of God you would know that what I have experienced is real, and that my conversion has been the result of finally being exposed to the truth."

The demon said, "Do you think your mother, who sits in heaven with Allah and gave her life for you, is proud of what you are doing? Do you realize that in your selfishness you are insulting her and adding to her pain? She is consumed with guilt and sadness, since she knows that your infidelity is the result of her not being present to raise you and teach you the right way."

Naturally, this was painful for Fatma to hear, but she knew that Satan and his demons dealt in lies, and she should not pay attention to it. It was still unsettling for Fatma to think about what might have happened to her mother's soul, as when she died, her beliefs were different than Fatma's. At least that is what she had heard from Ghassan and her aunt Reema. She asked for strength to deal with this attack, and responded, "No one has forced me to convert. I am following what resonates in my heart, and on top of that, the real angel that looks after me has revealed himself already. He has not come to judge me as you have, but to help me choose by opening my eyes to the truth."

The demon continued, "What makes you think he exposed you to what is *really* true? Have you not considered that maybe there are forces here that want to do you harm? It all seems very well coordinated, starting with the American teacher conveniently leaving her bible at the café, then pursuing you until you allowed her to contaminate your thoughts with her propaganda. Then, the impostor angels that did nothing to protect the IDF soldiers from their death. Don't you think there is something suspicious here? That is why I have come to you, so you can see where the truth really lies. I am here to save you."

Fatma did not buy his tactic, feeling an increasing source of strength as she listened to his speech, which made her trust her gut even more about the fact that he was lying. She also started to sense that the demon was getting frustrated, beginning to show signs of fear. He knew that his lies were not working on her. Whatever was making her feel calm and strong was having the opposite effect on him.

There was an awkward silence, and all Fatma wanted was to end this episode. She tried to will them to leave, concentrating on that thought in her mind, but there was no reaction. She wondered if it was possible that they could not only react to what she said but could not read her mind. Would she have to verbally command them to depart? She took a deep breath, straightened her posture, then said with an assertive tone of voice, "I have no idea who you are or what you want from me, but you are not welcome in this house. You need to leave. Now."

The demon saw this as an opening to reengage with Fatma. He started to move forward again, then went on to speak, this time in a pleasant and softer voice, "I am the angel Agariel, and this is my Legion. We are here to save you from the Hamas radicals that have been following you ever since you saw them commit that awful act of violence, which was inspired by those you saw that told you they were angels or messengers. I am also here to tell you to be very careful about a person that will be coming to your apartment soon. Don't be fooled by his appearance or peaceful demeanor. He is coming to betray you."

Fatma knew there were lies mixed with truth in that statement and immediately made a connection to the vision she had the day of the attack and the dark warrior she saw next to the two attackers. Barachiel had told her its name was Agares. She thought about responding to his attempt to deceive her, but her inner voice told her not to engage in conversation anymore. He was a fallen angel and probably possessed much more knowledge and intelligence than her. Engaging would be an opening to play his game, and likely just result in confusion. She wondered if Ghassan could hear and smell what she was experiencing, since adding to the non-stop motion and awful noises made by the demoniacs, she could still hear him trying to push and turn the knob of his door, yelling at her to help him open it.

As more time passed, the chaos and highly unusual circumstances started to erode her calm demeanor. She needed to anchor her thoughts in the truth she knew, both in her mind and in her heart. As she was starting to take slow deep breaths in an effort to calm down, she felt the intensity of the demoniacs increasing. To her surprise, she started to feel their physical touch as they floated closer to her. Her confidence was beginning to shake, the strength and control she had felt earlier was waning. Fear slowly started to take over! Fatma realized that she could not fight them alone and remembered a brief prayer Jenny had taught her for moments when she felt that her faith was fading. She slowly raised her gaze and hands in what looked like a pose of prayer, and whispered, "Come Holy Spirit." She took another deep breath, and this time said it louder and more assertively, with the full expectation the prayer would be answered.

Out of nowhere, she felt a rush of energy and warmth coming from within her that immediately freed her from the touch of the demoniacs. She noticed now that she was under an intense light, coherently surrounding her body, that acted like a shield. This helped her feel even more empowered, but instead of using that empowerment to retaliate, she continued her slow breathing, thanked God, and prayed for them to go away. The light lasted only a few seconds, but while she was under it, she felt a sense of connectedness with an infinite intelligence and power. A power that was on her side in the struggle against the demons. During that time, she became aware that there was indeed a person she was about to meet, not a local, but rather a visitor from America. The American was not coming to betray, but rather help her. In the presence of the light, the Legion's presence began to fade. As they were almost gone, Fatma heard the voice of Agares say to her, this time in Arabic, "We will be back...in due time ..." Then, the light left her.

Fatma found herself alone in the kitchen, with the food she had been preparing in front of her, as if nothing had happened. She initially felt surprised about her matter-of-fact reaction to what had happened, but it did not take long for her to start feeling overwhelmed. She was in the middle of a battle between strong spiritual forces of good and evil. The strength she felt came from an external source, not from within her, even though she still felt an incredible connectedness and gratitude toward the Holy Spirit who had just liberated her. But now Fatma also understood that this might be the beginning of a longer, more difficult battle that, somehow, she was going to participate in.

Deep in her heart she knew she was not being forced to do it, but she also knew this was the right thing for her to do. It was her purpose. While she felt totally committed to collaborate, the exposure to these massive uncontrollable forces started to make her fearful. She started to tremble, then broke down and started to cry, supporting herself with her elbows against the kitchen countertop and holding her head with her hands. She felt vulnerable and unprepared, but at the same time was conscious of how this last episode had ended, and the warmth and goodness she perceived as she was engulfed in that light. There was no room for fear or any negative thought during that instant, and she also noticed how the evil entities reacted to its presence. But her reality did not always reside inside of the light. She was still in a physical world were the influence of evil was very strong, an evil that for some reason felt threatened by her, and would continue to pursue her, directly and through people that unknowingly followed him.

As she continued crying, she had the presence of mind to say a prayer, this time of gratitude, but also asking for strength in dealing with this challenge that had entered her life. She also asked for clarity, so that she would be able to unpack what she had just become aware of and gain a better understanding of the role she was supposed to play in it.

Finally, Ghassan was able to open the door to his room and rushed to Fatma to make sure she was well. Fatma's relationship with Ghassan was one of love that was only evidenced in their concern and respect for each other. However, neither one typically showed much affection. He was always dependable, and unbeknownst to her, was immensely proud of what she had accomplished in school, as a leader and great student, as well as being an outstanding daughter. So, the next thing that happened came as a total surprise to Ghassan. She dropped the cutting knife and went straight to him to embrace him and cry on his shoulder like the child she felt like at the moment. Ghassan returned the embrace quietly, simply showing that he was there for her, expecting that she would eventually tell him what happened.

A FEW MINUTES earlier

As the horrific scene in Fatma's apartment was taking place, Nabil started making his way back from the safe house, only a few blocks away. He still had not completely thought through what he was going to do but had noticed there was an alley along the side of the apartment that could be accessed without being seen walking in front on it. His plan was to get close enough so he could hear what was happening inside, and depending on what he learned, he might try to force his way in. He also recalled that on the opposite side of the alley, there was an abandoned shop where nobody lived. As he was within fifty meters, he started to fix his sight on the front window of the apartment, which revealed only shadows.

All of a sudden, he saw a flash of a white radiant light, followed by a more subtle illumination of the inside walls, as if a spotlight was shining on a specific object and the light that leaked from the spotlight was enough to light up the rest of the house and even the side of the street where he was standing. He was too far to see the target of the spotlight inside the apartment. Then, within a few seconds, the light was gone. Nabil's initial reaction was to hide behind a car parked across the street, since he had no idea what was happening and who might be there. He waited there for a few seconds, and as soon as he thought it was safe, ran across the street and hid in the alleyway next to the apartment.

Once on that side of the street, Nabil walked to the only door that opened to the alleyway, the entrance to the kitchen. He remained next to it, close enough to the door to hear something inside. He initially heard a very faint sound of what sounded like a woman sobbing, not too far from the door. This was followed within seconds by the opening of an internal door and a brief exchange of which he only got bits and pieces, between the two people inside, both of whom appeared to be crying. The silence inside the apartment finally broke, when he heard the female voice say, "Thank you, Father" in English.

So, she lived with her father, and they spoke English at home. This puzzled Nabil even more. He had kept this entire mission to himself, as he was still unsure about Fatma's intentions, but was fairly certain that she would not turn him over to the police. He also did not want an innocent Palestinian college student to become another victim of Hamas' ruthlessness... unless it threatened him. At the risk of not responding to calls from his brother or Abdul, he decided to shut off his phone so he could not be tracked. He kicked himself for not thinking about this earlier but doubted they would be tracking him constantly.

He continued to hear the woman crying, and eventually catching her breath. Then he heard her say, "Father, there are things happening in my life. Things that are not normal."

Ghassan, who was still in shock and initially did not pause to reflect on Fatma's comments, responded, "What just happened here? No one is in the apartment and everything is in order, but when I was locked in the room, I could have sworn I heard many voices and sounds, as well as a louder voice of someone that seemed to be speaking with you? Where is he? Where is everyone that was here a few seconds ago?" He paused, then moved closer to her and hugged her again and said, "Fatma, what is going on? How can I help you, little girl?"

So, her father had experienced it as well? Even though her supernatural encounters registered with her as very real, this gave her an additional sense of validation. These things were happening to her for a reason, and not a random misfiring of neurons in her brain. There was still a lot to understand, but she also felt that she would be guided through that process as long as she trusted this new messenger that had pierced a hole into this world in order to get her attention. She also felt strength from knowing she was not alone in the physical world either, as Ghassan was finally listening to her and showing legitimate concern.

Fatma said, "Father, thank you for being here for me. Thank you for listening!" She then started to open up about her recent experiences. "This is the second time in the last few weeks in which I have a very real, vivid experience that...frankly, is not of this world. When I witnessed the killing at Makassed, time froze, and the veil of the physical world appeared to be lifted. What was revealed was other beings living among us. Spiritual beings...angels!"

Ghassan was initially skeptical, but he thought it was still possible, having lived through what he knew was a supernatural experience himself. "What did they look like?"

"The good ones had human-like features, and, uhm...were dressed as ancient warriors. Their armor had a live golden glow to it...hard to explain. It was continuously flowing, moving..."

As Fatma said this, Ghassan open his eyes wide, covered his mouth with his hand, and remained speechless. Had it not been for his experience at her birth, and what he had just heard inside the apartment, he would have thought that Fatma was suffering from some sort of mental issue. But...the golden glow! He saw its reflection on Fatma's face as a newborn but had not been able to turn around and see where it originated. It must have been the angel! Her angel!

Fatma admitted that she had caught a glimpse of the attackers, but her focus remained on the spiritual beings, good and evil, as well as the victims. She paused at the end of the story, then hesitated for a few seconds, but then decided to open up to him, "Father, there is something that was going on in my life before this episode. I don't want to upset you, but you must know the truth. You must know where my heart has led me."

Ghassan interrupted, "Little girl, I know I don't say enough, and that at times I appear...well, I am...distant. But I know you are very curious, just like your mother, and like her, you explored Christianity."

Fatma was totally surprised. "How did you know? And Mother...what happened? Did she convert? Oh, my God!"

"She did not convert, in part out of respect for her family...and me."

"I am so sorry, Father," said Fatma, "I don't want to bring shame to you. To us..."

"No, no, my dear. You will never bring shame. All you have done is make me bloody proud your whole life. I am not worried about that...at all. You know I am not the most devout, so any concern I may have has to do with you, not me. It will not be easy..."

"I understand." She paused, reflecting on how her life and worldview had changed in the last few weeks, and especially that day, then continued, "With the things that have happened to me recently, I sense that I will have bigger things to worry about than being accepted."

"Fatma, ever since your mother died, I withdrew into my shell and have been afraid to accept what my heart has experienced and being more open about it. I never told you this, but on the night that you were born, something magical happened. Yes, I lost your mother, and that was devastating...but, I was very close to losing you as well. When things looked hopeless, a lady appeared from out of nowhere to console Layla and allow the midwife to remain steady in the delivery. There was also another being standing behind me, emitting a golden glow..."

"Barachiel! He was there?"

"Maybe...if he is the one that appeared to you. Then, probably. I didn't see him, just the reflection of that...glow. All I know is that they played a role that night. Otherwise, both of you might have died. The lady's presence covered the room in peace and light. I will never forget that light and the serenity I felt, even in the middle of the tragedy of the moment. It made me feel that everything would be fine, even without your mother here. It also made me realize that there was a special purpose for you. The lady and the angel would not have walked into the physical world to help deliver you if it wasn't for an important purpose."

"That is beautiful, Father. Did the lady say anything to you? Did she say who she was?"

"No...her mere presence, and how the environment in the room changed, was enough for me to know she was special. I think it was the Christian Virgin."

Hearing what had happened to his daughter reinforced Ghassan's belief that there was a connection between this event and the events of the night of her birth. He realized that Fatma's purpose was beginning to unfold and was terrified about the attention it was already attracting. Toward the end she mentioned that in the last experience, while she was inside the light, it was revealed to her that someone would be visiting. Someone that would somehow be involved in and help with her journey...an American.

THE TIME WAS NOW 19:40, and Nabil had been hiding outside and following most of the conversation, as the window kitchen had been left partially open for ventilation. He now knew that her name was Fatma, and that the Makassed attack was still very present in her mind, although he did not understand the strange reference to angels. The brief mention of seeing the attackers was a big concern and got him thinking about the need to take action...soon.

Nabil's attention was suddenly interrupted by the sound of approaching footsteps. They appeared to be moving in the direction of the front entrance to the apartment. By then, it was already dark outside, with the light from the apartment being the main source of illumination on that segment of the street. Nabil peered around the corner of the building to see who was coming and saw two men approaching. One had the appearance of a friar, like those at the nearby church of St. Lazarus. The other was a middle-aged man that did not appear to be a local, dressed in typical tourist attire – jeans, running shoes, a long-sleeved shirt and a wind breaker. Nabil remained focused on the tourist, who walked up to the door and knocked. Meanwhile, he lost track of the friar, who mysteriously faded into the shadows of the night.

24

NICK'S MISSION

few hours earlier
Nick continued in his tour, seeing things differently now. It had been four days since his transformational experience in Cana, and each stop along the way had an even more profound impact on him. This was day six of the pilgrimage, and his group got up early to go the Jordan River for a symbolic baptism, and the nearby town of Jericho for lunch. After a long day on the road they would head in the direction of the hotel in Bethlehem where they would spend the next two nights, but on the way there, Father Dalton would squeeze in a stop for daily mass and a quick view of the Church of St Lazarus in Bethany.

The Arabic name of the town, al-Eizariyah, had its roots in Lazarus, an important character in the New Testament. He, along with his sisters, Mary and Martha, were close friends of Jesus. He is most famous for being the friend that died while Jesus was traveling, and a few days later Jesus brought him back from the dead.

There was still about a half-hour of sunlight when the bus arrived at the church, and the rays of the sun were shining almost horizontally against the small buildings highlighting the colorfulness of the historic village. Nick noticed that al-Eizariyah was a humble, yet vibrant Palestinian town with a healthy amount of retail commercial activity and quite a bit of motor and foot traffic. Along the way, Nick had seen a row of butcher shops that appeared to take great pride in their variety of lambs and goats, with various body parts hanging to draw in shoppers. He reflected on how different this culture was from the United States and how sterile the American culture had become. This type of display is now only found in certain markets, mostly in ethnic areas where the custom has been preserved. Nick mostly shopped for groceries at places like Whole Foods, which have the appearance and smell of a boutique, with heavily sterilized meat and seafood departments.

The bus pulled up along the road by the entrance to the church and Nick got off with Ewan and Denise. They walked down the alley along its side and into the atrium adjacent to the entrance to the tomb Lazarus. The church complex incorporated what is relatively typical in the Holy Land. There were two churches built in the twentieth century under Franciscan and Greek Orthodox custody of the property. Both were built over a sequence of buildings that were constructed, destroyed, and newer buildings built over the old ruins, in succession during the last sixteen centuries. The original shrine was built in the fourth century. Over time, several other places of prayer were built at the same site, including a convent, two different mosques, and later the churches and small Franciscan monastery that existed to that day. In any other location, the Catholic church building, designed by Antonio Barluzzi, would be the main landmark of the town, visible from a distance and protected from any surrounding development. However, in the Holy Land, two millennia of cultural, political, and religious history had resulted in the church being surrounded by other buildings, most of which make it difficult to obtain a full view of its scale and beauty from street level.

Many of the Christian Holy Sites that they visited during the trip had their roots in shrines and churches built by the Byzantines following the conversion of the Roman Empire to Christianity. The Emperor Constantine and his mother Helena played a crucial role in this development. It was unclear whether Helena's devotion to Christianity preceded her son's conversion, but it was historically known that once the conversion took place, she went on a pilgrimage of Palestine and ordered the construction of these places of worship. Sadly, because of the history of that area during the last two thousand years, none of those buildings existed in a way that resembled their original form. That included the Second Jewish Temple – the one standing at the time of Jesus, which was destroyed by the Romans as they regained control of Palestine after the Jewish Revolt in the first century AD. That history of successive changes in political and cultural control of the region, had resulted in a stacking of Pagan, Christian, and Islamic houses of worship throughout many of these Holy Sites. While tragic, it was interesting that they provided great archeological and historical evidence for the truth and accuracy of the writings in the New Testament.

Nick started to walk along the atrium on his own, admiring the design. He reflected on how the expectations he had of what he was going to see in the Holy Land were so unrealistic. He had expected to see a land that looked somewhat similar to biblical times, how they had been recreated for films. There were a few places that still provided that resemblance. The most striking one was Capernaum at the shore of the Sea of Galilee. However, the closer the group got to Jerusalem, the more of this stacking of history they saw.

Three priests in Franciscan habits came down from the monastery and crossed the atrium on their way to the church for the daily mass. The first two included the pilgrimage guide, Father Dalton, as well as the local pastor, Father Kutiero. The third one appeared to be a more junior friar based on the simpler habit he was wearing. This one was significantly taller, wearing the capuche over his head and walking several steps behind. He stopped by the portico entrance and waited there for the group to proceed into the church. Nick was one of the last members of the group to walk in, and as he walked by him, he tried to make eye contact with the monk, but he was wearing the capuche so low that all Nick could see was a shadow under it. As Nick walked in, Father Dalton was already bowing at the altar about to begin the mass, so he quickly sat on the last bench.

The daily masses during the pilgrimage were relatively short but would provide an opportunity to use scripture to reflect on the biblical and historical significance of the place they were visiting. That day's gospel reading came from the John, Chapter 11, which recounts the resurrection of Lazarus. Bethany, being a small village approximately two miles from Jerusalem, was a place where Jesus stayed during his trips to the area, and most likely where he stayed during the week of his Passion, now celebrated during Easter Week. Because of that, there are several stories captured in the New Testament about events that took place in Bethany. Nick thought of how incredibly fortunate and blessed he was to be physically present at that location. The feeling was hard to fully comprehend, as everything was happening so quickly, and the day had been a long one, leaving the entire group just enough time after this mass to check in at the hotel in Bethlehem, dine, and get some rest before another busy day.

After the gospel reading, Father Dalton gave a short homily reflecting on Lazarus and the type of relationship he must have had with Jesus, and the role he likely played in early Christianity. Ironically, during the middle of the homily, the Islamic call to prayer started to blare outside, coming from speakers mounted on the mosque next door, strategically pointed at the church. Father Dalton, accustomed to this mild form of harassment from the local Islamic leaders, simply continued speaking, undeterred by the distraction.

The mass then transitioned to the Liturgy of the Eucharist, where eventually bread and wine were transformed into the Body and Blood of Christ. This was one of those teachings of the Catholic Church that Nick had always struggled with, even now after having learned so much about the faith and feeling so much closer to God. He still did not fully understand the concept of Christ being completely present in the Eucharist. Present, not only in the moment – meaning his spirit is here now – but also physically. It was a leap of faith he was willing to take considering all the other experiences he had had, but certainly not something he understood. Eventually the group of forty-eight proceeded in orderly fashion toward the altar to receive Holy Communion. Nick was the last member of the tour group in line. This time he took the host inside his mouth, and before he started to chew on it, reflected on the belief that it was indeed Christ, now in communion with him. Christ, the same God that created everything we knew, with infinite knowledge and power, was physically there...now! He gave the host an imaginary hug, and at that moment felt a warm tingling all over his body. He came back to his pew and knelt for a moment of reflection and prayer and to fully take in the unusual warmth of the invisible embrace he was experiencing.

Up until the last few days, Nick's experience of God had been based on reason and knowledge alone, just what satisfied his mind. He had devoured the historical, archeological, theological, and scientific evidence. With those, he had laid a great foundation, but something had been missing. The real, intimate, personal relationship with God as a person that Nick wanted so much, had not played a role in his experience until recently. Nick knew that this was just an initial taste, but that there would also be a progression of his relationship with God in love. He also understood that love is not the feeling, but rather, selfless action, sacrifice, and likely, suffering.

It appeared to last an eternity, and Nick would have been happy to just remain there. It certainly felt like a powerful embrace, and he knew who it was from. The sensation slowly began to wane, and as he opened his eyes and started to survey the room, he noticed that the tall friar was kneeling right beside him. Nick turned and looked to make eye contact and acknowledge him. At that moment, the friar pulled back his capuchin and revealed his face. It was Zaphkiel! Nick was initially startled, but at the same time excited to see that he was back. Nick was about to speak when Zaphkiel put his fingers on his lips in a sign to remain quiet. Just as in the last encounter, no words were spoken initially, as the angel communicated to him by connecting with his mind. "Peace be with you, Nick."

EWAN NOTICED that Nick had walked out before dismissal. He did not think much about it, as Nick had already made friends with a few of the other members of the group, and he might have left earlier to find a better seat in the bus. By the time Ewan and Denise climbed onboard, they found the two seats where they had normally sat at the fourth row still empty and took them. Upon sitting down, they struck a conversation with the Abelsons, the couple across the aisle. Ben Abelson was a non-practicing Jew from New Jersey, who had converted to Catholicism when he married Linda. Ewan, Denise, and Nick had met them during lunch on the first day of the trip, and in a few days developed a good friendship. The conversation distracted them from any lingering concerns about Nick's whereabouts.

Once everyone was seated inside the bus, Father Dalton

started his customary headcount process. Two thirds of the way through it, he was interrupted by Anton, the driver, who needed a response from him regarding the next stop. Where they going to make a quick stop at Zion Gate, or would they be heading directly to Bethlehem? Bethlehem was the answer, as they were already running more than an hour late because of the traffic in Bethany, and still needed to check in at the hotel with enough time for the group to have dinner. Because of that, the father did not complete the headcount, not realizing that someone was missing.

25

LED TO DO GOOD

Nick had left the church early following the angel's lead. As they walked, Zaphkiel looked at him and this time opened his mouth and said, "That was a good homily, and Father Dalton raised some great questions. Have you ever thought about how Lazarus must have felt after his resurrection?"

Nick, who was already feeling like the entire episode was too much for him to comprehend, now thought, "This is a bit awkward, to be having a conversation about the homily with an Angel!"

He asked Zaphkiel for clarification, "You mean, in terms of how the body would feel after being brought back to life?"

"Well, that too. But I meant his mind and soul. He had crossed over to the other side, which is full of the presence and glory of God. Suddenly, he is asked to return because his mission on Earth is not over. His perspective on things must have been different, knowing with certainty that the world beyond exists, gaining knowledge that would increase his understanding of everything, including who Jesus was, and that he would be able to experience that infinite joy after his mission was complete. On the other hand, he came back to an existence of challenges and suffering, where the presence and influence of the evil one can be felt throughout. Not long after he came back, it is very likely that he saw his friend suffer through brutal torture and eventually death, nailed to a cross... naked. Yet, the gift of that experience would have made him fearless, full of understanding, and more importantly, full of love and ready to do God's will." The angel paused at that point, as they continued their walk, allowing Nick to let the words sink in.

This was a reflection that Nick had never spent time on. He thought that the mere fact that Lazarus was brought back to life was a fulfillment of his role, just to be the subject of a miracle performed by Jesus to make others believe in Him and His Divinity. He then said, "Not much is said in the Gospels about what Lazarus did after being resurrected...other than that some of the Jewish and Roman leaders wanted to kill him. I guess he was one more piece of evidence fueling the early movement of followers of Jesus. But the Bible does not talk about his... second...death, or about what he did while alive."

Zaphkiel responded, "Like many others that met and experienced Jesus during that time, he understood and loved, and because of that, he taught and helped with the conversion of many people throughout the region. His work for God did not end at the time of his resurrection. That is where it started." He continued, "Lazarus experienced Heaven directly and came back. In your case, you have experienced tiny and narrow glimpses of the Glory of God during a few episodes in your life as you experienced recently. Did the experience have an impact on you?"

"Are you kidding? It has changed everything! I am just sorry that I wasted so much time rejecting the message. I was extremely stubborn about it. I guess it did not fit my plans..."

"Maybe, time was necessary for you to learn something.

Maybe it played a role," said Zaphkiel, providing some additional wisdom that Nick thought he needed to ponder.

They walked along the main road in front of the church for two blocks, then turned left onto a narrow street that had a mix of small apartment buildings, empty barren lots, and a few local businesses. It was already dark outside, and he looked straight ahead trying to figure out where Zaphkiel was taking him. At this point, he was no longer concerned about his safety. He was now living a different and more complete awareness, one where he could overcome fear as long as he stayed strong in his focus and faith. So, Nick completely trusted Zaphkiel and walked with him down this deserted alley-like street as if he was walking down King Street in Old Town Alexandria at noon on a Saturday.

All of a sudden, he saw a flash of light coming from an apartment on the right side, about one hundred meters away. It looked like the flash of an exploding transformer, but with even more intensity, and lasting at least a few seconds. It was enough to reflect on the buildings across the street. He turned to Zaphkiel, but the angel was simply looking ahead, not acting surprised at all. Shortly after the light went off, he saw a figure or shadow moving from the left side of the street, across to the general area where the light had come from. They were too far, and his eyes were still adjusting for Nick to determine what it was. Maybe a dog, cat, or simply just a shadow. They continued walking a few more steps, and Nick heard an explosion of multiple voices shrieking, although there was no one to be seen, and then felt a strange smell and what felt like heat going through his chest. He then recognized the fleeting presence of Agares, who seemed to be more intent on running away from something that had instilled fear in him rather than attacking Nick. It was no coincidence that he was there, and that made him think that the purpose of this walk with Zaphkiel had to do with confronting this evil presence. Even so, he still knew there were other layers to the situation that he was still unaware of, and hopefully, about to learn.

They walked up to within ten feet of the front door of the apartment were the bright flash of light had come from, and at that point Zaphkiel stopped and turned to Nick. "There are three things you have the opportunity to do now. The first one is to reinforce your knowledge of God, some of which will involve facing the evil that had played such a big role in blocking you from the truth. Agares does not work alone and extends his evil tentacles through a Legion of fallen angels and lost souls that belong to him, much as slaves. They, in turn, work tirelessly to influence people in the physical realm. They will continue to torment and raise doubt in you, and you need to understand that through discernment. Ewan pointed you in the right direction with that."

Nick nodded in understanding.

"The second one is to add the most important dimension to your quest for the truth – love. You have advanced in the dimension of knowledge and reason beyond most, but one equally important element of your search has been neglected, and that is your relationship with God and those that surround you. You now have the opportunity to grow in love. The third one will come out of the fulfillment of the first two. By acting on your knowledge as you confront evil, and by loving, you will be a witness of the truth, and a change agent for God on Earth. If you choose to do this, you will be helping the young woman who lives here with her father. She is someone that will play an important role within the people of Islamic faith and has a few things in common with you...you'll know soon."

Nick then asked Zaphkiel, "You'll be staying, right? I don't think I have enough context here to even know where to start. Besides, I will be a stranger to them. Probably someone that they will be afraid of..."

And then, before Nick had a chance to finish his thought,

Zaphkiel faded into the shadows of the night with one last message, "You will be fine. We will not be far from you but pray...always."

Nick sensed that this would not be easy and wondered how he would figure out the role he needed to play, and whether it would be as evident as Zaphkiel indicated. He also had no idea who was behind the door, and being a woman in a Palestinian town, what her reaction would be to see him there.

After a couple of deep breaths, a very short prayer verse, and trusting that he would figure this thing out, he knocked on the door three times. After a brief pause, the door opened. A young lady that he thought might be in her late teens or early twenties stood on the other side with an expression that indicated she had been expecting him. He thought it was odd that she would not be a little more careful. Maybe a sign of his conditioning living in a major metropolitan area in the US, where he would have been suspicious about any unannounced stranger knocking on the door, and at least would want to ask them to identify themselves while the door was still locked.

Upon opening, the woman's greeting was even more odd. She said, "Good evening. You must be the American." She waited for a reaction, then asked, "Are you?"

Nick, not entirely shocked that she had been expecting him, extended his hand and introduced himself. "My name is Nick Aday...and yes, I am an American. I am not exactly sure what I am supposed to do here, but the one thing I know for sure is that I am supposed to be here, now. Sounds like you expected it was well."

Fatma's eyes started to well up in tears, and she looked at him as if she had known him for years, not exactly the reception that Nick expected, but something he was happy to see. He also started to realize that, in the same way that he was prepped by Zaphkiel about this encounter, she must have also been prepared to expect him at that moment.

"My name is Fatma Saleh, and I am very pleased to make your acquaintance."

Her English was as clean as he had heard, and her accent was British! Nick thought, "This keeps getting weirder!"

Fatma extended her hand and shook Nick's, her handshake firm and her voice and movement assertive. She was not wearing a full hijab, but still had a short veil covering her hair. She must have been no taller than five-foot-three inches, was lean, and had attractive middle eastern facial features, with beautiful black eyes piercing through prescription glasses. She had the presence of someone older, with more extensive life experience, not a meek and insecure college student. On the contrary, she had an air of self-confidence with a commanding, yet humble presence. There was also none of the nonsense of being concerned about what Nick's intentions would be in meeting her or worry about what the neighbors would say.

Fatma's concerns and focus were around matters of much higher importance and she knew that Nick had been placed there by a source that she trusted infinitely. Both had been called to perform some sort of function that was part of God's plan. They would need to figure that out together.

26

TRUTH

"Please come in and meet my father. His name is Ghassan," said Fatma.

Nick walked in and shook hands with a man that appeared to be at least five years his junior, and his facial expression did not demonstrate the same assertiveness and confidence that his daughter exuded. Ghassan's eyes said it all. He was scared and confused, and had no idea what was going on, much less what Nick was doing in his home and why it appeared that Fatma was expecting him. Nick locked eyes with Ghassan in a gesture that not only reflected the customary *pleased to meet you* approach but was also intended to communicate to him that everything would be fine. There was no need for fear, although at the moment he could not undo the confusion Ghassan felt, as Nick felt confused as well.

While Nick was still unaware of his role at the apartment, his leadership conditioning from many years in industry, and Type A, OCD-infused personality, prompted him to take the lead in the conversation and go with his gut. He broke the awkward silence with, "I am not sure why we are meeting, but I can only say that us getting together was arranged by a Higher Power." Nick was intentionally being very careful with the words he selected, assuming that Fatma and Ghassan were of the Islamic faith and could be offended to any Christian references. He continued, this time specifically looking at Fatma, "So, you were somehow expecting me here. How did you know?" That was enough of a leading question to get Fatma primed to start opening up.

"So, I've had two experiences in the last few weeks that have opened my eyes to another realm that exists in very close proximity to ours. A spiritual realm. The first episode was in front of the hospital where I am doing my internship. I met an Angel of God..."

"I am quite familiar with that...as of the last few days," said Nick.

"You as well?" asked Fatma, with a mixture of surprise and excitement.

"Yes, we have that in common, Fatma," said Nick as he yielded back to Fatma so she could answer the original question.

"So, I met an angel at that time. His name was Barachiel. He said he had been watching over me since I was created by God." Fatma paused, took a deep breath, then continued, "there was also an evil angel, a devil. His name is Agares..."

Nick's facial expression changed from interest to surprise, mixed with fear. He interrupted Fatma, "Are you sure the name was Agares?"

"Yes, why? Does that name...?"

"Yes, it rings a bell, uhm...sounds familiar. Unless there is more than one Agares, this is a demon that has taken an interest in my life as well. I guess that may be one reason we were brought together."

The realization also affected Fatma, but in her case, she saw it as something positive. She was actually excited about having more help in her fight against Agares. She then told Nick the rest of the story of her experience in front of Makassed Hospital, finishing with the moment at which she lost consciousness.

"Wow! I'm sorry you had to go through that, Fatma. At least nothing serious happened to you...physically. I assume the overall experience was...intense. No?"

"It was, but it also felt normal, and in a strange way, peaceful. I know the Israeli soldiers are fine. Their souls, I mean. But there is more."

"There is more?" said Nick, starting to understand the inner strength that Fatma possessed. She was not the average impressionable twenty-year-old. Fatma was a strong, very interesting young woman.

"So, today...just before you knocked on the door, I had a different type of experience." She proceeded to tell him, which in turn, raised many questions in Nick's mind, particularly about Fatma and her purpose. She was certainly special and was most likely going to play a crucial role. He just had no idea what it was.

When Fatma was done, she added that, before these episodes had started, she was in the process of learning about and considering a conversion to Christianity.

"Oh, so there is more. Fatma, you have lived an entire lifetime so far this year." said Nick, with an attempt to inject some humor in an otherwise intense conversation.

Fatma took the bait, "Ha! Ha! Yes, Mr. Nick. It has been... interesting! I have to say that these angels I have met and the embrace of light I experienced are a manifestation of the God that I always thought I was praying to as a Muslim, but now I know is the God of Jews and Christians." She paused, realizing that this had been a very long answer to Nick's initial question, then added, "In any event, the *living* light revealed to me that an

American would be coming to us, and to welcome and learn from him. So here you are. I don't think it is a coincidence." After pausing, she said, "Is it fair to assume that the *Higher Power* you reference is that same God?"

Nick took it all in and started to connect the dots. Ghassan, meanwhile, was overwhelmed and growing more concerned about Fatma's future. It had just become even more real with Nick's arrival, the re-telling of her experiences, and the realization they had a common adversary in Agares. He was neither disappointed, nor was he completely surprised about her conversion, but it was taking him some time to process all that he was finding out at the same time. After inviting Nick to sit down at the dining table, he followed and grabbed a chair.

Nick then said to Fatma, "Yes, it is the God of the Christians, but also the God of all people and all of Creation. It appears that there is something we need to accomplish together, and for that reason, He has decided to join our paths. In the same way that you have been visited by an angel, the same thing happened to me...all the way to the front door of this apartment."

After pausing for a couple of seconds trying to figure out where to go next, he said, "Fatma, regarding your conversion to Christianity, I assume that is not something that is taken lightly here, right? Like, uhm...whether it's your family, friends, or the community here in Bethany. Can you tell me a little more about that?"

Fatma took some time to collect her thoughts, then said, "Yes, it is not easy for that reason. I am not even sure what the process should be. I still have many questions, but in my heart, I feel that what I have learned is much more aligned with the truth. It just resonates with me. It feels right." She then told Nick and Ghassan her conversion story, starting with the doubts she initially had as a teenager, to her coincidental encounter with Jenny, and how much she had guided Fatma to gain an initial understanding of the Christian faith, as well as her trepidation to convert given the challenges she would face in her community.

Looking at Ghassan, she then said, "Anyway, those were some of the concerns I had when I decided that I wanted to learn more about Jesus, and that is one reason I never told you, Father, or Aunt Reema, or anyone else I knew. It was a secret that only Jenny and I knew about." Then, after a brief pause, "I am sorry, Father." Fatma fought back tears but regained the strength to continue. "There is one more thing. In the little I have learned, which has been enough to change my life, I also came to the realization that there is more within Christianity than the teachings of Jenny's church. Just as an example...I believe that the Virgin Mary has a special role in the salvation that came through her Son, and that she is indeed the Mother of God. I believe she deserves the reverence that exists in the Catholic Church toward her and do not fully understand how she was and still is abandoned by the non-Catholic Christians. At least, the few Palestinian Christians I have come to know are devoted to her as well."

Nick was fascinated with her story and what it taught him. This conversion had taken place against forces that were much stronger than those that led to his denial of the church as a young man. He felt a great sense of wonder in how God does not need all of that preparation in his people to be able to hit them with his truth! He also started to wonder about the number of people that are touched in a similar way, but don't have the courage or the help to be able to convert, particularly those in societies where converting would result in immediate alienation, shame, and possibly death. How easy he had had it, and how shameful that he had pushed God aside when he did.

"Well, it's your turn now, Mr. Nick," said Fatma.

Nick took a few seconds to organize his thoughts, and starting with his experiences as a child, he delivered a summary of his story. When he was done, he said, "So, I have spent a big part of my adult life learning about God, faith, and trying to understand how I should act on it. I also have many questions, and I suspect that for some, my mind doesn't have the capacity to understand the answer. One thing I can say is that I have a much better understanding than what I had when I was your age, Fatma. Still it feels like there is an infinite amount of learning that can be had. I can tell you that, in this short time, I have learned so much from you and I wish I could repay it somehow. I am not an expert in any of this, but maybe I can take a crack at answering your questions."

Without hesitation, Fatma asked, "OK, with all the choices you have where you live, why Catholic?"

The back and forth went on for a while, during which Fatma invited Nick to join them for dinner. Nick was on a roll, since this was a topic that he found fascinating. Fatma paid close attention to his story and his responses to her well thought out questions. It was as if she was listening to one of her college professors give a lecture.

"The more I learn, the more questions I have," said Fatma. "You were just talking about the different Christian denominations. So, if Christianity is so aligned with the truth, why does God allow it to be splintered into different churches?" She then went on a roll about her other objections, "And why has the Catholic Church been behind so much evil against Muslims, from the crusades to the expulsion of the Moors from Europe in the fifteenth century? Actually, there are examples from other religions, like what the Jews say about the role of Catholics in the birth of anti-Semitism and their support of the Holocaust. Also, the power abuses of the Pope and other church leaders, like all these scandals about sexual abuse of children? Some of these are similar to reasons why I started to question Islam."

"Well, I am not knowledgeable about Islam, but I assume the popular belief is more exaggerated and binary than what really took place. The same thing is true of the accusations against Christianity...but, just like you, these were also some of my questions and reasons for doubting when I was younger. I have been interested in these topics for a long time."

Nick then closed his eyes and took a deep breath, addressed Fatma's questions one by one. A central point in his answer was the existence of evil. "Just to give you an example, the factors that precipitated the Reformation where all due to human weakness and the evil that men...and women, allowed to enter the Church. It had to do with people and their behavior, not so much the actual Church beliefs and teachings."

Nick realized that he needed to provide more context. "Let me backtrack a little. First, evil is real and originates in a living entity. It is not only an abstract concept, but rather a *person* that chose to reject God, so his motivation is to do the opposite and destroy as much as he can of God's creation. He is substantially more intelligent and experienced than any of us humans, being in existence since before the physical world came to be. He uses many tactics in his mission to separate us from God and from one another. By dividing us, he gains influence. Ironically, I think his movement is doomed to fail in the long-term for that reason. There is no love, no trust, no real loyalty, so division may eventually take over."

Both Fatma and her father listened intently, and she nodded her interest.

"One of the most powerful and effective tactics he uses is to hide the truth. He can wrap a story around something that is true and appears to be good, to make us believe in something that is actually evil. This is mentioned very early in the bible. Do you have one?"

"Yes, I do. Let me get it," said Fatma as she rushed to her room and came back with the bible Jenny had gifted her.

Nick said, "Go to the very first book. Genesis. I believe in the second or third chapter, it talks about *The Fall*. Do you see it?"

Fatma, with a growing sense of excitement, sat down and said, "I have read the book of Genesis before. It has references to Noah and Abraham, who are both in the Quran, and so I was interested to see what it said." She opened the bible and started turning the first few pages, then said, "Yes, it says *Genesis 3, The Fall*. Where to now?"

Nick paused, trying to remember. "If you read from the beginning, it talks about the serpent telling *the woman*, that God had lied to them when He said they would die if they ate from the fruit of the tree of knowledge of good and evil, and so on. There is an important statement there that the serpent tells her. Can you read that out loud?"

She started reading, "'You will certainly not die,' said the serpent said to the woman. For God knows that when you eat from it your eyes will be opened, and you will be like God, knowing good and evil."

"That, right there," interrupted Nick. "Read the last sentence again and let me know what you think it means."

Fatma re-read the last sentence, then said, "The serpent, who is Satan, is telling them that once they eat of the forbidden fruit, they will have the same power that God has to *know* what is good and evil. 'Your eyes will be opened, and you will be like God, knowing good and evil'. Interesting, I hadn't noticed there is a deeper meaning when I read that before. God defines for us what is good and evil, and eating that fruit would give them the same power God has to know, to define, what is good and evil."

Nick jumped in with excitement, "Bingo!" not realizing whether that expression would have any meaning to her. "I mean, yes, that's it!" He was impressed at how quickly she was able to extract that interpretation. "When we are able to assume that power, then there is no need for God to be telling us what to do, how to behave, etc. It is no longer up to Him to define good and evil. We can define them individually or as a society relative to what we think or feel it should be. Isn't that what is happening today? The secular society that is now the norm around the world, with some exceptions, rejects any absolute rules, rights or wrongs that came from God in favor of a determination that is made by us humans based on our own assessment. According to their thinking, rules should not be absolute, but rather change relative to a changing world. In other words, *relativism*. It is not such a progressive or new concept after all!" Nick paused to let that sink in with Fatma, and interestingly enough, Ghassan, who was quietly paying attention and looked very interested.

He continued, "That book, Genesis, was written almost 3,500 years ago, and the concept of relativism as something that the devil wanted to tempt us to do was already there. Human nature hasn't really changed that much. Men are men, women are women, and both have differences that have always existed and will exist forever. Killing defenseless humans is evil, no matter what the justification. Taking from others – stealing – is wrong. We conveniently ignore that and keep trying to change or adjust the rules under the false premise that everything is changing, all in the name of progress."

Nick paused again, realizing he had gone off on a tangent... again! "Sorry! So, anyway, evil. It seems like there are entities like Agares pulling strings everywhere." He then went on to provide his thoughts on the various questions and objections Fatma raised, encouraging her not to take any of it at face value, but rather research the topics to draw her own conclusions.

The conversation continued on for hours, in what felt like a few minutes. All three were fascinated with the topic of discussion. Fatma, and in a very quiet way, Ghassan, were hearing from a voice that is not allowed to speak in their culture. There was no tolerance for Christian thought and belief, yet on the flip side, Nick did not once say anything derogatory about Islam and its believers. From Nick's perspective, he saw in them the same hunger for the truth that he grew up with, but a much stronger devotion and discipline.

Upon realizing that it was past midnight, Nick told Ghassan and Fatma, "I apologize for staying here so late and talking non-stop since I arrived. It has been wonderful to meet the two of you, but to be honest, I am not sure I was supposed to be here so late." Fatma did not need much of an explanation, as she also knew that there was a reason for Nick to be there, which would become evident to them at the right time.

Ghassan responded, "Mr. Nick, it is me that apologizes for not being more hospitable and offering you to have some rest. It is too late now for you to find safe transportation to meet your group, and I can offer my room while I sleep in the couch."

Nick quickly responded, "Please, there is no need for that. I was planning on getting a taxi or an Uber to the hotel in Bethlehem. It is all inside Palestinian territory and a relatively short drive, isn't it?"

Ghassan did not want to sound disrespectful, but he found Nick's assumptions to be somewhat funny. He said, "I wish it were that easy. It is already too late to find any type of transportation. Even if you did, it would not be safe for you to be out there. Maybe in Tel Aviv, but certainly not here. Please accept our offer to stay here tonight, and tomorrow morning I will help you rejoin your group, hopefully before they leave the hotel."

Nick was embarrassed when he realized how naïve his questions had made him sound. He tapped the side of his head and said, "I am sorry for being so clueless. I guess I have been in this bubble with our tour group...Anyway, I have already inconvenienced you too much. Please go to your rooms and rest. I will be fine staying in the living area. I'll take the couch..."

"No, Mr. Nick, you are our guest and I insist that you sleep in my room. It is clean..." Ghassan said with a smile. "I will sleep in the sofa and will be ready to go at dawn tomorrow."

27

NABIL'S MISTAKE

It was now past midnight, and Nabil had been hiding outside, between the living room window and the back-door to the kitchen, in the darkness of the alleyway. He had been able to listen in on the entire conversation, and the gratuitous lecture that Nick provided, which he found unexpected, shocking, and at the same time fascinating. His initial reaction was to reject what he heard, particularly things that contradicted the faith he grew up in. However, he also realized that his rejection was of the person delivering the words, as well as his background, not so much the message itself. Nick was an American. In Nabil's mind, likely someone that hated Muslims and thought they were all terrorists. Could he be a spy, or undercover police working in collaboration with Israeli authorities? Was he just softening Ghassan and Fatma so he could eventually get information on local Hamas radical cells? Was he a threat? In any event, he was not moving away from the area at this time, so the three of them were conveniently captive for the remainder of the night. He was struggling to decide what to do next, and a sense of fear overcame him, so he rushed back to the safe house.

Nabil arrived at the safe house a few minutes later, and found Fathi, who was angry over not being able to track him since sunset. It had been almost six hours since his location was not available. Fathi vented his frustration at Nabil as he usually did since they were kids, whenever little Nabil would not obey his brother's direction. Nabil had always had a mind of his own and was not concerned about fitting into Fathi's model. He also knew that Fathi was overly dramatic, would yell and scream at the slightest provocation, but never showed the courage to take things further. Nabil had conditioned himself to tune him out whenever he went on one of his tirades. This one lasted about fifteen minutes and was followed by an awkward silence, which served to calm down Fathi.

During the tirade, Nabil patiently waited for Fathi to finish venting, ready to move on to what he wanted to talk about. His mind was fixed on what he had just heard emitting from the apartment. On impulse and driven mostly by fear and hatred for the American and what he represented, Nabil told Fathi that he had found the girl's apartment.

"It is not far from here. You know, the street just before the roundabout? Up that street, less than three hundred meters from the main road. The woman's name is Fatma. She lives with her father, Ghassan. I did not see him but would not be surprised if we have seen him around town." He paused, still trying to decide if he should disclose the other key piece of information he learned, and then continued. "While they were getting ready for dinner, two men showed up. One was wearing a brown tunic, like the type that the Christian priests wear. The other one looked like a tourist. I later heard that his name is Nick. He knocked on the door, and before it was opened, I lost sight of the one with the tunic. Not sure what happened to him. The tourist one was welcome in the apartment. He is an American!" said Nabil with wide eyes to emphasize. "When I left, he was still in the house, and it sounded like he was staying. I am not sure whether he was a religious person of some type. He seemed to be preaching to them."

"Preaching?" said an incredulous Fathi.

"I don't know. Maybe he was pretending. Maybe that was his way of getting her to open up and talk about the shooting. Isn't that how someone from Mossad or the CIA would do infiltrate? I thought it could be that our mission has attracted too much attention, and that made me worried."

Fathi's frustration with the temporary disappearance of his brother was quickly replaced by excitement. He saw this as an opportunity to redeem himself in front of Hamas leadership, and without giving it too much thought, called Abdul.

Abdul lived in a town not far from Jericho and was in the middle of his sleep when the cell phone rang. He got out of bed, got his phone, and walked outside his room to answer the call. After cursing Fathi for waking him up, he listened to the update and realized the importance of the find. He also understood that, given the circumstances, they had the opportunity to turn the situation to their benefit if they acted fast. Before finishing up the call, Abdul was already in his Kia, heading over to the safe house. At that time of the night, with no traffic, he could cover the thirty kilometers in roughly forty-five minutes. He could not afford to attract attention, so he maintained a steady speed, within the speed limit. As soon as he disconnected with Fathi, he made an encrypted phone call to Hassan's cell phone.

After two long beeps, the voice at the other end answered, "Salam, Abdul."

Abdul responded, "Marhaban. I apologize for calling at this time, but it is important. I have some information that may be of interest to you. My people believe they found the apartment of the witness of the IDF attack. I am on my way there now and will handle the situation, but...I was told there is an American inside with them. Don't know why or what it means but thought you should know. Any ideas?"

Hassan remained quiet for a couple of seconds, then said, "Understood. Thank you for the information. Can you hold for a second?" Hassan returned saying, "Are you certain the American is there? Now?"

"That is my understanding. Yes. Nabil thinks he is staying in the apartment overnight."

"OK, I just woke up Ahmed. He was not happy either, but if the American is still there, he will go with you," said Hassan.

"Good. I did not realize this Ahmed would be willing to get his hands dirty. I thought he operated above us, and in stealth."

"This is different. He may want to be directly involved in learning more about the American. This is probably an experienced agent, so he may not want to take any chances."

"Good. How much time does he need?" asked Abdul.

"I believe he is on your side of the barrier, but much closer to Jerusalem...and al-Eizariyah. He can probably be there in thirty minutes."

"OK. The apartment is less than a kilometer from the safe house. Just tell him to meet us at the safe house in one hour. Can you give him directions?"

"Oh, he knows where it is," said Hassan with a tone of sarcasm. "He and his boss know everything about us. For all I know, he is listening in on our conversation...and probably knows the American by name."

"Well, we will see him there in an hour. Anything else?"

"No Abdul. Good luck. Yalla..." and Hassan hung up.

As Abdul and Ahmed were separately heading toward the safe house, Nabil started to argue with Fathi over the need to call Abdul at that time. "This is the equivalent of issuing an execution order for everyone inside that apartment! I think you needed to know, so much so that I came here to tell you I found them, but I did not intend for this to be handled as an immediate execution. There may be more we could have learned from them without getting Abdul involved."

Now that Nabil realized what he had set in motion, he started to reflect back on all he had heard from Nick, as well as Fatma and Ghassan's acceptance of all of it as truth. Was there something to that story that made it really true, even for a Muslim? The realization that he had made a mistake began to grow on him, and as soon as he found the opportunity, he stormed out of the safe house. His mind was in the middle of a violent storm. A truth he found difficult to accept was starting to tug at him without pause. His lack of maturity and impulsiveness had led him to make a grave mistake. In addition to the conflict and confusion in his mind, he felt alone. There was no one he could go to for advice. The people he grew up trusting were full of contradictions and driven by fear and hatred. With that he turned to Allah and prayed for clarity as he jogged back toward Fatma's apartment, clueless about what his next steps should be.

Abdul arrived just past three in the morning to find Fathi alone at the safe house. While he noticed that Nabil wasn't there, he was completely distracted and anxious about meeting Ahmed there in person for the first time. His primary concern now was to ensure that he and Fathi looked like they could be trusted and were effectively doing their jobs as field soldiers of Hamas. Abdul had only heard about him through Hassan as they were planning this attack. Every message and instruction were extremely short and focused, but reflected very sophisticated planning skills, so Ahmed was an interesting mystery to Abdul. Neither he nor his cousin Hassan were privy to the longer range plans that Ahmed and K, and their organization, had regarding their land.

At approximately 3:15 am, Abdul and Fathi heard the door lock to the safe house click open and a tall, athletic man with dark features wearing black Adriano Goldschmied jeans, a dark gray Adidas quarter-zip, and black Brooks running shoes walked in and shut the door behind him.

"Good evening, or should I say good morning?" said the new arrival, surprising Abdul and Fathi with his English accent and diction. This was in stark contrast with Newham, where Abdul had spent his early years, and the environment was borderline ghettoish. "I am Ahmed."

Ahmed Ossas was one of K's main lieutenants, and someone he trusted, not only because of his loyalty, but also because of his intelligence, education, and ability to operate in very diverse situations. His background was similar to K's, being the son of Muslim immigrants. His family migrated from Somalia to the UK, where he was born and raised. He also emerged from very humble beginnings to get an education that culminated with Finance at the London School of Economics. After several years working as an investment banker at Deutsche Bank throughout the Middle East, he was recruited by the government of Iran to help them with complex financing operations, all of which were clandestine and funded their proxy military and terrorist operations in the Syria, Lebanon, and Israel-Palestine region. In addition to his very strong banking and deal-making acumen, Ahmed had been trained by the Iranian Imperial Guard and Russian intelligence. During the last few years, he had gravitated more toward field work where he had an opportunity to hone his tactical skills and had become a ruthless, but very surgical terrorist. Both Ahmed and K had greatly benefited from the open, merit-based system of Western countries, but sadly had devoted their adult lives to destroy that culture. They were using radical Islamists, committed to jihad, as one of their fronts on that battle. To gain their trust, Ahmed had to pretend he was also part of the cause.

"As-salaamu Alaikum Ahmed. Thank you for making the time to come," said Abdul.

Ahmed responded, "This is important. I am not sure what

role an American would be playing in this situation, but it feels like they may be getting too close, so I thought I'd come." He paused, surveyed the room realizing that Fathi was also there, and said, "Let's start with a prayer." Ahmed was doing this for effect, as he was indifferent to the religious situation there, but saw it as a way to connect with the troops.

After the brief prayer, Fathi relayed what Nabil had told him. "The name of the witness is Fatma. He also mentioned that the name of the American is Nick. This Nick came with another person to the apartment, but Nabil could not see where the other person went. Nabil said it was dark, and it was hard for him to see while also hiding behind the corner of the building. The other person was dressed as a monk, probably a Franciscan. A few of them live at a monastery near the Church of St Lazarus, not far from here. I am not sure what an intelligence operative was doing with a monk...or maybe the monk was in disguise..."

Ahmed interrupted, "Interesting. Did Nabil get a good look at the American...this Nick? Did he describe him? Is Nick still there? Also, who else is in the apartment at this time?"

Fathi responded, "Nabil did not see the American's face, and was only able to listen in on the conversation from outside the apartment. According to Nabil, they were still at the house when he left, and there were no signs that they were going anywhere. The father of the witness invited him to stay. Also, Nabil mentioned that most of the conversation had little to do with the attack on the IDF soldiers and more about religion. They spoke about that for hours."

Ahmed asked, "Why are we getting the story secondhand from you? Can't I speak directly with Nabil? Where is he?"

Fathi responded, "He went home. He is not feeling well." The response made Ahmed feel uneasy. It was odd that Nabil was not present, as a minimum to get recognition from his superiors for the excellent surveillance he had performed and for finding the woman. Perhaps Fathi had pushed him out so he could be in control? Those questions would have to wait.

Ahmed asked about a few additional details and got the information he needed for now. He still felt that information about the American was incomplete, and that added an element of risk to the plan, as he did not know what to expect. Still, time was of the essence and Ahmed promptly devised a plan. "We need to move fast and act on two different objectives. First, we need to separate the American from the witness to ensure we get the truth. We have to take one of them away from the apartment. Perhaps the woman? Fathi and I will stay behind to interrogate and execute the American and the father and will set the apartment on fire to destroy any evidence we may leave behind and make it harder for them to identify the men. Abdul, you will bring the witness back to the safe house and execute her, but not before learning what she told the police and the American, or anybody else. We will dispose her body later."

There were a couple additional details that they discussed, and when Ahmed was satisfied that they had enough information and a plan, recognizing that they needed to work swiftly and under the cover of night, the three men got their gear and left. Fathi also grabbed his backpack for additional ammunition, a roll of duct tape, a knife, and a few black cloth sacks. As he was leaving, he also picked up a two-gallon jug, half-full of gasoline.

"Let's see how much information we can get, then erase this nuisance," Ahmed said coldly as they walked toward the exit door of the safe house.

28

EVE OF BATTLE

Ghassan, Nick, and Fatma had fallen into a very light and restless sleep. All three were tired but felt an unusual sense of anxiety. They did not feel completely safe, as if someone else knew that Nick was there. That did not allow them to get to a deep sleep and fully rest.

Nabil had walked back to the apartment and was hiding behind the side of the building, next to the kitchen door, still under the cover of darkness. Before he left, he had grabbed his knife. He decided not to bring a gun, as the inventory was carefully watched at the safe house, and he did not want to raise any suspicion with Fathi or Abdul. The apartment was totally quiet, and it sounded like they were sleeping inside. Nabil was tormented about the situation he had created by opening his big mouth.

While he felt a commitment to Hamas, it was familiar to him and knew he had a future there, he felt that Fatma was an innocent bystander and a human life that should not just be extinguished as collateral damage simply because it was cleaner if she could no longer pose a threat to them. He also started to feel a stronger connection to Fatma, even though he felt tormented by the thought in his mind when he had the illusion that she was communicating with him. Ghassan did not appear to be a threat at all, other than he remained too quiet during the conversation and what Nabil believed to be an indoctrination by Nick, something Nabil interpreted as being complicit and even agreeing with those ideas. Nick was someone to be concerned about, since he appeared to be there trying to influence and obtain information.

Nabil also expected the situation to turn violent once Fathi and Abdul arrived there and had still not decided what to do if and when they showed up. If he decided to confront them, that would be the end of his participation in a cause that up until now he had a lot invested in. There was also the concern about his brother, how he would react, which side he would take, and regardless of that, how this episode would reflect on him within Hamas. After all, it was Fathi that introduced him to the organization. All of this was cycling through Nabil's mind as he waited, trying to determine how to act. His mind told him to remain loyal to the cause and what he was familiar with. His heart wanted him to act on the side of the truth.

FATMA WOKE up abruptly by attempting to escape from a nightmare she had in her very light sleep. She was tired, but with all the thoughts going through her mind, had not fallen into a deep sleep. It was in this tormented state of consciousness that she felt a horrible feeling through her body, akin to having a fever, but much more unpleasant, and a deep feeling of sadness and despair. Upon waking up and regaining her full consciousness, she began to grow the unease she had felt before the episode she experienced in the kitchen, and this time sensed a dark and powerful presence that she had now become familiar with. She got up and walked outside of her room and noticed that Nick was wide awake but Ghassan was still sleeping. Nick was on the couch and Ghassan had stayed on the hallway floor immediately between her room and the kitchen.

Out of the corner of her eye, Fatma noticed a faint light outside the front window. It was a very dark night, with the moon at waning crescent. She could see what appeared to be light coming from the screen of a smartphone. Adrenaline shot through her bloodstream like lightning and her heart started beating at an uncontrolled pace. She looked at Nick with her eyes wide open, as if expecting an explanation from him about what was going on outside.

Nick returned the look with an expression of resignation but also strength. He whispered, "It is time. We are about to enter a battle being fought between good and evil, truth and darkness, and for some strange reason, we have been asked to participate in it. Be strong, Fatma..."

The relative quiet was suddenly broken by a thump-like metallic sound and the front door swinging wide open. Fathi rushed in and saw both men just to the left and within ten feet of the entrance, one on the couch and the other on the floor at the edge of the hallway. Ghassan had just woken up and was starting to get up when Fathi rushed him, pushing the dining table to the far-left corner. He quickly kicked Ghassan on the side of the head and knocked him back down. He then saw Fatma in the shadows of the hallway that led to the two bedrooms. He signaled to Abdul, pointing at her to let him know where the witness was hiding, and quickly rushed to the couch and grabbed Nick, turning him and putting the full weight of his body on his back. Nick resisted some but did not have the strength to overcome the attacker and was so startled that his reaction time was too slow.

Before he knew it, he had his hands behind his back with the wrists and ankles taped together, three straps of duct tape over his mouth, and a black cloth sack over his head. He was frisked to see if he was carrying a weapon, and in that process,

Fathi pulled his mobile phone from one of his front pant pockets. At the same time, Ahmed stood at the door, keeping an eye on Ghassan to ensure he remained unconscious on the floor. He had no intention to get his hands dirty unless it was absolutely necessary and did not care to be seen until both were neutralized and had their eyes covered. Even though they would be killed soon, he had a preference for remaining faceless in front of his victims. A combination of paranoia and cowardice.

After being done with Nick, Fathi went back to where Ghassan was lying to repeat the same procedure while he was still unconscious. He said, "I don't think any of them are armed." At that point Ahmed went inside and stood by Nick, who was in a fetal position on the sofa. Nick could not speak because of the tape on his mouth, but he was also careful not to emit any noise or movement in order not to provoke any additional violence on the part of the radicals. He felt like a lamb at the mercy of its executioners. It was not going as he expected. Evil was in control.

Meanwhile, Abdul cornered Fatma in her room. She did not resist. Instead, she said, "Please do not harm my father. If you are coming for me, please..." and before she could finish, Abdul grabbed her right shoulder with his left hand and swung his right arm violently hitting her with the palm of his hand three times until she momentarily lost consciousness. He carried her to the main living area where he also tied her up, put a sack of black cloth over her head, threw her body on his shoulder, and rushed outside to take her to the safe house, only a few blocks away. They were flawlessly executing the plan of separating her from the two men and interrogating each to extract as much information as possible without any deception on their part. They needed to know what she had told the Israeli police or any other party that could have an interest in exposing individuals within Hamas. In less than two minutes the three hostages were neutralized, and the woman separated from the other two, just as planned.

Nick felt useless for not being able to protect or stop their advance and the unnecessary violence on Ghassan and Fatma. If he was confused before about the purpose of his visit, he was even more perplexed about why it entailed capture and torture by terrorists. Still, he was confident that this was all happening for a reason, and eventually something good would come out of it. He knew that the forces he was aligned with were much stronger than anything they could be dealing with in this world. The abduction happened so quickly that he was unable to identify how many of them there were, and without his sight, was totally disoriented. He saw the one guy that rushed in with a scarf covering his face but heard other male voices after they put the sack cloth over his head. He also did not understand Arabic, and that is all he heard from the first two men that had forced their way inside the apartment. He was having difficulty breathing, given his chronic allergy problems, which kept his nose congested most of the time, and now he had duct tape over his mouth and face. In addition to the concern and pity he felt for Ghassan, he worried about Fatma and wondered about the horrors she would experience at the hands of these animals.

Ahmed surveyed the overall situation and was pleased at how efficiently they had been able to neutralize them. He also began to have doubts about the American, and whether he was truly a US or Israeli agent. He had been too easy to subjugate. Now they needed to execute quickly to get information from him and dispose the two men in a way that would not point back to Hamas. Ahmed pulled out his cell phone, which was connected to an external battery, tapped on the screen a few times, and placed it on the dining table. He then walked over to the sofa where Nick was still lying on his side with his knees together up to his chest, and hands tied behind his back.

Ahmed grabbed Nick's left arm to help him off the sofa and sit him on one of the chairs of the dining table. He then took the roll of duct tape and went around his chest and arms, and behind the back of the chair four times to fasten him to it and immobilize him in that position. Once satisfied that Nick was under control, he pulled the cloth sack up to Nick's nose and ripped the tape from his mouth. Nick took in a couple of deep breaths and was able to regain his normal breathing.

"Good evening," said Ahmed loudly in perfect Queen's English, as if to provoke a response from the American. "The first thing you need to know is that no one will hear you from this apartment if you scream, but if you do, you'll regret it." He then tapped Nick on the side of the head twice with his gun to put an exclamation mark on the message. "We are operating with limited time, so the sooner you cooperate, the less pain you, the girl, and her father will have to endure. We know that the girl that lives here witnessed the elimination of two infidel pigs at the hands of our troops. We are interrogating her at a separate location to ensure that you both tell the truth, and my people are waiting for my signal to drive a hammer into her skull, which will swiftly happen if you don't tell us what is going on and who else knows about this...or, if your stories don't agree."

Nick, who had been in silent prayer until now, was disgusted with what he had just heard and shocked at the fact this was likely someone that had grown up and received his schooling in the UK. This was a seasoned and hateful terrorist who was about to kill Fatma, and them shortly afterwards. There was no other way around it. Yet, this was certainly an English accent, making him feel somewhat familiar – an interesting and nauseating dichotomy.

Upon hearing Ahmed's comments, Ghassan began to shake, doing everything possible to break free of the tape that bound his wrists and ankles, and grew so anxious that he began to hyperventilate almost to the point of convulsing. Fathi grabbed him by the ankles and dragged his body to the other side of the living area by the hallway in front of the kitchen. When he got close to the wall, Fathi pulled up his legs and flipped him unto the wall. Ghassan landed on his collarbone, which immediately cracked upon impact. He shrieked and started to sob in desperation, and Nick could hear the muted sounds from the heavy nasal breathing.

Nick, who was upset, but remained relatively calm up until now, started to become angry and wanted to avenge all this pain that the terrorists were inflicting on them. He also felt a strong sense of guilt. It was likely he that led the radicals to the apartment of the witness they wanted to eliminate, and that he was an American would likely make things worse.

In the darkness and loneliness that he felt, he began to feel the presence of Zaphkiel and heard, "Do not fear and do not give in to hatred...or lies. Be in control. Be strong, and let the truth be your weapon. We are with you."

As he heard these words, Nick visualized Zaphkiel, along with tens, maybe hundreds of angels standing behind him. They were not physically in the room, but very much in the spiritual realm in a space that intersected the time and place on Earth. It was a gift for Nick to hear this, and it gave him great strength, even though all indications were that the situation would not get resolved in their favor.

Nick thought, "I am turning everything over to God. Act through me, Lord. I am your hands and feet in this world...even though they are tied right now." It was no time for humor, but he felt the irony of the situation. He then prayed for Ghassan to remain strong, as deep down inside he knew that regardless of how grave the situation was, they would somehow prevail.

As Ahmed spoke again, the angelic vision began to fade, but not their presence in Nick's heart and mind. He knew they were there for the duration. "It is a problem when outsiders come into this land to contaminate the people with their satanic beliefs, but when it is a local that betrays us, it is rather sickening," continued Ahmed, referring to what he assumed was a betrayal on the part of Ghassan and Fatma.

Nick responded, "What have they done to you, and how do you know they are betraying you and your people? This gentleman and his daughter are good people that had the horrible fortune of getting sucked into this cycle of evil that you and your organization are perpetuating..."

Ahmed cut him off, "The mere fact that they are hosting you is offensive. Before you continue pontificating, tell me, who are you and why are you here?"

Nick responded without hesitation, "My name is Nick Aday, and I am in Israel as part of a Christian pilgrimage group. How I got here to this apartment, I don't fully understand, and I am now afraid that it has been a death sentence for this family." He went on to explain where he was from and what he did in the US in a way that was extremely credible, something that threw Ahmed off balance.

As the interrogation unfolded inside the apartment, a black Range Rover made a left turn from Jericho Road on to Fatma's street and turned off its headlights. Inside were two men, a driver and a passenger sitting in the rear. The passenger was K, and he had been listening in on the conversation at the apartment since Ahmed called using an encrypted phone application a few minutes earlier. Ahmed had earlier shared the location of the apartment with K, and K's plan had been to listen from a distance, but not intervene. After dropping off Ahmed a block away from the safe house, they had parked the SUV nearby so they could be available to pick up Ahmed after he completed the executions inside the apartment. K did not trust the barbaric local Hamas agents and preferred to maintain his identity hidden from them, so they had dropped off Ahmed at the safehouse and maintained a distance from the activities that would ensue. But K had not counted on the fact that he would recognize the voice of the American hostage, whose identity was then confirmed once he mentioned his name. This made K curious beyond the point of reason, and he could not resist confronting him. Besides, his plan with Ahmed was to complete that night with a clean slate. Anyone that met them could not be allowed to survive to identify them later or leak any information about their role in Palestine.

Ahmed and Nick were still going back and forth in the interrogation, now turned dialogue, when Nick heard the front door slowly swinging back in, being pushed by someone who had been standing outside. Fathi also turned and looked. Once the door was open it revealed the outline of a man, someone that seemed overdressed for the occasion. He was wearing nice slacks, a Brooks Brothers long-sleeve button-down shirt, and a wool blazer.

K was still standing at the threshold of the door, which cast a shadow on his face, when he said, "Salam." While it was in Arabic, the voice sounded familiar, and it was evident that the person was known to at least some of the radicals that were already there, possibly their superior. He also detected an accent. Even though Nick did not know Arabic, the general intonation did not sound local. Nick thought it would be helpful if he spoke again, to see if he could make a connection.

Ahmed turned around slightly surprised, then responded, "Good evening. Thanks for joining us." Nick was surprised to hear Ahmed address him in English adding credence to his theory that the new arrival was not a local. Ahmed proceeded to update K on what had happened and his skepticism about Nick's story of being just a tourist.

"What is his name?" K asked, pretending to be unaware that it was Nick. After Ahmed's response, K continued, this time addressing Nick, "What would an American Christian pilgrim be doing here in this apartment? At this time? I am fairly certain that those groups stay at nice hotels and do not stray far from the rest of the group. What is your business in this apartment, with these people?"

Nick could not believe the familiarity of the voice he was hearing. It was certainly someone he had been in touch with recently, not more than a few months ago. Nick bought some time by answering the question, while at the same time trying to decipher who this was, "It is hard to explain, but I can assure you it is not for the reasons you might be thinking. The group I am traveling with was at the Church of St Lazarus, and as the mass was ending, a monk walked over to me and asked that I accompany him to this apartment." He knew it sounded almost insane, but it was the truth. "I know this question may sound awkward, but you sound just like people from the area where I live, in D.C. Is it fair to assume that you are not a local?"

With that question and offended by the ridiculous story about the monk and the attempt at small talk, K looked at Ahmed and made a gesture. Ahmed immediately understood and drove his knee into the right side of Nick's face. The impact was so strong that Nick tipped over and fell to the floor. His teeth cut into the inside of his lower right lip, and he started bleeding immediately. Nick remained quiet but was shocked with the unexpected and disproportionately violent strike on his face. It took a few seconds for the initial shock to subside, then he started to feel a throbbing pain on the right side of his face. The impact also seemed to jolt his memory, as he then made the connection that the secret voice was of a man that he had met back home, one he had specifically spoken with about this trip. It was Youssef Khoury!

29

THE BATTLE – ACT I

Nick's face was throbbing, but his stomach turned when he realized that indeed, it was Youssef. This shattered the image he had of him as a Palestinian Christian whose vocation was to support Christians in that area and throughout the Middle East. Many thoughts raced through his mind. Were there Christian Palestinian terrorists in that area? Was that even a thing, and could Youssef be involved in that? If they were connected to what Fatma witnessed, what was their motivation to target the IDF? He knew there was a history of friction with some of the more conservative Jews in the area, but in general Christians were accepted by the Jews much more than by Muslims in Israel.

After an awkward silence, Nick struggled to say, "I am sorry if I offended anyone or if it was inappropriate for me to be asking questions." He paused, and then went with his impulse, "Youssef, I know it's you. What's going on here?"

Youssef responded, "Nick, the one that should be answering that question is you. What are you doing here, in this apartment, at four in the morning? Now that you know it is me, it would be nice to stop BS-ing and tell me the truth."

"Youssef, I'm not lying. I don't totally understand the reason I came to begin with, but it has nothing to do with the shooting. I was not even familiar with the shooting. And yes, Fatma told me that story, not so much because I play a role in pursuing it, but because when it happened, she experienced something that she could not explain. It was something supernatural!"

"Supernatural? Nick, don't make the mistake of assuming you are talking to the naïve academic you met at Georgetown. What is happening here is a matter of life and death, and you are not helping yourself," said Youssef.

"I'm struggling to understand what your role is here. It appears that you are connected with this organization of radicals. What kind of organization is this? Unless you are here to rescue us, this doesn't seem like something the United Nations would be involved in."

Youssef made eye contact with Ahmed again, then pointed with his eyes in the direction of Fathi. He was concerned about Fathi listening in on this conversation. All this knowledge was likely going to make him collateral damage this night. They had no idea who Fathi was, and how valuable he might be to the organization, but they knew he was more of a field guy than a leader. That made him a peon, an expendable resource. There were many radicalized men in that area that could take his role without any disruption to their activities. Fathi remained motionless, standing next to Ghassan, pretending that his entire focus was on the hostage. Inside he was a little bit surprised about the initial exchange in the conversation. He had never met K before. Some in his circle of operatives had told Fathi about this character named K, who was very influential, not even a Hamas member per se, but actually above the local Hamas leadership.

After a few seconds of tension in the room, Youssef said in a much more forceful and serious tone, "What do you know about the United Nations? What do you *really* know about me,

Nick? The mistake that people like you often make is trying to view and judge the actions of the United Nations through the lens of your own values. Your belief in an absolute truth where an unchanging set of values come from. The world and its people are a living organism, not a static set of beliefs based on the knowledge that was acquired up through the last two millennia. What we are involved in is for the betterment and progress of the world. Practicing Jews and Christians, with their outdated and superstitious beliefs are standing in the way, and anyone that can help us neutralize or eliminate them is our ally...at least for now."

Youssef continued, "Before we go on, can you answer my original question? What is a retired IT executive doing at the apartment of a key witness in an IDF attack at this time of the night and six thousand miles from home? What was the purpose of your meeting?"

Almost as in cue, Ahmed grabbed the gasoline jug that Fathi had brought, opened it, and began to pour it on Nick's feet.

Ahmed said, "Can you smell it? This is petrol, and it should motivate you to speak quickly. We will start with your feet and move our way up."

Nick remained surprisingly calm. Torture is something he had expected, but somehow believed that he would find a source of strength and protection. He responded, "I've got nothing else for you."

Youssef, who was slowly strolling around the room to remain as calm as possible as his frustration was building, looked at Nick. He then reached into his shirt pocket, pulled out a box of Dubek cigarettes and lit one up. He knew Nick would pick up the smell of the match, and eventually the cigarette smoke. This was a subtle way of letting him know that he was ready to set his feet on fire if he did not cooperate. He then said, as he waved his right hand to put out the match,

"This gives new meaning to the phrase *holding your feet to the fire*. Anyway, let's start with your connection to this family. How do you know them?"

Nick responded, "Youssef, you are not going to get a different story just because you keep asking the same questions."

"You are making this more difficult than it needs to be," said Youssef, his frustration starting to show.

Nick quickly replied, "You are the one that got my feet soaking in gasoline and are threatening to torture and kill me. I am simply telling you the truth, sorry that it's not as exciting as you expected."

"OK, so you are saying that there is some sort of supernatural connection between you and the woman, and that is what brought you together. If that is the case, make it manifest itself here. Maybe I will believe if the evidence is there. In the meantime, I will make this more interesting," said Youssef, as he then signaled Ahmed to pour the remaining contents of the gasoline tank on Ghassan. "What you hear is the rest of the fuel being poured on your friend. We'll start with him." He then pulled the sack cloth from Nick's head so he could see what was happening around him.

Nick opened his eyes and surveyed the room. He saw a young man with a head scarf to his right. Youssef was three feet to the young man's right, and a slender tall dark man behind him, most likely the Brit, he thought. Ghassan was also to his right, on the floor and against the wall. His hands were taped behind his back, his head covered with another one of those black cloth sacks that seemed to be a standard tool of these radicals to instill fear. Ghassan was struggling to breathe, partly because of the broken collarbone, but also because his nose was congested with dry blood. Nick remained inexplicably calm again, even with what appeared to be a hopeless situation about to escalate even more.

Even he could not believe how serene he felt. He then pleaded, "Please don't do that, Youssef. The man has been through enough suffering already. He has done nothing wrong and does not pose a threat. If you want to take out your anger on someone, do it to me, but please leave Ghassan alone!" he paused, but there was no reaction. "Youssef, look at me. How can you inflict this kind of pain on an innocent person, specially someone that is part of the group you are supposedly trying to rescue from Israeli oppression?"

Youssef was getting more confused and frustrated as the exchange with Nick did not fit his expectations. He thought there was a possibility that Nick was playing mind games with him, but there was no reason to believe that he was indeed an intelligence operator. He simply did not fit the profile. Now, with that being the case, the question of why he was there was still a big conundrum. A feeling deep inside of him started to grow. Something he had not experienced in recent days – fear! There really was no logical explanation for Nick's visit there, so in a strange way, this intersection of fate could not simply be brushed off as a coincidence. Now that Nick knew he was involved with Hamas, he needed to continue executing his plan.

He turned toward Nick again and said, "OK, I can kill you first, but before we char your legs and the rest of your body, I need to know if there is anyone you are working with that knows what the woman told you tonight. If I am happy with the answer, I may let this Ghassan live." He paused to let the threat sink in with Nick. "Do you know that gasoline burns at almost 950 degrees centigrade? Oh, you are a Tulane guy. I guess for you that would be over 1,700 Fahrenheit."

Nick responded, "Thanks for the interesting piece of trivia, and the conversion from Celsius, which you came pretty close to nailing." Nick's fearlessness made Youssef visibly annoyed. He continued, "It only takes two seconds at 150 Fahrenheit to cause a third-degree burn, so I won't feel much of anything after that. You are wasting a lot of heat and money by using gasoline. There will also be smoke, and we are not exactly in a remote area in Syria, so your technique may not be the smartest to be using here, under these conditions. Boiling water would have been a better choice if all you are trying to do is cause pain." At this point Nick was buying time. He had no idea how he and Ghassan would get out of this, but he felt the presence of Zaphkiel in the room, and in his heart, he knew they would be fine. He was leaving everything in his hands and that of the powers that stood behind him.

Youssef was amused at how Nick, someone that had never been in a situation like this before, at the hands of people that would have no hesitation to torture and decapitate him, had simply engaged in this type of exchange. Maybe there was a way to torture him before his death in a way that would be much deeper, painful, and humiliating. Instead of physical harm, psychological. By undermining his hope. By demonstrating how the world was being transformed into a vision that he was opposed to, one he was probably fearful of. Besides, it was a great way for Youssef to stroke his own ego and demonstrate dominance, so he continued. "I am a little surprised about your attitude here, Nick. You are not in America, where the rules are different. You see the guy with the keffiyeh? His name is Fathi, and he is a hardened jihadist that probably feels I am wasting too much time engaging in frivolous conversation with a dead man."

Youssef paused to provide more emphasis with the silence, then continued, "You were asking earlier about the United Nations, but you would be surprised to know what *we* are involved in. The United Nations is just one of our assets. Our movement controls much more than that. The end goal is to obtain power, to control the masses that are asking for precisely that. The strategy is actually quite brilliant, almost as if it was conceived by a higher power. All you have to do is embed a set of ideas in the minds of the masses, reinforce them, and the rest simply flows from wiring in their DNA. They will act on them. The human mind is wired to find meaning, purpose, a mission, but it is also wired in a more primeval way to be motivated by fear."

"By the way, whether those ideas are based on truth or not is irrelevant. What is relevant is the creation of a strong following, and eventually activism behind a concept that can help us undermine the existing power structures. As those lose popular support, it allows us to fill that gap...that's how we gain power. The hard part is when outdated ideas still linger. Stubborn and superstitious people are the biggest friction we have to deal with." He looked at Nick in the eye as he said this to reinforce the point that he was part of this unfortunate group that slowed down their movement's progress. "Today, that battle of opinion has been won in most places around the world, except for the stubborn United States and small pockets of population, like parts of Israel."

Youssef was on a roll. He was pretty proud of himself lecturing Nick on strategy, and even corporate functions that he wasn't supposed to have a strong command of. He continued in an arrogant and condescending manner, "Nick, as I recall, you spent a lot of time during your career in the field of marketing. I suppose you know how we then *embed* these ideas into the collective consciousness." He was taunting Nick sarcastically, not really expecting or willing to wait for an answer. He went on, "There are great tools to promote and educate the masses on these ideas. That's where the marketing part comes in. We have a great concept, and now have to create awareness, trigger consideration, and eventually create a fanatical movement around it. What better than to educate them through the two most effective ways we have devised for society, by having trusted voices inculcate the message? There are no more influential voices than those of our educators and the media to deal with those massive groups of people. We have been able to activate the vast majority of those two assets in ways that can no longer be countered. Yes, it is true that some of the more stubborn people begin to question those beliefs as they grow older – I guess that is what happened to you – so we have made adjustments. Influence through academia is now much more forceful and effective than it was back in the 1980s when you went to school. We start much earlier – why wait for college when you can start indoctrinating in grade school? – and we have also created an environment in which it is much more difficult, actually offensive, to offer differing views. It is working. Then there is the media. Have you noticed how consistent and well synchronized we are? We are so much better than you at it that you should be embarrassed. What we have accomplished in the United States during the last few decades, but particularly in the last ten years has been masterful. We have enlisted millions of *useful idiots* that follow these ideas fanatically. The tide is turning, Nick. We are winning. It feels good to be on the winning side. Oh, and one last point that should give you pause, since you believe you are about to meet him...the tactics that your savior used were the same. He had a new set of progressive ideas that clashed against the power structures of the time, embedded those, and it spread like fire. How was he different than what we are doing? Do you see the hypocrisy?"

Nick thought of the irony that this was a perfect example of what he had been discussing with Fatma and Ghassan a few hours earlier. He finally broke his silence, "I should probably be impressed Youssef, but the feeling is more one of disappointment and sadness. You are a smart person, even gifted, and had a privilege that many people have never experienced, of being raised in a country that was built on and holds onto Western values. That country created the environment where poor immigrants like your parents could provide opportunity to their kids. A country where the Catholic Church has schools that provide a good education and an opportunity to learn about the faith. What a wasted gift on you! You owe the opportunity that was put in front of you by the same *power structure,* as you choose to call it, that you are now trying to destroy. If you would allow me to respond, I would love to offer my perspective." Youssef smirked, and nodded to allow him to engage in the debate.

"First of all, do you really believe in this?" asked Nick.

Youssef responded, "I believe in the need to shift power from the people that have been in control to a group that is more enlightened and deserving. If you are asking whether I believe in the approach or the messaging in the same way you believe in religion...well, you probably know the answer to that."

Nick then said, "You accept there is something guiding you, but you may or may not believe in the specific ideologies and certainly nothing supernatural. OK, understood. As a first point, you said this strategy is so brilliant it must have come from a higher power. What you have just described is the makeup of the antichrist. No one knows who the antichrist is, whether a person, country, or a more complex concept. In my humble opinion, it may not be one person living at a point in time, but rather a movement that has acted in waves during the last two thousand years. You don't believe there is a darker, more powerful force behind all of this? You also believe it is strictly the product of human *progressive thought*? Youssef, the biggest difference between the two of us is that at least I know who I follow, and why."

They went back and forth for a long time. Youssef being totally transparent with someone he knew was a dead man. To Nick, it was mind-blowing that this type of evil could exist, especially in someone he thought he knew well.

Nick made one final point, knowing that his time was

running out, "Youssef, I will say one last thing in response to your last comment about Christ. On the surface, most people will agree with your assertion that his *tactics* were similar, in terms of developing a *new* set of ideas that challenged the existing power structures and then letting them rip. However, there are some very important differences that chip away at your comparison. First, his ideas and messages were all based on an absolute truth that does not change with time or in relation to *where the culture is moving*. Secondly, there has been a lot of debate by biblical scholars about how progressive his ideas were, and the idea that he was a political zealot. The most recent research, a lot of which is based on historical and archeological evidence that has been found in the last few years, points to a different way of looking at His teachings. It suggests that He was more of a conservative, loyal to the original teachings of Judaism. He was more so than the Pharisees, Sadducees, and scribes that he constantly clashed with. The Pharisees had started to become an elitist class that defined their own set of rules. Those rules eventually became more important to their lives than the core teachings of the Jewish Bible...and they wanted to impose them on others. Doesn't that sound familiar? That is the group that you should be comparing yourself to, not Jesus. In reality, Jesus was much less a revolutionary than a force trying to appeal to their conscience to live by the more traditional and timeless teachings. Now, you will not find any of this in Easter or Christmas National Geographic TV documentaries. Youssef, what happened to you?"

30

THE BATTLE – ACT II

Abdul parked the Kia behind the building, got out and pulled Fatma out of the back seat where he had thrown her. He swung her body onto his left shoulder, carried her up to the rear door, and punched in the code. With the click of the solenoids that moved the locking bars, the door cracked open, and Abdul proceeded to throw Fatma on the meeting table. She had her wrists tied behind her back, and he proceeded to tie a rope to them on one end, and one of the legs of the table on the other. That would keep her on the table and not allow her to take her arms around her buttocks and under to bring them to the front. He pulled the black cloth sack from her head and gave her a couple of light slaps on her already swollen left cheek to bring her back to consciousness.

As she opened her eyes, she initially looked up and to her right side, before turning her gaze to Abdul. He removed his keffiyeh, revealing an expression of hatred that was beyond description. His intentions were not only to extract information from her, but now that he knew she was harboring an American in her apartment, he wanted to make her suffer and repent from her infidelity to her religion and her people before killing her.

He spoke to her in Arabic, "How can you explain the presence of this American, Nick, in your apartment? How are you connected?" He then ripped the duct tape from her face, paced around the room to defuse his rage and focus on getting the information first, then sat down, waiting for an answer. "The longer it takes for you to tell me everything, the more pain we will inflict on your father. We will burn his body one part at a time. If you want him to be able to walk again, you better tell me everything now."

The threat on Ghassan and the ruthlessness and hatred with which these people operated made her very anxious, but her experiences that night made her feel confident that, somehow, they would be fine. Fear had not broken through, not yet, and that surprised her. This enraged Abdul even more, since he could not believe that after all the violence and threats, she was not showing signs of breaking down.

She then started to speak in a soft and deliberate tone, "I don't know who you are or who you represent, but I think you are mistaken about my father and me. I am a student at Al-Quds and my father is an electrician that works on construction projects in the Bethlehem and East Jerusalem area. We are not involved in any type of radical political or religious movement, and we are certainly not tied to law enforcement in any way. The American man is someone that we met tonight, and he is simply part of a group on a religious pilgrimage in Israel."

Abdul interrupted, "You witnessed the killing of the two IDF pigs a few weeks ago, didn't you?"

"Yes, I did," answered Fatma, "It was a horrible experience, as I was standing very close to the two of them. I assume it was you and your organization behind the attack, and that is why you have been trying to figure out who I was. If that's the case, you should know that all I told the police is that I saw two men in the van but could not identify them. They were several meters away in a moving car, and it all happened very fast." This was consistent with what she had told the police, although through some power she did not understand at the time, she had been able to zoom in and see their faces, particularly the driver's. Of course, she did not share this with the radical, since it would get her killed faster.

Abdul started to get impatient, as he felt that she was hiding something and the threat of burning Ghassan had not worked yet. He got up again and started pacing. They continued to go back and forth with questions and answers for several minutes, with Fatma directly answering each question with what she knew to be true. This frustrated Abdul even more and his rage continued to build until he finally snapped and walked over to the table where she was sitting, grabbed her shoulders and started yelling at her, "You don't understand what is at stake here! You keep playing games with me, providing me no real information about what you have told the Israeli pigs or this American. For your arrogance, your father by now is fried from his waist down. You have done this to him and you are next!" The frustration of the moment and his absolute hatred for anyone standing in his way made him lose focus on the mission – extract information from the witness, then terminate her. He now wanted to make her suffer. He reached for the roll of duct tape, cut two straps and firmly covered her mouth again. Fatma was now so shocked by Abdul's rage, and the thought of Ghassan being tortured in such a hateful way, that she started to cry in desperation. Abdul started to rip open her jeans at the waist.

Fatma felt the pressure of the tugging around her waist and fingernails deeply scratching the skin in her pelvic area. She knew she was a about to get raped, and most likely killed after that, by what felt like a rabid hyena clawing at her. She could barely breathe with the tape over her mouth, trying to suck air in through her bloody nose. As she fully opened her eyes, she saw Abdul on top of her and tried to swing her hands at him but could not move them as both were taped behind her back. She was helpless, and at this stage, felt abandoned by the same beings that had given her strength before. Something must have gone terribly wrong for her and her father to be going through this agony.

With her eyes wide open, and in the darkness of the room, she could now see the shadows of the Legion of Agares behind the attacker. Abdul continued to act, unaware of their presence. They were connected to and pulling the strings of his soul, though he was oblivious to it. In her desperation, Fatma noticed how they were moving chaotically, in what appeared like euphoria, yet emitting miserable and desperate sounds. There was no joy, just darkness and emptiness, mixed with chaos - the same type of visual from watching a shark feeding frenzy. Chaotic motion, but an absence of emotion or feeling, just empty eyes.

Her feeling of desperation and loss was very intense now. Her mind was moving so fast that she felt Abdul moving in slow motion, slower as it went on, to the point of him being frozen in time. While time appeared to stop in the material realm, the euphoric motion of the Legion demons continued to accelerate, this time projecting a sense of disorientation, and eventually fear, among them. It was then that she saw, directly over her, Barachiel, and behind him, an army of countless soldiers dressed just like him. His gaze made Fatma feel peace, that she was not alone, and the realization that in the chaos of the moment, somehow things were going to work out. The Legion did not even attempt to confront them but started to move even faster and more chaotically as the collective light the warriors were emitting filled the space of the spiritual realm around her.

Fatma's moment of peace came to an abrupt end when time

in the physical realm started to elapse, and all the pain came back from her swelling face and the tugging of Abdul as he continued to pull her jeans down her hips. She gasped for air, but could not take any through her mouth, and attempted to cough, with more blood spraying out of her nose. Fatma thought to herself in desperation, *Is this how Jesus felt when all seemed lost, violence was chaotic, and death was inevitable?* Barachiel had just been there with an army and had vanished the Legion but did not do anything to block the attacker from continuing on. This time, it would have to be done in the physical world, and she was unable to even move or breathe. She could not understand how any good could come out of this moment, as she was being overpowered by this violent attack, one that she could not return physically. In addition to the immediate physical harm she was suffering, sadness and desperation were consuming her. This was the darkest place she had ever been in, with all hope lost, resigned to the fact that these were her last breaths and moments on Earth.

At her lowest point of despair, Fatma heard the rear door's solenoids click, followed by the sight of a sliver of dim light filtering through and painting a narrow line on the floor, originating at the door. Abdul stopped and took a step back, looking confused. He was standing with the waist of his pants down below his buttocks, in front of her, looking surprised about the circumstances and the fact that he had gone so far outside of the mission, which was very simple and should have been carried out without distraction.

All of a sudden, out of the corner of her eye, Fatma saw a body flying from her left and landing on top of Abdul, knocking him to the floor. Nabil wrapped his left arm around Abdul's neck as both wrestled on the floor next to the metal armoire. As they struggled, Abdul uttered, "Are you fucking crazy? What are you doing, you ignorant idiot? I am going to kill you!"

Abdul was kicking and swinging his elbows wildly, as he eventually connected with Nabil's ribcage, cracking two ribs and temporarily releasing the grip he had on Abdul's neck. This was enough for Abdul to turn sideways and punch Nabil in the same area, causing Nabil to lose his breath and completely release him.

As soon as he was free, Abdul pinned the younger and lighter Nabil to the floor, put his knees on his chest, and proceeded to strike his face and head, swinging both fists violently in succession. Blood from Nabil's nose was spraying in the direction of each strike on his face, getting all over the floor. Nabil was still conscious, and with one last burst of energy, managed to swing his left knee forward, kicking Abdul from behind and making him lose his balance, rolling to the side. That gave Nabil enough time to lunge at Abdul, stabbing him with his knife just below the sternum and under the right side of his ribcage. The knife went through, severing Abdul's liver, which started to bleed profusely.

At first, Abdul was able to slide and get out from under Nabil's grip, but it was too late for him. He was losing blood too fast, and even with the rush of adrenaline going through his system, weakness took over and he was unable to move. His face turned pale, and his last act on this world was to look back at Fatma and say, "Damn you, infidel whore!" Then he gasped for air one last time, and his eyes rolled backwards as he left the misery he had been living on this Earth.

Nabil and Fatma locked eyes. His expression was one of shame, combined with the shock of the moment. He moved closer to her and lifted his right hand that was still holding the bloody knife. In his mind he heard a loud, *Please don't!*, but continuing to move forward, he said, "It is OK. I am cutting the tape and the rope. I know you have no reason to trust me, but you will see that I am not going to harm you." After her hands were freed, he helped her pull the tape over her face and mouth, and said, "I am very sorry for what I have done, to you, and the IDF men and their families. I guess to your father, and the American too. I have become something that I don't like, and now I have also killed another man."

Once her mouth was free of the tape, she was able to take a couple of deep breaths, then started to cough and gestured with her hands for Nabil to wait. After a few seconds she was able to breathe normally. "Thank you! I don't know what to say. Thanks for saving my life!" She took another breath, the continued, "What you did with the IDF men was horrible...just wrong! But what you just did was in self-defense, and in the process, you saved my life. Why did you do it?" She then got up, surprised that there was no pain in her legs and body and went to the industrial sink next to the table to wash her face. "Are there any first aid supplies here?"

Nabil turned around and walked over to the cabinet against the wall to get a first aid kit. She tended to the wounds in her face and Nabil's bleeding nose and mouth. Then he said, "Thank you. And again, I am sorry for everything. The last few weeks have been intense for me and have tested my beliefs and the way I look at life. You planted the seeds with the question that somehow you communicated to me...and I still don't understand how that happened." He paused and collected his thoughts, "Anyway, I interpreted what I heard from you as a license to learn and question my beliefs. I thought what I believed in was true, but now I see they were rooted in fear and hatred."

Fatma was shocked about the admission, although something had to explain his change of mind in coming to her rescue. She said, "Wow! I planted seeds? I communicated to you? How?"

"I heard a voice immediately after the shooting...at the same time you saw me. I think it was you," said Nabil.

"What did the voice say?"

"It asked...*why did you do this?* I know...cryptic. Maybe I read too much into it, but it made me question everything, how I got to that point..."

"Wait, you heard it?" Fatma asked, and Nabil nodded in affirmation. "I must have been standing fifty meters away, and just whispered..."

"I heard it as if it was said right next to me," responded Nabil, then continued, "I thought I had followed you to your house today because I wanted to turn you in and eliminate the witness that could undermine our operations in the West Bank. But the truth is that I followed you and listened from outside because I was intrigued and obsessed. I came back here just now because I feared for what Abdul would do to you." He paused again, this time with his eyes starting to well up with tears. "I don't know who your visitor Nick is, who brought him here and why. Everything he said felt like he was speaking to me. His words resonated within my heart in ways that I did not expect. I initially rejected it, again, out of fear and hatred for him...what he represents. But when I came back and saw all this evil done by Abdul and Fathi...and the other man, I realized that I had been on the wrong side all along."

Fatma was still unsure what to do or say. The shock from all that she had experienced during the last few hours was over-whelming. Still, in the middle all these emotions, she remained focused on what Nabil was sharing. She wondered how it would be possible that she could influence such a transforma-tion in someone that went from a hardened radical to a full rejection of that world. Before drawing any conclusions, she asked, "Are you saying that you believe that what Nick said was the truth? Are you open to learning more?"

After a brief hesitation, he said, "Well, I don't know yet. I feel like I have opened my mind and soul to a different way of looking at things, but there is a lot I need to learn, and I am still skeptical. I also worry that, after what I did, I will not be allowed to be a part of it anyway."

At that point in the conversation, Fatma remembered her father and Nick, and her anxiety started to take over. "Where you there when these men came in and took me away?"

He responded, "Yes, I was hiding behind the rear entrance to the kitchen and heard it when they forced the door. I then went around and saw Abdul carrying you out of the apartment and into his car. As I was about to leave, I then saw a man I did not recognize standing outside the entrance of the apartment. He appeared to be texting on a cell phone. He was wearing the types of clothes you would normally see foreigners wear. He walked in only after the commotion inside was over. Then I saw Fathi, my brother, walk up to the door and close it from inside. They believe there is a connection between the American being at this apartment and you being a witness of the shooting, like he is part of some anti-terrorist force, or Mossad, or CIA, or something like that. Well, that's also what I thought..."

Fatma said, "I doubt he is involved in any of that. He actually came into our apartment and did not even know why he was there, and never asked about the attack. Well, it sounds like you heard most of that conversation anyway. Do you think he is CIA or some sort of threat to your group?"

"No. Not anymore. I agree. I don't think he has anything to do with intelligence or law enforcement or spying. I do think... anyone who speaks like he does is a threat to them."

For a split second Fatma considered calling the police, but was also hesitant, as it would take time to explain everything that had happened, and it would certainly neutralize any help she could get from Nabil. She did not feel great about helping him hide, but at the same time sensed that he was telling the truth and that he might be able to help rescue her father and Nick. She needed more time to decide what to do about Nabil, but that would have to wait. For now, she needed to get back and do something to save her father, needed to have some form of backup.

As they were about to leave the safehouse, Nabil told Fatma, "I realize that you want to go, but this is for me to fix. I was the one responsible for them finding out where your apartment was. If you go, it will give them another opportunity to abuse and kill you." He took a deep breath, then said with a surprised tone, "I do not recall ever having flowers in the safehouse. All of a sudden there is a very strong smell of roses."

Fatma had also felt it, even though there were no fresh roses in the safehouse or anywhere near it. She knew it must have something to do with Barachiel and possibly a message. She responded, "I am not surprised it smells like this. A lot of unusual things have been happening to me lately...and this smell sometimes pops up before they do. Also, I appreciate your concern about my safety, but something tells me I need to be there as well."

With that, Nabil opened the rear door, and they walked out. In the darkness of the street, Fatma saw Barachiel standing within ten feet away, waiting as is he had been there for some time. His glow was as intense as it had been before, and within seconds she started to discern, one by one, the warriors standing behind him. He and his army of warriors were waiting for her. They had never left!

"Wow! Thank you!" she said as the angels floated up above them and started to move in the direction of the apartment. In the distance, Fatma could see a dim red glow in full motion above the general direction of the apartment. Just looking at it gave Fatma a feeling of sadness and despair, just as she had felt each time she confronted the Legion of Agares.

"Wow, what?" Nabil responded, and then repeated turning toward Fatma, "Wow, what? What's going on?"

She realized that not everything she could see was visible to the people around her. "Are you sure you do not see anything? Do you want to see?"

Nabil thought her last question was unusual. You could either see or you couldn't, but the concept of *wanting to see* something that wasn't there was interesting. After turning his gaze up above to the night sky, and in his heart and mind asking *I want to see*, he said, "Well...I am starting to see a very dim glare above us, with a yellowish...no, a golden color. It looks like a low cloud, flowing north and east, in the direction of your apartment. Wait, in the distance I also see a dark ghoulish looking cloud, red and black, swirling like a vortex. It is hard to distinguish it from the darkness of the night, but I see something there. Maybe the reflection of a fire?"

Then he turned his focus to the golden cloud again, since it was closer. He followed its direction toward the vortex and noticed that the clouds were actually groups of individuals in motion. He could see now that they looked like humans, except that they could fly gracefully on their own and were wearing some sort of ancient military uniform. Their torso, parts of their arms and forearms, and lower legs were covered in a glowing armor that looked like streams of light flowing constantly in many directions. There were more details that he could not figure out because they were moving fast and appeared to be crisscrossing each other in a deliberate way to get to an attack formation. Their target was in or around Fatma's apartment. Nabil looked at Fatma in total amazement and said, "Had you seen them as well? Who...what are they? Are they on our side?"

Fatma said, "They are angels of God. The good ones. So yes, they are on our side. I saw some of them for the first time at the scene of the shooting. One of them is assigned to me. You probably have one too..." She looked at him with an amused stare, then continued, "The name of mine is Barachiel. They live in a different realm – a spiritual one. In that realm there are also evil ones, which to us are what we call devils or demons. I think those are hovering like vultures in the distance, above my apartment."

Nabil was absolutely amazed with this most recent development, which was now even more amazing than listening to the voice of Nick in what he thought was a message directed at him.

"I saw them as we walked out of the warehouse, but I now know that they were with me all along," said Fatma, "They are ahead us going to the apartment. Maybe to fight the next battle. I hope it is to help my father and Mr. Nick? Let's go."

She felt the strength that flowed from Barachiel's team, and she could also feel it emanating from her. She was in good company, and while she had no idea what to expect upon arrival, she knew they would succeed. They were on the right side, on the side of truth. They were on the side of God.

Nabil was now in a state of bliss from just watching this manifestation of the beauty and power of God. However, he was also conditioned to be a little paranoid about those on the physical world, particularly the characters that were at the apartment. He said, "Stay about ten meters behind me, walking on the shadows as much as you can, and do not make a sound. We should be there in less than ten minutes."

31

THE BATTLE – FINAL ACT

5:27 *am*

The debate between Youssef and Nick continued on, adding a strange sense of normalcy to the violent and awkward situation that they were in. Youssef had planned to make this a very short visit, extract information from an American he suspected might have ties to Israeli police, IDF, or Mossad, and quickly exit while having his people do all the clean-up and leave a false trail of evidence that would place the blame on other parties. His timeline was extended by the discovery that it was Nick and the temptation to engage in a discussion about topics that he was secretly passionate about with someone that he knew would challenge him intellectually. He wanted to exert dominance physically, as well as mentally, and humiliate him by demonstrating that he was the one on the right side of history. What he did not count on was on Nick piquing his curiosity with a couple of pieces of information that challenged his understanding of the issues. It was an understanding acquired mostly through academia and activism, his primary known sources of truth. Nick's last question was unexpected, as was Nick's complete calm in the face of potential torture and death.

Youssef responded, "In the United States, there is a certain persona I have to live within, and that is why I have continued to play that role. My *Christianity* is faked to add credibility to my anti-Jewish sentiment. Within my circles in academia and even the UN, it is safer and more credible for that commentary to come from a Palestinian Christian than a Muslim. It is true that my heritage includes that label, but I reject it. By the way, my time at Georgetown Prep, pretending to be a Christian, was miserable. I never fit in…never wanted to…and the constant exposure to the faculty and Catholic kids just made me hate them even more. I also hated that cheap, antiquated and hypocritical religion. I am more about hating Jews and Christians and wanting those beliefs exterminated from the face of the Earth, than I am about any religious ideology. As a matter of fact, I am not a believer…in anything outside of the natural world. This has just been a very convenient alliance, because we have a common enemy. They are somewhat useful now, but eventually we'll get them out of the way too."

Youssef paused, and within a second, the brief silence was broken by the Fajr call to prayer blaring from the speakers along Jericho Road. Youssef looked at his watch, and saw that it was almost 5:30, less than a half hour before sunrise. Their window of time had closed, and now they needed to move swiftly to eliminate the hostages and exit under the cover of night. He abruptly got up and said, "Well, I believe I am done here," and made eye contact with Ahmed, who was waiting for his signal to execute the plan they had laid out. They would leave no one alive and sacrifice any low-level operatives that happened to be in the apartment with them in an effort to frame the American. That casualty happened to be Fathi, who was completely unaware that this would be his fate. In addition to him fitting well into their plan to frame Nick, Fathi had heard too much during the conversation.

Fathi was still standing over Ghassan, literally with his left foot on Ghassan's neck. Ahmed made eye contact with him as a sign that he could set Ghassan on fire, and Fathi obliged immediately. Ghassan, as if perceiving that his end was near, began to shake again, unable to kick or move his arms, as Fathi dropped a lit match on his gasoline-soaked clothes. Flames took hold on his pants near the ankles and started to spread quickly, eventually covering his entire body. Shockingly, as soon as he started burning, the desperate grunts he had been emitting through his nose were replaced with what sounded like a peaceful chant. Fathi moved across the room toward Ahmed, initially back-tracking to distance himself from the flames, but then turned around. He was shocked to see Ahmed point his gun directly at him.

Nick had been observing in awe what was unfolding in the room, something that apparently no one else was experiencing. Earlier, when Youssef had finished speaking and got up, Nick began to feel a dark and deeply sad presence, followed by loud collective groaning and a vortex-like motion emanating from the top of the room. The vortex was formed by the circular flight of tens of creatures of a reddish dark color, reminiscent of embers, who were coming in and out of the room. Nick was able to follow and even made eye contact with a few of them. He could identify two types of beings. One had the shape of a human body, and their faces, while in agony, looked also human. These humanoid creatures were smaller and appeared to be subordinate to the other type. The other beings were less defined in their shape, which seemed to morph as they flew around, but generally included elements of a beast – big clawed paws or hoofs instead of hands and feet, big canine teeth, tails, horns, and in some cases, wings like those of bats. Both types of beings had facial expressions that showed fear combined with a hyper-ecstatic feeling. They seemed to be feeding off the human cruelty in the room and the anticipation that more evil was about to be committed by men. But there was a sense of anxiety in their expression and the way they were moving, conveying a feeling diametrically opposite of peace.

As Fathi lit up the match, Nick had seen their speed accelerating and suddenly heard a loud rhythmic thump of flapping wings, immediately followed by a golden light that entered the room through the ceiling. The light came in as a lightning bolt onto Ghassan's body and surrounded him. Once the motion of the light settled, Nick saw that it was a human-like figure, wearing an ancient warrior's armor that glowed in a golden light. It was the same armor as Zaphkiel's, so Nick knew it was one of the good angels. The angel hugged Ghassan, covering his entire body, as his clothes were completely engulfed in flames.

The passage of time in the physical world started to slow down again in Nick's perception, and he was now more in tune with what was taking place in the spiritual realm. One by one, the dark creatures began to attack the golden warrior, but were deflected by the light around him and the arrival of a handful of other golden warriors that began to fend off the attackers as they formed an impenetrable circle around Ghassan. The light itself appeared to be their weapon and main defense.

The dark creatures could not penetrate it, and it was painful for them to come near it. The scene continued to deteriorate as more of the creatures continued to appear, some coming through the ceiling, and some from the ground below. They surrounded, but still could not penetrate the defense of the warriors. Nick realized that his senses had become much sharper than he had ever experienced in the physical world. Now he could clearly hear the overwhelming sound of the groaning and wailing that the creatures were emitting. He could also sense a very strong smell of sulfur and feces that was even stronger whenever one of the creatures flew close to him.

He then felt the air around him become colder until it felt that there was an absolute absence of heat, even with the fire around Ghassan's body next to him. It was then that he saw a creature of more than three times the size of the others floating in from his left and approaching him. It was Agares, and he had his eyes fixed on Nick's as he said, "Everything you think you have learned is a lie. In your quest for knowledge, you have sunk deeper in ignorance and that will translate to despair. Same thing with that whore you appear to be obsessed with. Aren't you too old for her?"

Nick looked back at him and knew not to react or engage in conversation. In the middle of that drama, he had a sarcastic thought - he would have expected a little more elegance from a high-ranking demon. He knew this was all about deception and also felt the strength of knowing that Zaphkiel and an army of angels were near him. He thought, "It was never a quest for knowledge. It was a quest to connect with and get closer to God, something that was part of my wiring ever since I remember having any type of awareness."

Then Nick scanned the room and each of the characters in the drama that was unfolding in it. Every single one, but specifically the radicals, were unaware of the evil presence around them. They were being influenced by Agares and his legion to the point of torturing and killing other human beings that had done nothing to them and were clueless about who was pushing their buttons. Nick thought, "I don't think they have any idea who they are serving. How could anyone in this world choose to follow that path?" It was incomprehensible to him. Instead of feeling contempt for Youssef and his gang, at that moment he was saddened at the tragedy of Youssef losing his soul. He simply felt sorry for him.

Nick then heard the familiar voice of Zaphkiel say, "Anyone

who denies the truth and leads with lies is being influenced by Agares or his peers and their master, Satan. Some may do it in a less physically violent way, but they are equally as wicked and destructive."

Nick had also noticed that Ahmed was lifting his gun and pointing it at Fathi's head. Time in the physical realm was elapsing even slower now. Mixed in with the chaos, Nick began to detect a familiar smell that did not belong in that setting. It was a clean smell that reminded him of visits to Shannon's grave. Roses! Along with that, a growing feeling of peace enveloped him. This must be what it feels like when you die, he thought, taking in the juxtaposition of the darkness and evil of what he was experiencing with the feeling that now over-whelmed him. Ahmed started to squeeze the trigger, when suddenly, the room lit up as if a brilliant spotlight had been switched on over them. At the same time, a burst of energy accompanied the loud sound of thunder and blew off the flames on Ghassan and threw the three radicals to the ground. As Ahmed fell to the ground, his gun was knocked out and slid more than three meters away from him.

The front door also flew open revealing Fatma and Nabil about ten meters away running to the entrance. At this point, Nick's perception of time started to roll at the same pace between the spiritual and physical realms. He looked around the room to assess the situation and find out what was going on. Ahmed was lying on the floor to his left along the wall of the living room. He was completely startled and shocked due to the intensity of the light flooding the room. The light over-whelmed him, and the expression in his face showed frustra-tion over whatever was happening that had disrupted their plans. Youssef, who was also in shock and fearful of the powerful presence of the light, got up and ran out the front door before Nabil and Fatma arrived, sprinting for the SUV parked outside. Ahmed and Fathi would have to fend for themselves.

Fathi had dropped to the floor next to Ghassan and was absolutely shocked and confused. He was still in disbelief over the betrayal of Ahmed pointing the gun at him and started to see that Ghassan's clothes were intact, without a trace of the fire that he thought had been consuming him for the last few seconds. Ghassan was also free of the duct tape that had been rolled around his wrists, ankles, and over his mouth, and was turning to look up at the source of the light.

As Nick's pupils began to adjust to the intense light, he began to distinguish shapes within it. By then, Fatma and Nabil had reached the threshold of the front door. Inside the living room and close to the source of the light, Nick saw two of the angels. Suspended on air, just above them, there was a woman looking down upon the entire scene. He also saw two other men moving forward toward him, wearing IDF uniforms, and in their name tags, *Moshe Bitton* and *Jacob Dahan,* respectively. They were both inside the glow that surrounded the woman and had a peaceful and joyful expression on their faces as they turned their gaze to Nabil. Their eyes conveyed a message of forgiveness that needed no words.

The source of the light was behind the woman, radiating and illuminating the room as if it was sunlight. She was dressed in white, with a light blue veil that went down the length of her dress. The veil was of a material that did not look manmade. It had texture and light that was in constant motion, and as Nick focused on it, looked like the sky, full of stars that were shining brilliantly.

The woman was of indescribable beauty. She was looking directly into Ahmed and Fathi's eyes with an expression of love and compassion. There was no judgment or condemnation in her stare, yet they knew that she was saddened to see them behaving like animals, allowing evil to pierce through into this world. The sight, and apparent focus on them, did not fit in Fathi's paradigm of faith and the spiritual realm. Partly, this was because it was a woman, but also because she did not fit the description of what he believed in. He thought it could be the Christian Virgin, but he dismissed that idea as blasphemy. In the shock of the moment, and not fully understanding what was going on, he got up and rushed out of the apartment yelling, "Allah, save me from this demon!"

Ahmed, who up until now had just been watching the entire scene in disbelief and fear, got up and ran out immediately behind Fathi, leaving his gun on the floor. At the same time, a collective loud shriek could be heard in the room. In the middle of the shrieking, a deep voice said, "Get away from me, woman! No! Nooooo!" And in an instant, that hellish noise was gone, replaced by a quiet and peace that was extremely rare in al-Eizariyah.

Nick also noticed that the demons that had made up the constantly moving reddish vortex above them were quickly moving away. That was except for one of the human-like entities, who had slowed down enough to stop at the threshold of the hallway, and for a second seemed to be bending its left knee to touch the floor, before suddenly rushing out and disappearing.

The first indications of daylight were starting to be seen in the light purple and orange hue of the eastern sky, and not even the loud sound of cicadas in the nearby fig trees could be heard. This sudden, peaceful silence also muted the loud sound of the morning call to prayer, which had started less than a minute before. The world was suspended upon the presence of the Holy Queen and her companions, and the Legion of Agares had departed from the apartment. Their fear was deeper and darker than ever, as the presence of this amazing woman was too much truth, goodness, and light for them to withstand. They had also come to understand that Fatma was a special being, blessed with an incredible closeness to God and His family in Heaven, and would not be afraid of them again.

Fatma and Nabil felt compelled to kneel as they both looked up and admired in awe the beauty and power of the vision in front of them. Deep in their hearts, they also knew who it was. Not a goddess, but as she was called locally, Mariam, the young Jewish woman who was the human Mother of Jesus. Through Him, she had adopted everyone, believers or not. Her closeness to God and His light of truth made it impossible for any evil entity to be in her presence. The two angels standing below were also glowing, but not as brilliantly as her. Mariam's gaze was now directed at Fatma and Nabil, and for the first few seconds, not a word was spoken, just a loving motherly gaze and reverence on the part of the two college students.

Nabil, who was still haunted by the guilt of having been involved with Hamas, broke the silence and addressed the Virgin saying, "I have done a terrible thing. I beg for God's forgiveness..." He was experiencing the most important event in his life but did not feel it was deserved. At that moment, in his heart, he knew that he had committed some horrible acts against what he now understood were his brothers. The murder of the IDF soldiers was a horrible act, and there was no way that his participation in it could be justified. He knew it at the time, even if he had been told that this was Allah's will, and he would approve of it. If there was one God, it was the one he experienced now in that light surrounding them and Mariam, and this was a God of Life, not death.

Mariam turned to speak directly to him. "Nabil, what you did was terrible, but God's capacity to forgive is infinite...as long as you repent, and you are confessing that repentance now. Though you may have to make reparations for this very grave sin, I am sure He is prepared to forgive you. Turn to my

Son, Jesus, in humility, and He will live in you, and you will live in truth."

At that point, Nabil broke down crying like a child. He was able to summon enough strength to say, "God of Life, Living God, I know you are here and can hear me. I am not worthy of forgiveness, but please know that I am forever regretful and ashamed of what I did. I beg for Your Mercy!" At that moment he felt a vibrant rush of warmth flowing through his body and knew at that time that he had been forgiven.

Fatma was in awe witnessing that conversation unfold, and amazed that there was no intent to avenge the death of the IDF men, who after all, were children of this God. This was the God of the Christians, but also the Jews, and while they were not aware of it, people of other faiths or no faith. It was the God of all in this world. And this God offered infinite love, and was moved to provide mercy to someone that, through no fault of his own, had been indoctrinated in a destructive sub-culture that Fatma was very familiar with. Fatma was also thrilled to see that Nabil showed sincere regret and humility. The sobbing on his part was contagious, and Fatma began to cry as well. Fatma's physical pain from Abdul's beating had paused momentarily, and every ounce of her body fell into a state of bliss, an immense, peaceful joy. She was now enveloped in the embrace of the energy that emanated from the light and did not want that moment to end. All the suffering, angst, and death that she had experienced during the last few hours were irrelevant, not important in the present moment.

Mariam then spoke to her, "Fatma, how good it is that we can be here together. Your courage and the desire of your heart to find the truth have pleased Our Father, and His love is being poured out on you through the Holy Spirit. You have responded to His call and have acted with love, even though you were initially fearful. God gave you strength, and through your actions and sense of compassion, you allowed Nabil to move closer to understanding the truth. This is your gift."

Mariam paused to let her assimilate those words, and understand that along with that gift, there had to be a responsibility to put it to good use. Then another unexpected thing happened. Mariam addressed both Fatma and Nick, "Before I depart today, there are two things I want to do. First, I want you both to be at peace with something that has been giving you sadness and anxiety." After a brief pause, "Fatma, your mother, Layla wants you to know that all is well, that she loves you and is always near you, and that whatever your difficulties or suffering, it will all be resolved in the end."

Fatma remained calm and felt that she was not deserving of this beautiful sign of love from God. Her eyes welled up in tears, and she simply said to Mariam and the infinite source of goodness that she understood was God, "Thank you!"

Then, turning to Nick, "I know you have been going through a very a difficult time, but you should know that Shannon is fine. I also know you are still trying to understand why you were here in the first place. If you had not come, Ghassan and Fatma would be dead, and a young, confused man would not have had the opportunity to come back home. There is a lot you that you have learned here in the last few hours. It is your turn to continue on your mission to *get closer to God*, and let the truth come out. Isn't that what you feel in your heart?"

At that, Nick felt an intense mix of peace and warmth, combined with the realization that what he had been searching for his entire life could be summarized so simply and beautifully with that phrase – get closer to God. The feeling also stemmed from the knowledge that Shannon was fine, which immediately replaced the painful image and memory he had of her during the final days being consumed by cancer.

Mariam then continued, "I also want to share something to

give you a better understanding of how both of you can use the gifts that you have received."

At this moment, time in the physical world came to a pause, with only Fatma and Nick and those in the spiritual realm continuing in the conversation and the images that started to emerge in front of them. They felt like they were ascending over al-Eizariyah and could clearly see the entire land of Israel below. There they saw what looked like military encampments, the concentration being around Jerusalem. The soldiers in those encampments all had the dark aura and moved just like the demonic creatures they had just witnessed in the fight at the apartment. Their numbers were overwhelming. As the vision began to quickly pan to the west, they could still see patches of these encampments, but smaller ones and not as active. That was until they could see in the distance, the East Coast of the North American continent. Not only were the numbers exponentially higher, but there was a continuous red glow along the entire coast as if their presence was uninterrupted. They continued to move west and saw the entire country blanketed by this glow, as if they were preparing for and engaging a big battle. Their adversary could not be seen. Nick remained speechless, trying to understand and process what he was witnessing.

Fatma was confused and said, "There are no warriors on the side of God to counter this. Is this hopeless, Holy Mother? Have we lost the support of God?"

Mariam then brought them back in space suspended above el-Eizariyah, still paused in physical time and told them, "God is always there. He loves his children too much to abandon them, but it is true that there is a battle taking place, and the enemy has made big advances in recent time. As you saw, Israel and the United States remain the biggest battlegrounds. That is because those are the places where the devil and his legions face their biggest resistance. It is where they are focusing their energy. Where you saw less of them is where they think they already have a beachhead and are in control. They can only act on the world by influencing humans, but as you should have guessed, they cannot use the same approach as God – an approach of love and truth. Because of that, they have developed a strong religious following of people that don't even know he exists. Those who fall in the sins that Isaiah 5:20 so clearly articulates are doing homage to him and committing the gravest of offenses against God. Many of them are more committed to that religion than what most Christians and Jews are to their respective beliefs."

"In the same way, God has chosen that His angels be there to support and strengthen humans in this battle, but the battle has to be fought in the physical world...by men and women. This is where you can make a difference and where you can put these graces of God to work." As Mariam said that, the intense light that had been surrounding them made them feel the intense presence of truth, goodness and love. They knew it was the Holy Spirit, and within that light, they saw what appeared to be an infinite army of Angels and Saints. Zaphkiel and Barachiel were in the front of the group, closest to them. Mariam then said, "Children, may you have peace in the Holy Spirit. This army will always be with you, fighting in the spiritual world. But remember, your battle must be fought where you are. Do not be afraid, live as Jesus did and taught, and always pray. We will be at your side." With that, the Virgin, along with her companions, began to gradually fade, the light of the Holy Spirit replaced by a sliver of daylight from the sun.

Fatma remained in prayer, overwhelmed with what had just taken place. She then understood that, even in a small way, she had passed on the blessings she had received from Jenny in exposing her to the message of Jesus. Jenny and then Nick had helped in her conversion, which she was infinitely grateful for. But the most amazing thing, and what Fatma thought was a miracle, was Nabil's conversion. It showed an openness to learning and seeking truth that was missing in Youssef, Ahmed, and Fathi, all of which had witnessed the awesome show of power of this apparition. There was much more for her to learn, and she felt that there would also be many burdens to carry, but this was as real and true as she had ever experienced, and there was no doubt that she was being called to continue spreading this message, particularly in the community where she grew up, something that would be extremely difficult and risky.

The pain in her body from Abdul's attack now started to come back, as if she was coming back to full consciousness after being in a trance. The reality of the moment now began to sink in, and her thoughts turned to Ghassan. She got up and walked to him, still on the floor and now sitting with his back against the wall crying. He was still having difficulty breathing, as he was starting to catch his breath again after the tape had been removed from his mouth, but he was also gasping from all the crying.

Ghassan looked at Fatma and was surprised to see her bloody and bruised face in front of him. Even in her broken state, he was still elated to see her alive, breathing and functioning fully, since he had expected the worst once he realized the radicals had taken her out of the apartment. He whispered with the little strength he could summon, "Fatma, you are alive! My baby is alive! Thank You God, for bringing good out of all this pain!" He paused to catch his breath, then softly asked, "Are you OK, little girl?"

Fatma responded, "I am fine, Father. It was horrible, but in the end, we were all saved. I am a little sore, but that is something temporary that I will recover from. I hope that whatever injuries you have are not serious."

She then proceeded to assess Ghassan's condition, quickly finding that he had a broken collarbone and some bruises in his face and body. While she did that, Ghassan started to regain his strength and slowly stood up. He was still feeling a sharp pain near his right shoulder, but aside from that, was fine.

In between gasps, he said, "I thought I was burning. I thought...I thought I was going to die." It was tears of happiness and from an overwhelming feeling of being loved, not of sadness or fear. He saw the lady that was present the night Fatma was born. He prayed, thanking her for everything she had done for his daughter, then and throughout her life, but also for saving his own life and reassuring them that Layla was well. He was overwhelmed emotionally and had felt like a child in her presence.

There was now enough daylight filtering into the apartment, which allowed Fatma to notice the black smoke stain on the wall. At the bottom of the stain, the original white color of the wall showed a well-defined profile that had the shape of a man with giant wings. Ghassan's clothes were untouched by the flames, even though they smelled of gasoline and smoke.

All four, while feeling pain from minor injuries, were still in a state of tremendous peace. It was a great victory and source of celebration for all of them and a reaffirmation that the forces of good are infinitely stronger than the forces of evil, particularly in the spiritual realm. The physical realm provided a more level playing field for the dark forces, and they took advantage of that. Nick and Fatma also had developed a clearer understanding of the battle that is constantly taking place in humanity, both at a macro level, but also within each individual. The battle has to be fought on both fronts, and whether each individual likes it or not, they are participating in it.

Nick's planning instincts started to kick in, and he began to anticipate what his next steps needed to be, considering that they were all in danger and needed to leave the apartment as soon as possible. How would he gain a more specific understanding of what he was being asked to do going forward? His natural drive was to plan and act, and the mission still felt too broadly defined. Then he caught himself not living in the present. He shook his head, looked up and smirked, realizing that this present moment was a gift that very few people would have the opportunity to experience. His thoughts then shifted to what surrounded him.

He looked and saw Fatma and Ghassan crying tears of joy. Nabil, still near the entrance, on his knees, appeared confused but in awe of what he had just experienced. Nick had a clearer understanding of the reason for him being there that night. Fatma was definitely someone special that would play an important role in this battle, and he had unexpectedly deflected the focus of the radicals that night, which in the end, allowed her and Ghassan to survive. The experience had also solidified his faith. He had experienced the spiritual realm and now knew it was even more real than the physical one. He had also started to learn about forces on Earth that were directly influenced by evil spirits, even if unaware of it. He knew there was a role for him to play in exposing and fighting them, but would need to figure out how, over time.

Questions started to pop up in his mind, which he saw as a good sign and an indication that more specific direction was forthcoming; What was Youssef's role in this battle of good and evil? What was this vaguely defined, yet powerful organization that he represented? Why did that dark creature stay behind at the appearance of the Holy Virgin, while the rest of them, including Agares, fled in fear? What was the implication of Zaphkiel's last message?

Anyone who denies the truth and leads with lies is being influenced by Agares or his peers and master, Satan. Some may do it in a less physically violent way, but they are equally as wicked and destructive.

As the sun was coming out, Nick walked up to the main entrance door to ensure that the radicals had all left. From the threshold of the door, he could see that the street was deserted. They were gone for now, but would definitely come back, and this time there would not be any dialogue. He stepped outside and realized that the temperature had dropped a lot overnight. He took in a deep breath of the crisp morning air, reflecting on how being aware of the gift of a breath is one of the simplest, most powerful ways to *be in the present*.

He then slipped his hands into the pockets of his jacket to keep them warm and felt a small piece of paper in the right-side pocket. He thought it was probably a receipt or credit card slip as he pulled it out and unfolded it. It was from a small notepad, and on it, in his wife's handwriting, *Thinking about you. Love, Shannon.*